A Song Below Water

Also by Bethany C. Morrow

Mem

should probably give you some media coaching, since I'm basically a master now."

"Your mom showed me your channel online."

I freeze. So he does know. I'm not just going for hometown hero. I'm going for siren activist. I'm joining the fight to free Camilla Fox, and I'm petitioning to get Lexi taken off the air, and I want to teach the world that we have a right to use our voices. No taking the name "siren" and erasing the ones who actually exist.

"You know?" I ask, but I'm back to looking at his hand on the railing instead of his face.

"Yeah. Your mom was right. You have a . . . presence. A real way with words."

"I *am* a siren." This time the smile's impossible to hold back, and so is the way my breaths are coming faster now.

"Yeah." Dad smiles too. "Maybe that Priam boy'll want to give the two of you another try now."

My breathing doesn't just slow down, it stops.

"No. I doubt it." Immediately I remember Priam in the courtyard, and usually I'd excuse myself to my bedroom without saying anymore. But Effie's not there today. When I get up to the attic, her bed'll still be there and it'll only make it feel more lonely. I could call her, but I don't know how good the reception is in the Narnia-tent. Anyway, it wouldn't be the same.

Dad's looking up at me. It might be the first time in years we've spoken this long without my mom as a buffer. And it hasn't been en*tirely* awkward.

"I saw Priam at prom," I finally say. It sucks the way Dad's face lights up. "I asked him if he regrets the way he treated me."

Now Dad shifts on his step, leans against his hand like he's really interested to hear the answer. Or that Priam didn't treat me well. At least not at the end.

"I asked him if he still hates me."

Now his eyebrows cinch.

"He said he doesn't. He just wishes we'd never met."

First Dad's skin creases even harder and then, abruptly, his brows relax.

"Well," he tells me. "I was never really a fan of that kid."

"No?" I laugh.

"Not really, no. Sirens deserve better."

"Yeah," I say with a smile. "We do."

Bethany C. Morrow

A Song
Below Water

TOR
TEEN

A TOM DOHERTY ASSOCIATES BOOK
NEW YORK

A SONG BELOW WATER

A Tor Teen Book
Published by Tom Doherty Associates
120 Broadway
New York, NY 10271

www.tor-forge.com

Tor® is a registered trademark of Macmillan Publishing Group, LLC.

The Library of Congress Cataloging-in-Publication Data is available upon request.

ISBN 978-1-250-31532-8 (hardcover)
ISBN 978-1-250-31531-1 (ebook)

Our books may be purchased in bulk for promotional, educational, or business use. Please contact your local bookseller or the Macmillan Corporate and Premium Sales Department at 1-800-221-7945, extension 5442, or by email at MacmillanSpecialMarkets@macmillan.com.

First Edition: June 2020

Printed in the United States of America

0 9 8 7 6 5 4 3 2

To Jennifer, my Effie

A Song Below Water

I

TAVIA

It feels redundant to be at the pool on a rainy Saturday, even though it's spring, and even though it's Portland, but maybe I'm just more of a California snob than I want to be. Back home I went to the beach on more than one cloudy day. I'd stand on the cold sand, burrowing my toes beneath the surface as though there'd be some warmth there, and I'd listen. Just like I'm doing now.

I always close my eyes, and today's no exception. It's never made a difference but it's part of the ritual, and I guess it must mean something that I did it even before I knew there was a way for living sirens to listen for their dead. It was one of the first things I learned when I finally found "the network," so despite my lack of results thus far, I close my eyes now too.

The problem is I don't know exactly what I'm listening for. The story goes that sirens originated by the water, that once we used our calls to damn seamen, and that when we die, our voices return to the sea. If the mythos is to be believed—and as far as any nonmagic people are concerned, most of it isn't—I should be able to hear my grandmother here.

Here, Portland; not here, the Southwest Community Center, specifically. I mean, I'm at an indoor pool with all its colorfully elaborate water features that nobody is enjoying because my play-sister's the only person doing laps. Even if sirens' voices really do

9

return to the water, they probably don't go to chlorinated bodies of it.

The problem with mythos is that it varies too much for any one interpretation to be believed. Do sirens' voices return to the body of water near where they were born, or close to where they died? Do sprites have a physical body and are they just too quick to see, or are their forms entirely ethereal? Do elokos *have* to be self-obsessed phonies, or have I just been lucky to know that exact type?

Who knows. I guess it depends on what movie or song or TV show shaped which decade. It doesn't really matter when what the world believes about you isn't a matter of life and death. And it isn't. Unless you're a siren.

Anyway, I have another problem: I wouldn't know Gramma's voice if I heard it. We lived in neighboring states my whole life, she in Oregon and me in Cali, but we never met. If what the network taught me about how a siren listens for her ancestors ever worked, I still wouldn't know when I'd found her. I've got no lullabies, no loving nicknames, and zero turns of phrase to confirm her identity. Just my hope that like recognizes like.

The community center receptionist did me a solid and let me accompany my sister, Effie, free of charge, since we're here for Effie's conditioning, and I never get in the water. I always hang way back so the girl doesn't think I'm trying to sneak a swim, so when I find I've gotten close to the pool's edge, I pin my arms behind my back—no one dives with their hands behind them!—and take a break to watch Effie for a while.

Beneath the water, she's got her feet hooked together, one leg behind the other so tight that not even the water can get between them. This is how she swims when she wants to go fast, when she's done her breathing exercises, and her underwater twirls and arches and hypnotizing glide. She doesn't look like a mermaid now. For one, she's abandoned the dramatic dolphin kick that her audience so loves. Right now, she looks like something sleeker. Something that cuts the water instead of dancing in it.

To clarify, Effie's not a real mermaid, she just plays one on TV. By which of course I mean at the Renaissance faires. (Obviously, play-sister means we're not actually related by blood either, but "real" doesn't apply to family.) With her tail on and with the way she swims—and if you ignore basically everything known about mermaids—it isn't hard to believe she's legit. Every time I see her slip into character, I believe. And I wish I were something else.

Anything else.

A wave of chlorine rushes me and the smell is so intensely antiseptic that for a moment I'm back in the sterile hallway of a hospital I haven't seen since my parents finally got me the hell out of Santa Cruz.

I must've closed my eyes again because when the shock of that memory recedes, Effie's almost out of the water and her sopping wet twists cascade over her shoulders to hide her face while she reaches for her towel. She keeps it on a plastic chair so close she can be covered before anyone gets a good look at her skin, which never looks as parched as she thinks. The lifeguard I'm not supposed to tease her about takes the opportunity to check on the other end of the pool, verifying that it is indeed still uninhabited, and I nod. Good boy.

Effie catches my eye and gives me one of her smirking smiles, like she does when I describe her as golden-brown instead of whatever criticism she's just given herself. She's heading to the showers now; she'll be back in five or so minutes (longer if she gets distracted trying to lotion away her dry patches), and then we can head home. But I don't trust my mind to keep me company anymore, so while I wait, I pull out my phone to catch up on my favorite vlogger.

I've been watching Camilla Fox's eponymous YouTube channel for the past two years. I've studied her wash-and-go technique, I've acquired a small kingdom's worth of natural hair products at her recommendation, and I *still* have not cracked the secret of her bounce and style preservability. In the tutorial, she cuts to a later date and—through the magic of the satin bonnet and silk

11

scrunchies (and the patience not to bunch her hair haphazardly into both)—her two-day-old wash-and-go always looks better than my day one. Of course, if we could crack her secret, she probably wouldn't have three and a half million subscribers. There's something she knows that we don't, or she's a muse (if they still exist), or anyway she's just hair divinity walking among us.

She's my patronus. When I can't deal with real life, I escape into her virtual space, where everything is perfectly lit, perfectly coifed, and perfectly accompanied by neo-soul music I never hear anywhere but natural hair videos and the beauty supply shop.

But something's off. Not with the perfection that is Camilla Fox; I haven't gotten to her channel yet. It's the fact that, because I'm a subscriber who watches little else these days, Camilla's face should be the first thing I see when I open the app. Except under "Recommended," there's another familiar face staring back at me. Another Black girl—a woman—from southern Oregon. Only this one's dead.

I recognize Rhoda Taylor even though she hasn't been in the press much. Her picture showed up on the evening news the weekend after her live-in boyfriend murdered her, but only because social media had been circulating it and demanding to know why no one seemed to be saying her name. Now there's a BREAKING NEWS banner under her picture—and it isn't a picture I've seen before.

I shouldn't open the video and I definitely should've muted it first, but it feels like there's a tornado in my guts and I'm not thinking straight. My throat feels hot, like someone's striking metal against a flint.

Rhoda Taylor.

Recent murder victim.

Suspected siren.

I only catch fragments. It doesn't matter; I already knew. As soon as I saw the thumbnail photo, I knew. There's only one reason a dead Black woman would suddenly make the news, only one reason her boring HR employee photo would be replaced with one where Rhoda's eyes are red from the flash and her mouth is open like she's in the middle of talking. Or moaning. However they're implying we entrance our hapless victims.

The defense is saying the deceased was a siren.

Which means maybe she wasn't a victim after all.

The video has captions, so when I realize the community center has great acoustics, I finally mute it. It doesn't stop the familiar, unsympathetic voices from blaring in my head.

Sirens, they say, and anyone listening knows it's a dirty word.

Danger, they report, and they're talking about the danger she posed, never the danger we face.

The world is closing in on me, and in the community center, I feel the wall at my back. There's a wet echo all around, and it's sad, but I'm relieved when I remember that I'm alone. The news people, the talking heads who for once will all agree with each other, they aren't talking about me—at least not as far as they know. My chest is jumping with a jackrabbit pulse and it's beginning to hurt.

But no one knows.

I'm still safe.

I must have slid down the wall because soon I find myself sitting on the floor. If it's damp, I don't notice. If I've lowered myself into one of the many wayward puddles decorating the pool area, I can't tell. What matters is that no one can look over my shoulder. No one can see what I'm seeing—even though according to the viewer count, literally thousands of people already have.

I turn off my phone; this is something not even the iconic Camilla Fox, naturalista goddess, can fix.

Because Rhoda Taylor was a siren. Like me.

I think I'm going to be sick.

II

EFFIE

There's nothing like being in the water.

People ask me if it's quiet, if that's why I like it. It makes sense; I'm quiet, I must want the world to be the same way.

Tavia asks me that; Tavia is people.

The thing about being underwater is that it's not—quiet, I mean. I can't hear what's happening above the surface, but when I'm totally submerged, I hear the water. I hear its song, the way it sings to itself and anybody who comes below to hear it. I love the way it never changes, and the way I'm always different when I'm here.

Sometimes I bring my head above the surface when I don't need a breath, just so I can duck back under and hear the song start again. That's all I mean to do when I crest between laps, but this time I feel a pair of eyes on me.

I can always tell when I'm being watched. I guess when you can never shake the feeling, you've gotta be right sometimes.

There he is. He's leaning back in his seat, wearing a white community-center polo shirt with his red shorts, tanned brown hands interlaced on top of his buzz-cut hair. He lifts one my way and I can't help but smile—even though I immediately hide behind my heavy twists when I wave back.

Last week he said his name is Wallace, and now I hear it replay inside my head.

We only just introduced ourselves (finally), but he's been coming to the pool for the past several years and I feel like we've built up a rapport.

Hey.

How's it going.

The water feels fine.

Okay, a very vague rapport, but I'm not a great conversationalist—which he probably reads as disinterest like everybody else. (Joke's on them, I'm just super uncomfortable.) Sometimes I don't say anything at all, just make a nonverbal hello.

With the faire coming up, it's the gesturing that makes me feel a little guilty. Like outside of me and Tav, signing should belong to my life in the mermaid tank. And to Elric, the boy I'm betrothed to when I play Euphemia the Mer.

Whatever. Wallace told me his name but nothing else. He's the strong, silent type, I guess. Emphasis on the strong. I used to think he was a lifeguard (his arms are built for heaving people out of an unforgiving sea, trust) but despite being a walking ad for the community center, he's never on the lifeguard stand.

When I climb out of the pool, he's looking away, smiling with a mom who just got foot-checked by her overly enthusiastic toddler. A moment ago, it was just us—the way I like it. As if Tav knows the sight of a mother and child'll be a trigger, she chooses that moment to look over, but I play it off.

It's the one downside to Ren faire season returning. Knowing Mom won't. Most years it's a passing acknowledgment. Just the truth, crappy but not crippling. This year feels different.

Tavia's not in the lobby when I'm done showering, so I double back through the locker room and find her standing in a corner on the far side of the pool. For a moment, I think maybe she finally heard something in the water. I don't know exactly what she's been doing the last few times she's come with me to the pool;

I'm not a siren. I just know what I pick up from Tav, and she's not totally sure she knows how this whole searching-for-siren-gramma ritual is supposed to work. All I know right now is that she looks more traumatized than victorious. Like, even before I get to her, I can tell something's really wrong. She might be trying to be*come* the wall, the way she's pressed into it.

"They said she was like me," Tavia signs when I get closer.

When she defaults to ASL, I know there's a problem. It means her siren call is close to sliding free—or she's afraid it is, anyway. It means the safest thing for her to do is not to speak. When that happens, I try not to speak either; we sign. I've got my swim bag in one hand, and the other one's still checking that all my twists are safely bound inside my wrap and completely out of sight, so I have to respond out loud.

"What?" I ask, and even though it isn't my voice that has power, the sound of it makes Tavia shiver and she waves me even closer.

"They said she was like me," she signs again, and when she swallows I can't help but remember how she said it feels when she's scared to speak out loud.

The inside of her throat must be burning. It must feel tight and tense, like a rubber band stretched too far. She told me once that it's like choking on a rock of fire that refuses to melt down, and that must be why she's teary-eyed.

"Who did?" I ask when my hands are free, but I mouth it too, the way I do at the Renaissance faire when me and the few other cosplay mermaids are in our tanks.

Tav reaches out and pulls me in before spelling Rhoda's name against my chest. When she's done, she just stares at me with these pleading eyes. Like I'm the strong one. Like she's not the one teaching *me* how to keep it together.

Like I haven't been waiting all day for the right time to tell her I'm having nightmares again. The swim was supposed to give me the courage, because the water's the only thing that does.

But now *Tavia* needs *me*. So I do what I do best; I sputter. I open my mouth and just make generally unintelligible sounds like I sometimes do in class, hoping someone bails me out before I shrivel up and die.

Tavia knows my tricks.

She mouths my name once, then widens her eyes for emphasis—and that's when I remember who Rhoda Taylor is. That her boyfriend's going on trial for her murder, and that no one's ever mentioned her being a siren before. They've barely mentioned her at all.

"Is she?" I ask her. Like an idiot.

C'mon, Effie. That is *not* the point.

I expect Tav to gesture wildly, sign that she doesn't know or that I'm a jerk for thinking it matters. Instead she does something worse. She deflates, shrugging one shoulder like she doesn't have the energy to lift both.

"C'mon," I say, weaving my fingers through hers, and walking my sister around the puddles and the pool. I don't do a last sweep to find out if Wallace is still around. Tav and I just walk straight through the lobby, into the light rain.

We don't even break into a half-hearted jog or cover our hair. Mine's already in a wrap, but Tavia doesn't squeal or throw her hands up like they'll offer any substantial shelter. If the flax seed gel isn't enough to keep her coils from frizzing, it'll be okay. Her top knot'll still slay. Camilla taught her well.

When we're sitting in my car, we're holding hands again. Tavia sighs so I know she feels safe to speak.

"Does it still hurt?" I ask her.

"A little," she says, and almost grimaces. "But it's probably in my head."

She's touching her keloid so I'm not sure she's even talking about the fire in her throat. The scar is definitely too old and too healed to cause her pain anymore.

"This sucks."

"Yeah," I whisper through an exhale.

"This *sucks.*"

She wants to say more than that, but even for a nerd like Tavia, there probably aren't words enough to do it justice. She could write one of her monster IB essays just on what havoc the revelation might wreak in her relationship with her dad, citing her childhood isolation from her paternal grandmother and the crisis that precipitated the Philipses' move to PDX as necessary historical context. (I might've read one or two of her assignments.)

I've only lived under his roof for three years and I know Rodney Philips well enough to be worried about how things'll play out for Tav when we get home. My gram, Mama Theo, is a force to be reckoned with—or, preferably, not—but Tavia's dad might be her match. Part of the reason we immediately glommed onto each other must be that we know what it is to feel like there's something wrong with us. And like our families know it. I didn't know anyone else understood the sting of love mingled with obvious disapproval till I saw Mr. Philips with Tavia.

And still sometimes I envy them. Because at least there's blood between them.

At least they know what Tavia is.

At least she knows what her family disapproves of.

"He's gonna wanna scrub my online presence. Again." She's talking about her dad too. Sometimes I honestly think she can read my mind and I don't know if that's a siren feature or just a Tavia feature. "He's gonna tell me to delete the video from my history log and search my social media accounts for any mention of Rhoda Taylor or 'say her name.'"

"Yep."

"Anything that links the two of us, or shows I ever had an interest in or connection to her. Which'll accomplish nothing. And look paranoid and suspicious. And I'll do it."

"Yep," I say through another sigh. "And you'll apologize."

"And I'll apologize. Even though I'm not sure how I should've known." She's crying now. "Because if I was somehow supposed to have divined that a dead woman no one's ever heard of was a siren despite the fact that the defense only just suggested it, then who does he think *we're* fooling?"

She looks at me, tears streaking her pretty face, and I smirk because I can't help it.

"This sucks, Tav."

As usual, she makes it seem like my fumbling is enough.

"Yeah." She nods and turns back to look out the windshield again. "It really does."

A moment later, she fishes her phone out of her pocket and at first I think she's gonna watch a tutorial. I slide closer so we can watch it together, the way we always do when things feel over-whelming. Living with Tavia's taught me there are better ways to deal with stress than picking at my skin or hiding behind my twists. For instance, twists can be manipulated into sweet updos, or faux-bobs, and learning how is a lot more distracting and fun.

But instead of queuing up Camilla Fox's latest, Tav goes into her history and deletes the breaking news video.

"Drive aimlessly so it takes forever to get home?" I ask as I pull myself upright again and finally start the car.

"Sounds about right."

"I hope you got gas money," I say, and as she melts down in the passenger seat, letting go of my hand so I can drive and she can hug herself, Tavia sort of smiles.

I take her everywhere, pretend she's brand new to Portland and shuttle her around like a tourist. We cross bridges just be-cause, zigzag from one side of town to the other, listen to the radio because my car's too old for an aux plug.

Eventually we decide we're playing spot the Fred Meyer, and by the time we climb the hill toward home, we're laughing like Tav's identity isn't being used to justify a woman's murder, and I'm not dreaming of childhood-destroying sprites again. All we have to do is make it through the front door, up the stairs, and into our bedroom without incident, and we're golden.

I'm thinking this might just work.

Except before Tavia can reach for the knob, the front door flies open.

Her dad is standing on the other side, frowning. He steps out onto the porch and cranes his head to look up at the roof.

"Dad, what're you—" Tav starts before following his gaze and going quiet.

I look too.

There's something on the roof, a large something. Made from stone, it's a hulking figure that's crouched and gripping the edge with long talons.

Hello, gargoyle.

Mr. Philips does not look happy when he gestures us through the door.

"Get inside."

III

TAVIA

"You need to take that thing more seriously, Tavia," he's saying, one finger pointing at the ceiling as though maybe the gargoyle's in our upstairs rather than perched on the roof.

I barely have time to get in the house before the lecture begins. Earlier I'd been relieved not to have to see my dad all day, but really that only made it worse. It's meant that in the background, everywhere we were and no matter what I was doing, I kept imagining his response.

Not his words, but the way they'd make me feel.

Effie did her best to keep me occupied, but all day all I could think was, Dad's gonna be pissed. No, that's not it. I know better.

Dad's gonna be scared. Again.

Now I know that I was right. All my unease—the palm sweats and acid reflux—was because I know my dad well.

He probably saw the same breaking news I did, and then the gargoyle returned to roost tonight, the way it's done for the better part of three years. It all mixes together and makes my dad terrified and angry.

"Do you hear me?" he demands with a raised voice.

"Rodney." My mom just has to say my dad's name and his eyebrows buckle. Like if she weren't there, he could spin out easy.

21

Like she's the only reason he won't. He grabs hold of his neat, black beard like he's pulling himself together for her.

"I hear you, Dad." I drop my eyes and wish I had a curtain of twists to shield me like Effie does. Instead my twist-out is pulled up in a top knot that felt really stylish this morning but now makes my forehead feel like it's liable to split and—worse—leaves my face completely exposed.

"It's like he's a beacon, Geneva," he's saying to my mom like I'm invisible, like I didn't preemptively clear my history to make him happy. Whenever he gives up like this and only talks to her, I feel like I've physically shrunk. Like if I keep it up, one day I'll disappear. Like maybe that's what he wants. "Three years he's been roosting here. You don't think the neighbors are wondering why? What about our house is different, what makes a gargoyle choose us, what's he protecting?"

Effie's right beside me, and there's no way she speaks up in a situation like this, but I know what she'd say. Something totally sardonic and hilarious, but only to me—which is fine because she'd only say it to me anyway.

If I were her, I could get away with smirking and saying, *I don't know, Dad, Hillside's a pretty desirable neighborhood. Plus we've got that spire.*

Which I obviously don't say.

"No, I don't think the neighbors are wondering why." My mom is being gentle with him, like my dad's the one who needs consoling today. "I think they're envious—and who says gargoyles are protectors?"

He doesn't have an answer for that, but what does that matter? We've got a secret, and as far as my dad's concerned, everything threatens to give us away. The fact that anyone else would be excited to host a gargoyle is beside the point. The fact that gargoyles are ridiculously rare, are the only nonhuman magical beings beside sprites, and therefore—and most importantly—have zero connection to sirens doesn't matter.

"And even if they were protectors"—I hate when she does

22

this—"not every siren has a guard." My mom doesn't go one step further and remind him that *no* siren does. That's why there's a network in the first place.

"These people don't know that, Geneva!" He keeps saying her name like he wants to be sure I know he isn't talking to me. "They're not supposed to know which of us are sirens and which aren't!"

"And they won't, honey, if you keep your voice down."

The room is suddenly quiet, and of course now is the time for the gargoyle to curl his stone talons tighter so that they scrape the drainpipe. When my parents' eyes lift, mine close.

I hate that beast.

The four of us are standing in a circle, Effie and me side by side. We've only come just beyond the foyer, but none of us move to the living room or try to take a seat. When the beast on our roof is done adjusting, my parents pick up the conversation where they left off.

"I'm gonna get rid of him, Geneva."

"All right, honey."

"I have to!"

None of us ask him how, or why three years later he thinks it's going to work. When the thing first arrived, or when a week had passed and we accepted that our house wasn't just a rest stop on his way somewhere else, my dad had tried blocking his perch. Whenever the gargoyle was away, he'd climb out my bedroom window and onto the roof to put something in its place, I guess in the hopes that gargoyles are severe creatures of habit and it would have no choice but to flee. Or maybe it wouldn't recognize the house, I don't know. I don't know any more about them than he does. None of us do. The only gargoyle mythos I've heard is that they're created, chiseled by a master out of solid stone. Which, full disclosure, I saw in a cartoon when I was little. No one ever disputes it, but who would. Other than the odd publicity stunt that turned out to be a load of crap, there aren't any known gargoyle masters chiseling new beasts to life, and as far as anybody knows, gargoyles don't speak for themselves. Who knows if they even can. What we know is that there's one gargoyle in Portland, and he chose us. According to the news crew that eventually showed up and that my dad couldn't bar filming it from the street below ours, this gargoyle's the first one to perch in the city in a very long time. So I'm pretty sure it has nothing to do with me. But that doesn't matter. According to my dad, everything's my fault.

Well, his, since it's his fault I'm a siren at all.

"And then the doggone news today, Gen," he's saying. "They're calling it a modern-day Siren Trial."

I don't say anything because they're standing closer together now. The circle's collapsed. We're not a group anymore; it's my parents and then Eff and me, and my sister's pretty occupied digging under her wrap to scratch her head. So we're putting up a pretty united front, too.

Between her persistent dry skin and a tingling scalp that no amount of oil treatments or tonics ever seems to soothe, I can't blame Effie for being distracted. I could've done without the way she's just ripped her headwrap off. Guess the itch got overwhelming. She's so adorably weird; I'd smile if I weren't totally miserable.

"These kids don't think past their hashtag activism." Dad's just shaking his head now, like he disapproves of everything. "They've been demanding the media pay attention and now it turns out the girl was a siren. She's dead, but what about those of us who can still get hurt by this? But everybody wanted a spotlight and now white folks are gonna give it to them. What happens to those of us who knew better than to call attention to ourselves? We get caught up with the rest of them."

My eyes shoot up to look at my father and my vocal cords turn to flint for the second time today.

"Her life mattered," I say, but the heat is building in my throat and I have to sign the rest.

"Whether she's a siren or not," Effie says in my place, translating for me while her twists protect her from my dad's disap-

24

proving glance. "No one should get away with murder because of what we are."

Effie's fingering her skin looking for dry patches. She doesn't want to be in the middle any more than I want to waste my breath. What else is there to say when someone still thinks they can prove anything to the rest of the world. When they think there's a way to behave to avoid being brutalized.

And why bother when all I want is for my dad not to be upset with me anyway.

When it's obvious Effie has nothing left to translate, my mom squeezes my dad's shoulders, nodding at him after a moment.

"We'll talk about this later, Tavia," he says through a sigh. "Just stay away from this whole mess. I'm serious. Nothing any of us do or say online is a secret."

"I know," I reply, because nonsensical or not, if my dad says I can't watch the news, I won't.

Mom ushers him off to the kitchen and blows me a kiss over her shoulder. Only a tiny part of me wants to follow her, ask her for a real hug. Instead I start up the staircase until Effie interrupts.

"Hey. Dinner."

"I'm good," I say. I know there's no way my dad's done talking, and I almost ask Effie not to engage, but I can't. They're her parents now too and I don't wanna mess that up, so I trudge the rest of the way to our bedroom.

I just want this day to be over.

~~~~~~

When Monday morning finally arrives, I have choir first period, and today I really need it. After a weekend involving multiple instances of my throat overheating, it's a good thing there's a small group competition coming up. It means that instead of working in the main room with the whole class and the clutter of tacky music-program posters taped to every surface, my gospel ensemble gets to sequester ourselves in one of the soundproof practice rooms.

As soon as the door is closed, and despite the fact that the outer wall is half-window, things get serious.

"You okay?" Tracy asks, and all eyes are on me.

Gospel choir is my hallowed ground, the one place at school where I'm safe. The reason we moved back to my dad's home-town, even though he never intended to. We didn't come back just for this collection of eleven girls—ten, at the moment—but because they're part of the network that's been here for decades.

In a remarkably monochromatic city in the unsuspecting Pacific Northwest exists one of a handful of networks. They are communities inside the Black community, where sirens are known and protected. As usual, though, the community isn't actually just made up of us, and neither is this gospel choir. Yes, nine of our twelve members are Black, but Tracy, for one, is a white girl and she still knows about me. More than that, she's trusted not just with my secret, but with the mandate to mask for me. They all are, including anyone with a magical identity of their own. While they sing, my call blends safely between their three-part harmony so that I don't have to live my life in silence. The rest of the school—even its small community of Black students—aren't privy to my identity except for Effie, who isn't in choir because (surprise!) she isn't much for stage performances.

"How're you holding up?" Tracy asks.

"My dad's frazzled," I say because that's the part that matters. "And I'm not supposed to watch the news or go online, I guess."

That gets everyone. Eyes roll, an assortment of snorts and clucks clutter the medium-sized practice room, outside of whose window the rest of the choir's running through scales with Mrs. Cordova. I can't hear them, but Landon McKinnon is doing that overenunciating thing he always does during scales, and it looks like he's going to unhinge his jaw and behead the petite girl in front of him. She's seconds from being cannibalized and she doesn't even know it.

"Anyway." I return my focus to our room just as Tracy squeezes my hand. I squeeze back to let her know it helps.

Or it usually does, anyway.

I'm supposed to let everything out here, according to Mom. This is how we make sure Santa Cruz never happens again. And I'm more than grateful for them, but there are just some things that not even the network would understand. That nothing short of knowing how it feels to *be* a siren would explain. As evidenced by what someone says next.

"It's the Siren Trials all over again." It's Porsha, the smallest one in the ensemble, and the resident charmer. Even though to me it seems super cliché when she turns out to be our mind-blowing soloist, the judges are always thrown. They somehow never see it coming. Looks can be deceiving, they say. Over and over again.

"How do you mean?" I ask. "How is it like the Siren Trials?"

"Just how, in the 1960s, sirens were being outed and informed on, and when they were killed their murderers were never brought to justice."

It's a painfully concise description of the era that spawned the very network Porsha's a part of. And leaves out the part where even the Black community quieted down pretty quickly following the acquittals, so as to keep the movement from losing steam and focus. After all, there hadn't been a record of a non-Black siren since the Second World War; we were too niche a population to deserve extended support or attention.

"Right," I say to Porsha, careful to keep my voice as light and breezy as possible. "But the first sirens to be targeted during the Civil Rights movement were activists. When they were accused, they opted to confirm their identity."

"That's true," Tracy says. "Rhoda Taylor is just suspected of being a siren. She might not even be one."

She says it like *that's* the injustice—that a non-siren is being called one. Not that the suspicion was raised at the murder trial of Rhoda's live-in boyfriend. And by the defense. Not that the whole world seems to agree that, yep, it matters whether she was a siren or not.

Because maybe she Compelled him to hurt her. Maybe it was suicide-by-boyfriend and he couldn't have stopped himself.

"A siren made me do it" is a pretty strong defense, I guess—even if the siren's the one who ends up dead.

"Anyway." I take a deep breath and look back out the window. "He hasn't gotten away with murder yet."

I don't say that I've always hated the way Siren Trials makes it sound like sirens were the perpetrators and not the victims. Despite my mom's advice, I don't tell the group how my stomach's too upset to eat solid food either. I don't tell them that even though we're intentionally saying her name and refusing to join the media in repeating her killer's, I'm already starting to cringe at the sound of Rhoda Taylor's name, and how that makes me feel like human garbage but I can't help it because I'm terrified of what could happen to me if the wrong person finds out what I really am.

I also don't bother saying that I've been looking for Gramma, or why. That it's not the first time I've tried to silence my siren voice, and that last time didn't go very well.

Why bother. Why get anyone else's hopes up when I still don't know what finding Gramma would accomplish. I don't know that there's a way to purge my voice of power, or if she'd even approve. After sirens lost their lives lending their voices to a cause, maybe my grandmother would be disappointed in me. I haven't thought that far ahead.

I swallow everything I'm not telling them and rejoin a conversation that's shifted to the upcoming competition. It's not long until, through the wall made equally of window, I see our missing member crossing the choir room to the emphatic delight of the class, whom Mrs. Cordova gives a bit of leniency until Naema has acknowledged them and disappears behind the solid door of our practice room. A rapping follows, and then she lets herself in.

"Sorry, sorry!" Naema's entrance here is received pretty much exactly as it was by the rest of the choir. There's no need to bat her naturally curled eyelashes or bat aside some of her unnaturally straightened hair. "I am so sorry," she says, and she beams this perfect smile over us like she knows she doesn't have to be. "Did we already warm up?"

"We wouldn't start without you," Porsha says through a beaming smile.

"I am so sorry," Naema says again, only now she's holding the small silver bell at the end of her necklace with both dark, berry-brown hands. It's pretty obvious what she's about to say, or what the subject will be, anyway. "Principal Kelly asked a couple of us to welcome a new eloko, and I just completely lost track of time."

"There's a new eloko student?" Porsha is practically bouncing, and even those with more self-restraint have wide, wonder-filled eyes.

"One more for the roster," Naema says, sliding her bell charm back and forth along her necklace chain as though to make sure we haven't forgotten that she's one, too. "We're taking over!"

And everyone laughs. Which is the opposite of how they'd react if I'd said it. They're my network, but none of us are immune to the public distrust of sirens. Even though I depend on them to help me stay safe, to give me a place to siren call, I still don't think that joke would've gone over well coming from me.

My problem is that for a long time sirens have been Black women. Not just mostly. Exclusively. Now that it's just us, the romance is dead. Instead of inspiring songs and stories, now our calls inspire defensive anger. Our power's not enchanting or endearing anymore; it offends.

Once on par with elokos, all that changed long before I was born. Now the consensus is clear: the world is better off when we're silent, and if the system skews toward making that happen—if Rhoda Taylor's just another in a long list of victims whose pain or death seem justified by her identity . . .

Well. Everybody's safer for it.

Sirens might be exclusively Black women, but all Black women aren't sirens. We're not even *only* sirens. Naema, for instance, is a different kind of different—one that manifests in any and every racial ethnicity, which is probably why despite having a pretty creepy mythos attached to them, elokos are still thoroughly adored. (The mythos is untrue, of course, but then so is mine and that hasn't changed anyone's mind.)

"I'm sorry, Tavia," Naema's saying. "Did I interrupt?"

"Nope." I smile because no one will mention how her elokoness comes up in every rehearsal. Today it's a new student, but it's always something. I'm not at all fooled. "We were just about to get warmed up."

"Let's do, then."

And it really isn't fair, but when I crinkle my nose to match her exuberant expression, I consider using the power in my voice just one more time.

~~~~~~

I'm always glad to put Monday behind me, like whatever happened—Naema being the worst, my dad's attitude shifting whenever I entered the room—was only because it was the first day of the week. It's ridiculous, but I can't help hoping Tuesday'll be better, and the next afternoon finds me in Mr. Monroe's classroom, the lone student already in my seat and patiently waiting for the bell to ring, and meditating on the way that junior year was actually going pretty well before a maybe–Siren Trial threw a wrench in it. High school, in general, really—Mondays and first heartbreak aside.

There's this thing called sunshine, and even though Portland doesn't grasp the concept for full seasons at a time, it seems like the last few years there's been more of it. It's more than that, though. After all, there was plenty of sunshine in Santa Cruz, the beach town where I was born, and I hated my life.

Mr. Monroe teaches IB Social and Cultural Anthropology and IB English 3, and if we were discussing it in the latter, he'd explain that when I say "sunshine," I'm really speaking figuratively. He'd say I'm talking about things like "illumination" and "warmth"—things that help me see more clearly and feel more comfortable in my own skin, and he'd talk about how those are things that bring "growth." In short, he'd say that what I really mean by "sunshine" is my network in the choir, my own personal sense of agency, and my sister-friendship with Effie, all rolled into one.

I mean, that's what he'd say if he knew about any of those things besides Effie being my play-sister. And coming from him, I'd really consider it.

There's a reason I adore Mr. Monroe, and it started in anthro, the day he asserted that there's no such thing as cross-cultural empathy without cultural competency. Not only did he acknowledge "dog-whistle politics," but he knew how to demonstrate it in a classroom. Legend.

He had three students each stand on a stack of books at the front of the room. I was one of the chosen three, but I didn't get the slip of paper; Altruism did—which is literally someone's name because this is Portland.

Anyway, Mr. Monroe had the three of us stand there while he gave a short, seemingly harmless presentation, but every so often Altruism took a book from her stack until finally she was standing flat on the ground and me and the third kid were towering above her.

See, every time he said something related to whatever he'd written on that paper, she got demoted. Beside me, she just got smaller and smaller, and it was strangely difficult to watch. It was hard to have the class's eyes on me while I processed that someone understood. When it felt like I might be ready to cry, I imitated Effie when she doesn't want to look someone in the eye and I found a focal point. I fixed my gaze on the speaker right beside the classroom door until the swell inside me passed, and by then Allie had both feet on the floor.

Mr. Monroe gave us a chance to guess what he'd written on the paper, but we couldn't. Even when he reread his presentation and Allie indicated which parts of it brought her down, few people got it. Only Allie understood that he'd been talking about her.

He made something plain to a room full of mostly white kids, and it meant I didn't have to. He was the teacher, so, at least on *that* topic, I didn't have to educate my peers. He became the best teacher I've ever had with that one class period, and I seriously doubt anyone's gonna top that.

Still. As much as I think the real Mr. Monroe is everything, I'm not sure I agree with his imaginary analysis of my "sunshine." There's a lot he doesn't know. For one thing, that "agency" we're always debating in fictional characters? I displayed mine by concocting a story to hide behind. I figured out that *not* using my siren calls at all is not an option. I tried that. It almost cost my family everything. But I also can't always have a choir entourage, and sometimes the call rises, replacing my human voice, and if I open my mouth, it's coming out.

So, I took a page from my parents. Without my consent, they came up with a cover story to explain the belt I tied around my neck in sixth grade; I came up with a cover story to explain why I sometimes lose my voice. Why I need to use ASL sometimes, and why I need an interpreter.

I got what I wanted when I stumbled on a disorder called spasmodic dysphonia, but . . . I'm not sure that counts as agency. And it sure doesn't feel like "sunshine." It doesn't feel like "illumination" and "warmth," not always. Most of the time, it just feels like surviving.

As random as it sounds, it's Camilla Fox that makes me feel both awake and at peace. She was the first natural-hair diva I found when I decided to take my hair care into my own hands (literally), and she's still my favorite. Her perfect lips are always some gorgeous matte, her septum piercing is real and forever gleaming, she basically looks eternally like some envy-inducing photo from Afropunk, and I am obsessed.

She's everything I want to be when I grow up, everything a lot of Black girls want to be.

She deals with her fair share of drama, *and* she taught me the L.O.C. method of hydrating my hair, so if "agency" is breaking the rules, I'm gonna use it for Camilla. For my sanity, really.

I've already pulled up her latest video when a few more class-mates wander into Mr. Monroe's room. I glance up and give an acknowledging smile to the two Jennifers and Altruism.

"Whatcha watching?" Allie comes around to peer over my shoulder. We're not close anymore, but when I moved to PDX the summer after sixth grade, Altruism was my first friend. Back when she went by Allie. It was easy then; her dad's Latinx, so even though her mom's white, they were the only other family of color in our neighborhood, and no one had to tell us what that meant. We just knew it was nice to see each other on the hill.

Nothing happened, we just made other friends and grew up, and while her world can get as big and unwieldy as she wants, I've got to keep mine under strict control. While she can date whenever and whomever she pleases—even if it's just the same person repeatedly, which in her case it is—I've seen how close I get to telling on myself when I'm in love.

Or whatever I was in.

"Hair vid," I say because no one in this room, or maybe the entire IB track, would know Camilla Fox's name.

"What's a hair video?" one of the Jennifers asks, and both of them join Altruism behind me.

"It's a video tutorial that teaches you how to do your hair," I answer while we all stare down at Camilla, who's talking about how she got two perfectly symmetrical braided buns while wearing rainbow overall shorts over a flowy-sleeved crop top.

Ugh. She's so dope.

"That's wild." It's a Jennifer again. "I didn't know people needed to be taught how to do their own hair."

"That's because all of mainstream media has been a white-girl hair tutorial all of your life," Allie says. "It's invisible to you."

"Wait, is that for real?" A symphony of bangles chime before a finger jabs in from behind me and accidentally pauses the video. "She legiterally has millions of subscribers! She's famous!"

"Yeah." I unpause it. "She's kind of a big deal."

"I've never even heard of her!"

33

This is apparently really mind-bending for the Jennifers, but I refuse. I'm not up for educating anyone on how many things exist that they don't know about or support, even if we are basically friends. Camilla Fox time is me time.

I scroll down to "like" the video and leave a supportive comment, but I immediately regret it.

The comments section that's always been the happy exception to the never-read-the-comments rule is bursting at the seams. It's always a hub for conversation and generally gassing each other up (while of course giving all praise to Camilla, too), but the huge bricks of text and deep threading of replies has nothing to do with her hairdo or her outfit or the product she briefly reviewed.

I can feel the three girls breathing behind me, and I wish I'd listened to my father. I scroll faster, hoping they won't see the name, but it's everywhere, no matter how far down I go.

Rhoda Taylor.

Rhoda Taylor.

Rhoda Taylor.

"They're doing minute-to-minute updates from the courthouse now," Allie says, almost gently. However loudly we were all speaking before, it's like this new subject is sensitive and she knows it.

I should close the video and change the subject. Clear my viewing history again, just in case. No, I should say something to keep from arousing suspicion. No one would believe I don't know about the trial, or that I don't have an opinion on whether or not the allegation is true.

And then, as though to prove it, the bangle-less Jennifer asks.

"Do you think it's true? Do you think Rhoda Taylor was a siren?"

"I don't think that's okay to ask Tavia," Altruism says. Because I'm the only Black girl in the classroom. In most of our IB classes.

"I wasn't just asking you, Tavia, I was asking everyone."

"I know." But I didn't and I don't believe her, so I don't know why I say it. But it makes for a good transition, so I take the opportunity to close my phone.

"Are you okay?" Allie asks when I stand up just as most people are coming into the room.

I nod and smile big. Too big, if sincerity mattered. By the looks of it, the Jennifers are satisfied that I'm fine and they can move on. Only Altruism keeps her eyes on me while I pass Mr. Monroe in the doorway, assuring him I'll be right back.

In the bathroom, I turn on the water and unnecessarily wet my hands.

Nothing happened; I didn't do anything wrong. I just saw other people discussing something *everyone* is discussing. Something my classmates are discussing, in every hall and at every lunch table, and the teachers are no better.

Before they only seemed to know the defendant's name, but now Rhoda Taylor is branded in their brains. I've heard it a dozen times today—but this isn't what we mean by "say her name."

None of that changes the way my dad would look at me if he knew I'd been involved. That I'd gone online.

I stare at the thick stream of water I can't feel running over my hands.

Gramma . . .

This is ridiculous. I'm, what? Looking for a siren soul in faucet water now?

I'm getting desperate.

IV

EFFIE

The dream's getting weirder.

And crowded.

Instead of me and four other kids the way it was in real life, now Mom's there, and Tav. So two people who couldn't have been, and oh yeah, a trick my eyes played on me. The "water mirage" I call it, the few times I've mentioned it aloud. It's this rippling hallucination that moves across my vision and just generally adds to the eeriness of the whole ordeal.

As if anything could make that day worse.

I'm in the park, but it's darker than it was. (I mean, who plays "Red Rover" at twilight. Kids are creepy, but they have their limits.)

The usual chorus of voices chants as I crouch down, one of my knees almost touching the damp grass.

My friends are lined up across from me. They're gripping each other's hands and swinging their arms. I can't make out their faces, and something tells me if I could, they'd freak me out. I just hear them, chanting on a loop.

Red Rover, Red Rover, send Effie on over.

Nine-year-old me rocks back on my heels and readies myself like I'm heading into battle.

Red Rover, Red Rover, send Effie on over.

36

Mom and Tav are standing clear of the action, but I just . . . sense them.

I'm the last one called. Again. Even though this time, Red Rover was my idea. My grandfather Paw Paw had always said not to read too much into being called last, that they knew they weren't strong enough to take me until they were all together, but I still felt left out. So I always ran a little faster than the time before, and I always pushed my shoulder into them a little harder, even though Ashleigh said I almost broke her wrist once.

She's always the weakest link. In the dream I can see her hands shaking, even before I take off.

And then it's like everything slows down.

I'm running, flying toward my friends, and my twists are streaming behind me. (Even though I shouldn't be able to see that.) I'm like one of the knights in the jousting tournaments, charging with no fear.

I zero in on Ashleigh, like always. She was already shaking, but when we lock eyes, she actually starts to vibrate.

That can't be right.

"Don't let her in!" she squeals because she can't feel the way her whole body rattles. Because this is a dream and my mind keeps finding ways to make the memory worse.

The game goes on, and I veer toward Ashleigh and Tabor.

She's bracing herself and I brace myself too—but when I finally make impact, I feel like I'm smashing into a wall, not flesh and bone.

There never was any sunlight (at least not in the dream version of events), but now everything is gray. Including my friends.

When I crash into them, their locked hands shatter.

Literally.

Shards go flying, striking me all over.

That's when I wake up and, as usual, I actually have to remind myself where I'm at.

I'm safe. I'm in my bed. I just have to get my head straight.

Things are different now. Mama Theo and Paw Paw aren't

down the hall and I'm not a kid anymore. I'm living with the Philipses, in the house on the hill, off of Macleay.

I'm not in the park (and I'll never go back), but that's exactly where four kids will stay. They're still stone statues that I can't forget used to be flesh. They're still in that park and I can't get over leaving them behind.

I don't get why the dream is never completely true. It always shows me crashing into them (which didn't happen), and—until today—it never showed the mirage (which did).

I guess the truth isn't the point. Torture is.

That's when the guilt sets in.

My life is anything but tortured now. I'm the Philipses' kid, and I live on the hill. Sure, I can't have gluten or soft drinks unless I eat out, but I like the way they eat. And sure, when they took me furniture shopping, they said everything was totally up to me until I chose an antique-y wrought-iron bedframe. They got really quiet then, and Miss Gennie, Tav's mom, asked if I had a second choice.

It made sense later on when I found out what twelve-year-old Tavia had done.

The point is they adopted me. (Basically.) Now I'm in a bedroom three times the size of the one at my grandparents' house, and I get to share it with someone who shares everything with me.

That's what the guilt's about. Tav's who I should be focused on. The nightmare she's living, not the one I already survived.

So when I can't find my keys this morning, I try not to lose it. Not right away, at least. I tell myself I must've been more tired than I thought last night. I must've forgotten to put my keys on the hook next to the bedroom door.

I check the room's nooks and crannies. Twice.

Sprites.

"Calm down," I tell myself through clenched teeth. But Portland is a hub of sprite activity and I don't lose my keys. Ever. Not since Paw Paw handed them to me.

Plus. Well, this isn't the first time I've been caught in the middle of their game.

Red Rover, Red Rover . . .

I slide to a seated position on the floor.

Do not overthink this.

Except I can't help it. Everything takes me back to that park, and that might be PTSD, but this time it's warranted. Another sprite has chosen me for its mischief, and I'm taking such shallow breaths that I'm getting light-headed.

"Sprites aren't thieves because they always bring things back."

That's what Mom used to say. When I was younger and all my doll clothes disappeared one night and I was crying against her breasts, she said that to me in a singsong voice. It's one of those things that gets passed down, from parents to their children and then to theirs. Mama Theo wasn't Mom's birth mother, but she taught it to her just the same.

Tavia'll come back from the bathroom any minute, so I get up off the floor and check everywhere again. And I find my keys at the bottom of my swim bag.

I'd checked it at least three times already and I know I was thorough, so I stand there clutching them and feeling like there's a stone in the pit of my stomach. This is the type of mischief everyone pretends to find amusing so they don't have to think about the time sprites went too far. I know better.

Tav's brushing her teeth when I get to the bathroom. I keep my face as blank as I can.

"Find 'em?" she asks around her toothbrush.

I let them dangle from my fingers. "Swim bag. Must've forgotten to take them out yesterday."

She spells out H-O-O-R-A-Y instead of using the gesture and I laugh.

"Hoo. Ray." I echo, and let the keys clatter onto the counter. Grabbing my toothbrush, I suds up, distracting Tavia from my mood with a heartfelt compliment. "I see you, baby-soft heather-gray cowl-neck turtleneck, perfectly draped."

Tavia blows me a kiss through the mirror. If she's wearing it to cover the keloid, it's too flattering to raise my suspicions. That and few people in Portland know how she got the scar in the first place, but. Maybe she hides it from her parents. Or herself.

"Thrifted these," she says, giving her broken-in black jeans a pat.

"Noice." She's got hips where I don't, so the pants won't do me any good, but luckily we wear the same size shoe. "I've got next on those brogues," I tell her, and she nods.

That's when I catch a glimpse of my own reflection and genuinely wonder why I try.

"But this hideously dry skin, though," I say through a sigh. Tav nudges me for dragging myself. "A flare-up is the very last thing I need."

"It'll pass," Tavia promises and runs her fingers through my twists reassuringly.

I'm not so sure. I'm poking and pulling at my face and it seriously feels almost scaly. Miss Gennie's dermatologist said it must be eczema, but she said it like she didn't want to lose a patient for not knowing what it really is. So I've got what must be eczema, what most definitely is stress-induced (which is a diagnosis that works on legiterally anybody over the age of ten, I'm sure), and what is most certainly not a sign of being cursed.

Miss Gennie held my face in her hands and chuckled when I suggested that. But I wasn't kidding.

Mom's been gone eight years, and ever since she died I've wondered if I am. Even when I alone managed to survive the sprites a year later and people started calling me lucky, I found it hard to believe. Lately I believe it even less, and it's like my skin agrees: something is definitely wrong with me.

"Here." Tavia hands me a small bottle of olive oil and I mumble my appreciation before pouring a small amount into my hand and massaging it into my face.

I *will* exfoliate properly when I get back from the fairground tonight, no excuses. For now, oil hydration'll have to do.

The gargoyle is still on our roof when we leave, which explains Miss Gennie's parting instructions. First she wishes us a good day (like always) and then, right before we open the front door, she whispers something about "acting natural."

Like Tavia or I could draw any more attention to the stone monster on our roof. Her words just make it harder to walk nonchalantly to my car, especially when I can feel his granite eyes following us.

"I almost want to have some of the Ren faire guys over to study him," I tell Tav.

She grunts. Tavia's not a regular on the fairegrounds like me, but she's seen the cosplay gargoyles once or twice.

They're mostly young guys in silver paint, sometimes with prosthetics to extend their arms so they can mimic the perch, but it's far from enough. Tav's bodyguard has a presence I'm not sure we'd want to emulate even if we could, and that includes the gray guards who keep watch outside the hallowed Hidden Scales. Those are just more men in gargoyle costumes, but they're the "chosen." The ones whose entire storyline involves keeping the rabble from ever clearing the pavilion flaps. The Hidden Scales tent is made of cloth like all the others, but the flaps are double layered for extra security (and mystique).

Anyway. The gray guard isn't that much more convincing than the rest of them. Sure, they've got way more expensive gear (dyed leather wings, grills to make their mouths protrude, and gray contacts for effect) but now that I'm familiar with a gargoyle in the flesh (so to speak), nothing compares to the real thing. What can I say. Living beneath an actual stone behemoth has ruined me. The rest of the Ren world is as real to me as it was to Mom, but. Those guys are just strong men painted gray.

Tav and I manage to keep our cool until the monster's out of our rearview and then she looks back.

She didn't make any broken-down lawnmower noises or poke fun at the way my car struggles up the hill, so I didn't get to ask her when we can take that super-sweet ride she doesn't own. Our morning banter's totally thrown off.

"How do you think Dad's gonna get rid of him?" she asks.

"I have no idea." He's out of sight, but I glance back anyway.

"It's not gonna work," she says, and I incline my head. That's a given. I just hope he isn't considering hurting the thing. If that's even possible. "Is it weird that I want him to stay? Kind of? I mean, I only really hate him when Dad's lecturing me about the way he sticks around."

"Or maybe you only really like him cuz he pisses your dad off."

"You make it sound cliché, but at least it's not *me* pissing him off." And then, "Is *that* weird?"

In the three years that the gargoyle's been coming and going, I've gotten used to the sound of him settling in above my head. He's been with the Philipses almost as long as I have, and as far as I'm concerned, he just comes with the territory. Anyway, if he were offering protection to me, I'd want him to stay, too. How many people have their own personal bodyguard, let alone one literally chiseled from stone?

"It's not weird," I tell Tavia, and then it gets quiet and my pre-gargoyle morning comes rushing back.

I'm trying not to mention the "s" word, but eventually I can't stop myself.

When we stop at a red light not far from school, I say, "Hey. Have you heard of any sprite sightings lately?"

I keep my eyes on the road, but I know Tavia's looking at me. I avoid this topic like the plague, so there's no pretending this is normal. She knows there's a reason.

"The mirage again?" she asks. "It's just a game your eyes play on you because you spend so much time underwater."

She can be so optimistic when it's not siren-related. Like having a huge watery distortion in my vision when I'm nowhere near my tank or the pool is gonna be explained away.

"It's happened a few times since the park, right? And nothing bad's happened?"

"Yep." I seal my lips and nod earnestly. Only four of my friends ever turned to statues. The mirage *must* be harmless. Thanks, T. "Never mind."

We don't talk for the rest of the drive, and neither of us switches on the radio. It's the kind of silence a nerd like Tav might call "pregnant" . . . and hell if it ain't uncomfortable.

"Hey," I say when we've parked and the engine's quiet.

"Hey." She cuts her eyes at me, which is totally fair. I'm the one who made it tense, so I'm the one who has to make it better. I can tell by the way she waits patiently that she's not even upset. These are just the rules. Whoever acts like a jerk gets to stumble awkwardly around for the other's amusement or something.

"I just freakin' love you, sis."

"I just freakin' love you, too."

"So hey, wanna come set up with me after school?"

Sometimes when I'm lamenting my crappy skin and itchy scalp, Tavia compliments what she calls my "big, bashful eyes," so I widen them on purpose. Bat my eyelashes a few too many times.

"No foolin'?" she asks, too intrigued to comment on how I probably look like I'm having a seizure.

"No foolin'. Finna cross state lines," I say like I'm trying to get hyped.

Tavia squeals. "Today's the day!"

"Today's the day."

I'm not fooling anyone trying to play it cool, so after a moment, I squeal too.

~~~~~~

Ever since first grade, I've been a mermaid. For two glorious weeks a year, I've appeared at the Portland Faireground, a temporary exhibit reconstructed every year under St. Johns Bridge. But starting this year, Euphemia the Mer will be on display in Vancouver.

The big time.

It makes almost no sense that the permanent exhibit of the Ren faire is in Vancouver, Washington, instead of PDX, but sometimes you have to throw people a bone, I guess.

The important part is that Vancouver is home to the sacred tent of the Hidden Scales. And I'm getting closer.

Mom was a main-stage character before I debuted.

Minerva the Chosen. She was a pirate captain and she was so important that she was allowed entry to the Scales, where stories are born and decided. I thought that must be why I was given a story—a betrothal to the royal blacksmith's son—but Mom always said it was all me.

The audience loved to watch me in the Mer Cove. I mean, I get it. A little Black girl swimming—in a mermaid tail, no less! But when they were oohing and aahing and maybe gawking for all the most annoying reasons, I was working on my craft. I was earning my story. I was working on my breathing exercises during the off-season so I could stay underwater for ridiculous stretches of time. I was defying my introvert tendencies and smiling widely, learning to drape my body the way Mer Shirl did. The chain-smoking matriarch entranced me from the start, the way she would disappear from the Cove and turn up at the river's edge, half her body submerged like the water really was her lifeline.

The only mermaid at the faire for a long time, Mer Shirl got promoted to Vancouver when I was just starting out, and I made it my business to fill her fins. Every year for the beloved two weeks, I basked in the sun if it was shining and bathed in the rain if it wasn't, and no matter what the PNW weather had in store, I practiced sign language so I could speak underwater, just like Mer Shirl did.

I realize I'm white-knuckle gripping the steering wheel and ease back.

"It's finally happening," I say through a shudder.

I don't have to hide my excitement from Tavia. She's not part of this world, but she gets it. She's the only one who doesn't think it's corny, who doesn't feel the need to remind me I'm the only Black girl in the faire now that Mom's gone. She's the only one who seems to get that the fairegrounds are the one place it feels like Mom still exists. Where no one shies away from calling her Minerva, like Mama Theo always has. Even when Mom legally changed her name, Mama Theo insisted on calling her Minnie.

"How are we gonna put that huge tank together?" Tav asks, and her voice sounds just as energized as mine. I love it.

"Oh, we don't actually have to construct the tank itself, just make it home. Oversee the tech guys replacing Mer Shirl's with mine so the Vancouver Cove doesn't get cluttered up."

"Mer Shirl's retiring?"

"No, but—okay, you're not supposed to know this." I glance at her briefly. "I only know because I'm headlining now."

"Secret," she says. "I swear." Like I wasn't gonna tell her anyway.

"So Shirl's transforming this year, on opening day."

"Shut up."

"Right?"

"How? To what?" Tavia asks, rapid-fire, and I know I'm beaming. I can't help it. I wait all year for this, and now opening day is only two weekends away.

"A mage wedding."

"So, what? She's just not a mermaid anymore?"

"She's being enchanted by her intended, doy. She's becoming a land-liver, if you can believe it."

"I cannot. All her Captain Jack wannabes lavished gifts on her just to lose out to a magician. But the poor kids! They love that old bag; she's an institution."

"Right, but now they have me."

At that, Tavia turns to face me completely and proceeds to punch my arm excitedly, and repeatedly.

"Speaking of enchantments," I say through a flinch, pointing toward the glove compartment.

As intended, her attention is immediately diverted. Inside, she finds my kit and hands it over, settling against the passenger door to watch me prepare. If she were anyone else, my scalp would be on fire and my skin would feel parched to cracking. It's Tavia, though, so under her watch, I apply my scales.

I don't wear makeup—I've never beat my face to the gods or whatever—but I don't set foot on the fairegrounds without a hint of Euphemia. I won't be in the water today, and there'll be no audience, so instead of my appliqués, I brought along my scallop stencil and highlighter. Within seconds, Tav's cooing and wiggling in her seat.

"Not too much for setup," I say, dusting my cheekbones and temples a couple of times before handing the supplies back and gesturing for the final piece.

"Your potion, m'lady," Tavia says when she hands over the jewelry.

"Mer-lady," I correct her, and Tav bursts into laughter the way basically no one else ever does when I make a joke. At this rate, my face is gonna be sore from smiling.

I clasp the chain around my neck and then hold the mini apothecary jar between my finger and thumb. The label is yellowed, but the calligraphy is elegant. I can't help but sigh at the sight.

It's land-walking potion. A gift from Elric, so that we can spend time together outside the Cove. Anytime I'm not wearing one of my tails, I'm walking the grounds with my betrothed, wearing a simple white peasant's dress—and my bare feet.

When Mom gave me my first land-walking potion, I broke character. I was so shook by the suggestion that I gaped at her, reminded her how she told me only white kids are allowed to run around barefoot.

That was in the real world, she told me. "Out there," which is what she always called it. Like in our hearts we were always in the Renaissance faire, and only the two of us knew it. (Besides, the grounds are mostly plush, lovely grass, and I always end up back in the water.)

I uncork the bottle and take what amounts to four drops of sugar water on my tongue.

I'm ready.

The park is beautiful. The grounds are so green, they look ripe. Tech hands are wearing present-day electric tools in their belts, but underneath them are long skirts or men's boots that rise to mid-thigh.

I smile when I hear my name—Euphemia—and I sign a few greetings, like my voice isn't land-ready yet. (I always try to keep them wanting.)

Really, I'm looking for Elric. I spy his father's storefront, a polished wood frame with an open roof above the forge. Attached, the matching wood of a vendor's counter, and beside all of it, the blacksmith's tent.

There's a temporary addition to the wood-burned sign.

"And son," I read the cloth out loud. I'm holding my potion jar before I notice. "Elric's made second smith."

I always enjoy the story of Euphemia and Elric, but once I'm on the fairegrounds, I get downright swoony. I haven't even been to the Cove yet, but I grab Tavia's hand and take a spin around the fairegrounds. My excitement is only slightly deflated when I've snaked between the stands and tents and back and forth along the main way and there's no Elric to be found.

"I guess we missed him," Tav says.

"I guess."

"I bet he left something for you at the Cove."

I give her a smirk. She knows him almost as well as I do. Now that we live together, she's gotten to see every gift he's left on our doorstep and every letter I've received in the mail. It starts up about this time every year, two weekends before opening day. He always makes sure our paths don't cross, but Elric leaves notes, potions, or handmade gifts on our porch before stealing away into the night. They'll all come to live here, come opening day. I'll bring my cassone to display beside my

47

tank, a gorgeous carved and polished chest for my keepsakes. Or dowry, technically.

"Should we go check the Cove?" Tav asks, her brow cocked to entice me.

"In a minute. First things first."

I don't think Tavia's ever been to the Vancouver grounds, and there's something she has to see.

"This is the Hidden Scales," I tell her when we're standing in front of it. "This is the tent where everything's decided. It's the epicenter of the faire and our stories."

She takes in a breath and it feels so appropriately reverent that I can't help looking at the pavilion with her, taking it in from top to bottom like I haven't seen it a thousand times before.

The scallop trim around the circular top, the thick green stripes against the white canvas.

"It's so . . . modest," Tav almost whispers.

"Yeah."

"But like . . ." Her forehead creases when her eyebrows do.

"I know," I answer. "There's something about it. It's nothing compared to the queen's double-belled wedge tent with the elaborate awnings. I mean, size-wise, it's barely bigger than the fortune-teller's." I gesture down the main way, and neither of us look. "But this one has a skirt of fog. This one has secrets. Secrets Mom knew. And one day I will, too."

We stand in silence for a moment or two, letting the cold fog pool at our ankles. There's definitely an ambiance that comes with the thick white smoke constantly coiling around the tent's base. It makes me wonder whether there's anything inside but a rickety table, a ledger, a quill and accompanying ink, and a fog machine.

Even in the off-season, I don't dare peek inside. Some things are just sacred.

"We'd better get to work," I say after one final sigh, and Tav seems just as reluctant to leave as I am.

We both glance back at the striped tent, but only I see it.

Only my view is interrupted by an annoying (and worrisome)

water mirage. The distortion blurs the space just in front of the flaps, and keeps me from looking away for a moment.

I grab Tavia's hand, but I don't mention it.

The sprites have never come to the fairegrounds.

As far as I know.

No. Eff that. This is my safe place.

Nothing bad happens at the Ren faire.

V

TAVIA

My dad doesn't hear Effie and me come home. I know because he doesn't change the channel until we've locked the door behind us, walked through the foyer, and are starting up the stairs. They curve away from the living room, which opens wide to the left of them, but we can still hear the TV.

It's some prime-time procedural now, but I would recognize the previous jingle anywhere.

Lexi on a Leash.

My foot connects with the stair in front of it and I almost trip, but I don't stop climbing. Not even when he's suddenly standing at the bottom.

"Hey kids, have a good night?"

"Yeah," Effie answers, slowing down. I can feel the way she looks between us, like she doesn't know which way to go.

"Everything on schedule for the big day, Effie-dee?"

F-E-D, get it?

She's smiling now; I don't even have to check. In her phone, Dad's saved as CeeBeeAy. It's their thing. A dad joke turned nickname that earned him one from her.

What I wouldn't give for dry skin and a pitiful past that makes fathers reach out instead of holding me at arm's length.

I'm biting the inside of my lip so I don't crumble. I don't want to be this person who thinks horrible things about my sister just because she has something I can't.

I don't want to be this person, period.

In my bedroom, I lean against the closed door for a moment and close my eyes even though I never turned on the light.

I'm high on the hill, but I listen for signs of water anyway.

Nothing.

If pitiful's what I'm going for, I feel like nothing less when I collapse onto my bed, fully clothed, in the dark.

"Gramma," I whisper. Or maybe not. My vocal cords vibrate but only faintly. "I wish you could hear me."

My eyes open, but it doesn't make much difference. The space above my head is so dim I can barely make out the crisscrossing beams. Even the light outside the balcony door comes in dark enough to look almost blue.

That feels melodramatic even to me.

"I just wish you could tell me there's a way out of this," I whisper into the bluish darkness as though it's deep water. "I don't want to be estranged from Dad like you were. I don't want him to think he's better off without me. I don't want him to love Effie more than me."

I don't know when I started crying, but it only makes the hurt worse.

"I just want a normal voice."

But that isn't all. I also want to know why—if Dad hates sirens so much—he was watching Lexi. Of course, I know why, or I think I do.

Lexi's respectable. She's found a way to silence herself—or accepted law enforcement's way, which is to wear a call-dampening collar at all times.

I guess I could always do that.

I close my eyes again, but the blue is there, too. Only heavier somehow. There's a feeling, too—a sensation of buoyancy, like I'm really underwater, somewhere in the middle of the deep. My whole body gently bobs and sways, and it's like I'm back at Natural

51

Bridges in Santa Cruz, riding the tide and barely needing to tread water. And something tells me the longer I stay here, the harder it'll be to get free.

It's like schoolwork when you're tired. If I have a paper due the next day (because I procrastinated) or a presentation or I need to study for an exam, I can't devote time to thinking about how tired I am or it'll get worse. I'll never get the momentum back. Better to get up and move around. Shake my legs, get some fresh air.

That's what I do. I get up off my bed, wipe my face, and head for the door.

Effie and Dad aren't on the stairs anymore, but they're not far. I hear sounds of family and feasting from the kitchen, but I don't investigate. I consider looking for my mom, asking her what I can't ask my father; whether she knows anything about how to find Gramma's voice so I can get rid of mine. But if Mom were on my side in any of this, I figure she'd have said so by now. So I speak to no one and head right back out the door.

On my porch, I breathe in the night's chill. I pull the cold vapor into my lungs and look up and down my street before heading into the well-lit night. When I'm heading further up the hill, I glance back to see the house and our iron fence, and he's there. The gargoyle. The claws that make up his feet are curled around the attic's spire and it just really doesn't look comfortable, balancing all those muscles and limbs and wings on something that looks like it should break beneath his weight.

Maybe it's easy to look steady when you're made of stone. Maybe if he animated right now he'd fall.

That's when his head turns, slowly. Steadily. Like it's on Mama Theo's lazy susan, something mobile and separate from the rest of him.

I wish I hadn't checked to see if he was there, but I'm glad I stopped walking before I did. Now that I've taken the time to really look, he is not the kind of hulking, menacing, nightmare-inducing creature I want chasing me down. I just want to get some fresh air. I want to get further into the hills, up an incline, away from the asphalt and streetlights, up the steps that lead between the trees and over the mulching groundcover. There are paths all through the neighborhood; they're frequented by joggers and by cyclists with bikes so thin they almost look flimsy, their wheels so narrow I can't imagine how they have any tread at all. But right now I'm standing in the middle of my street, not blinking because the gargoyle hasn't. His head is still turned toward me and his chin is sitting on his shoulder like he can keep this up all night.

"I'm just going for a walk," I say out loud. Can gargoyles hear well? How effective are stone eardrums? So I hold out my hand, flat palm facing him. Which is how I've seen people command dogs to stay, not the way I would sign to Effie. I don't know whether that offends him, but he turns his head forward again and I guess that means I can go.

I'm up the street, onto the beaten path, and halfway up the concrete steps when I sit down. There's a light on the street above, where this path lets out, and it shines down on me and the grass and the bramble and my own street below.

The Pacific Northwest is very season-fluid, and even though it's spring, the chill hangs persistently in the air, nearly visible. I close the gap between my chest and my knees, aware of the strip of skin left exposed between my cuffed skinny jeans and my brogues.

The last time I was up here at night, I wasn't alone. I'm not sure I wanna think about him, but I guess Priam is as good a distraction as anything else.

We came up here once or twice during the whole three months we were maybe-together. I'm less and less clear on that as time goes on, whether we were officially dating and I'm supposed to call him my ex. Now I think of Priam as my almost-ex, but that sounds like we're together until I find a painless way to break it off. And I was definitely not the breaking-it-off party.

I was with Priam when the sprite touched my hair. We'd gone to a park near his house that evening, and I was sporting French braids.

"Can you teach me how to do that with mine?" he asked across the space between our swings.

"How to what? French braid your hair?" I must have asked with an obvious skepticism because he angled his head at me and mocked my surprise.

"Yeah," he said while we laughed. "I feel like I can pull it off."

"Priam."

"Tavia."

I remember my face getting all warm then, and for a moment even though I couldn't stop smiling down at the woodchips beneath the swings, I had to fight the urge to touch my neck. I wasn't self-conscious about my keloid around Priam, and it wasn't always my siren call flaring up, I told myself. A girl could get flushed because a cute boy said her name just right.

And then my ear was against my shoulder, one of my braids yanked so hard I heard my neck crack as it yielded to the tug. I might have yelped, but it was so high-pitched and sharp that it didn't really sound like me. Priam told everyone he was sure it'd come from my sprite admirer and I couldn't be sure it wasn't true. Ever since then, I wear my hair up when I visit parks, or elementary schools, or basically anywhere kids—and therefore sprites— might be. And Priam liked those hairdos, too.

"See, high buns are for me, man buns should be directly at the back for you."

"That's so expected, though," he had argued, touching the mole above my collarbone and staring at it like the black circle on my otherwise deep brown skin was emitting a Compel call of its own.

When I was with Priam, I sometimes wanted to use it. Not Compel, though. Appeal. If Compel bends someone to a siren's will, Appeal bends the siren to someone else's, even though she's the one in control. It's the call a siren uses to endear someone to her—that's the way my mom describes it, anyway. (She's the only one who does.) Basically, it makes the siren attractive to the subject, whatever that means in the moment. It changes the way the person sees her so they think *she's* been changed, and then it tells on the person. Like if I used Appeal on Priam, I would know how he wanted to see me, or how he wanted me to act or think in order to satisfy his idea of the perfect me.

The effect doesn't last forever, but it's still tempting—and not just with Priam. (Sometimes I think I should use it at home . . . but I don't need Appeal to know how my dad wants me to be.)

I hadn't liked anyone the way I liked Priam, and I haven't since. I think that's why, no matter how obvious he was about being into me, I always wanted him to like me more.

We were on this step up the hill from my house when I reached up and undid his hair, untying the strip of leather he used instead of a more traditional hair tie. He watched me the whole time and I didn't even mind his smug smile.

He had a mole, too, beneath his right eye, except his wasn't raised. It matched his dark eyes, standing out from his pink-beige skin just like they did, and it reminded me of some period drama where people gave themselves fake beauty marks. It was almost too perfectly placed. Maybe it was that—the perfection of his mole, his dark blond hair loose, the ends flipping and curling beautifully against his shoulders. The way he was totally comfortable and confident. All of it. It made me want to tell him the truth, and I thought it'd be easier if I brought up his trait first.

"Can I hear your bell?" I asked, settled on the step beside him, content to sit so close I could hear him breathing and see his pulse in his throat.

He broke into a smile and without breaking eye contact, dug the charm out of his pocket. This wasn't the first time a girl had asked to hear his eloko melody, that was for sure. But we were sitting close—like, almost intimately so—which meant I wouldn't hear it naturally, the way people do when an eloko first enters their presence.

Every eloko I know carries their melody in a charm like the one Naema wears around her neck, at least all the ones at Beckett High. They're gifts, usually given at a child's dedication or christening or some early milestone, and they're an eloko's prized possession.

Priam held it between thumb and forefinger and blew on the bell. I don't know if that was just for effect, or if it really activated the charm, but a three-note melody tinkled into the air between us and enchanted the hillside up the street from my house.

"That's my song," he said, and closed the charm in his hand.

I was supposed to say that I wished I had one. That's what people always say to elokos. I'd planned to tell him that I *did*. I had a song. And when I told him, it was gonna be life-changing, for both of us. He was going to get this look in his eye, and just be in awe of me and my call and the melody of it. But I thought I heard gargoyle wings, and when I finally looked from the sky above to my street below, I saw Effie waving. My parents wanted us to come back to the house. They liked Priam—which for my dad was actually an understatement—but I was sixteen and wandering the neighborhood with a charming eloko boy after nightfall. They're only human.

My dad was happy while I was with Priam. All three months of it. At first I thought he was just glad I was dating like a normal girl, and then I realized it was because of what Priam was. Dating an eloko made me stand out in a good way, he said.

"Not like your signing." He'd been watching TV when I came in that day, too. Now Dad snapped his head to look at me, like he hadn't meant to say that part out loud. "It's not like I don't want you to stand out, Vivi, you'll always stand out to me. I just don't want it to be for things like made-up disorders and—"

"Being my grandma's granddaughter." I hurt myself nibbling on the inside of my mouth and held my tongue against the wound, the taste of copper growing stronger by the second. "It's not a made-up disorder, Dad. It's spasmodic dysphonia, it's a real thing. It makes people's vocal cords spasm, and it can change their voice or keep them from speaking."

"And you don't have it."

"Well. I also didn't try to kill myself, but that doesn't mean it's not written down somewhere in a file in Santa Cruz."

"It's sealed."

"Like I was during that 5150." And then I shut my mouth. Like, I curled my lips into my mouth and sealed that puppy shut because I could not believe how far I'd gone.

It always seemed so easy for him to forget—and it still does. Not that I'm a siren and how badly my life can turn out. That stays right at the fore. Somehow he forgets how horribly he responded to what I only did because I knew how much he hated my siren call. I was eleven years old, but he should've known better. So as much as I want to be fixed for him, I'm keeping my not-fake-but-not-mine diagnosis and my sign language, because I need them. At least until I get rid of my siren voice.

"I was just trying to tell you how happy I am for you, Vivi," Dad said. He'd let me get all the way to the staircase before speaking again. "Priam's a good guy."

I turned back and gave him what felt like a really weak smile. I liked Priam, too. I just wanted my dad to like me regardless.

Anyway, Priam's long gone, so nobody sends Effie for me tonight. I come back down the hill alone, and not even the gargoyle's watching. He's got his neck curved like he's trying to see the front door from his roost, and when he does glance up at me, he looks right back down, so I follow his gaze.

Elric was here.

There's an envelope on the doorstep, and it says "Euphemia" in beautiful, dark script.

Effie's waiting on the staircase for me when I come inside. Before she can sign or ask me anything about why I was out in the cold, I flash the envelope and a smile, and we race up to our room.

It's her thing, so we drop onto her bed to read it, even though she hates when anyone gets too close to her sheets. Which she shakes out and changes obsessively so as to rid the bed of her dry skin flakes (some of which are totally imagined, btw). Which means her bed is always made, unlike mine, so I get comfortable, leaning up against the wall and offering the envelope.

"You wanna do the honors?" she asks me with a smirk.

"Don't be stupid," I tell her. "You know I do."

I take my time opening the envelope, and not just because I'm being careful with the thick material that I'm guessing is meant to be reminiscent of medieval parchment; it's because of what a difference a sister makes. A few minutes ago, I was feeling pretty sorry for myself (with reason, I might add), and now I'm genuinely at peace. Effie didn't do anything but let me be part of her Elric and Euphemia story for a moment, but it's just . . . her. The fact that she's here. She makes it better.

"What does my beloved say?" she's asking, leaning forward and making me lean back to keep her from reading over the top of the pages.

"It's not a letter," I say, skimming quickly, and flipping through the few pages to make sure. "It's fan fiction. Handwritten." I gape at her. "So cute."

"So cute!"

"Is it one of the stories from the Hidden Tales?" I ask, still skimming, and referring to the online forum where the Ren faire fans elaborate on the stories and characters they love, or else write themselves in. Hidden Tales, like Hidden Scales, get it? You get it.

"I don't know because you're not *reading*!"

"Okay, okay!" I yank them out of the way so Effie can't steal the pages from me. "I'm reading." But I give her a moment to get situated first. She settles on her side, propping herself up on an elbow, and taking a deep breath before nodding for me to go on.

"*Euphemia had been away for so long this time. Her glittering tail-fins hadn't crested in more months than Elric had ever been without her, and now his chest felt heavy. His steps, too, so that he lumbered to and from the forge, his eyes cloudy with distraction despite the brilliant fire.*

"*He looked for her at the water's edge, and quieted the worry within that this time she would not return.*"

I glance up at Effie, whose eyes are closed for a moment, a small smile at the corner of her mouth.

"He thought he saw her once, but it was the moon reflecting on the water, and not the shimmer of her brilliant scales. Not the glisten of ocean froth against the dark beauty of her skin, not the light multiplying in the perfect orb of her midnight eyes."

That part makes both our eyebrows raise, Effie opening her eyes and exchanging acknowledging sounds with me. It's sad that it matters so much, but it's unusual for the fan fiction to thoroughly describe Euphemia or any beauty not directly connected to her tail. The fans can go on and on about Elric and his charm and his hair and his eyes, but somehow they never get around to waxing ad nauseum about Euphemia's physical beauty. She's a mermaid, that's the part they love. Some stories even go as far as whitewashing her, cursing her with some disease that made her skin pale, and Elric professing that he loved her all the more. Once, her spirit was taken from her body and placed in the form of another Ren character. She's Elric's OTP, so they can't outright get rid of Euphemia—but occasionally they get creative.

Effie usually shrugs and skips to a different story on the forums, and I bite the inside of my lip to keep from saying anything. We know why it happens; no need to belabor it with lengthy discussions.

"Fandom routinely sucks for us," Effie sometimes reminds me with a snort. But this isn't some TV-show ship, where we don't know the Black woman being slammed because she has the gall to be attached to the hero; this is Effie's story. She deserves to be adored. At the very least to be wished well.

I don't know him like that, but I love Elric for this.

"He never left the shore anymore, though his father sent young ones to collect him, to remind him of the forge, and his duty. But if Euphemia did not return, he sent word back to his father, then neither would he. Neither could he.

"And then one morning, she found him lying in the sand, the morning

tide dragging him a little ways and then nudging him back as though he'd been shipwrecked and washed ashore.

"Euphemia pressed his hair from his eyes, and when he opened them, the sunlight danced behind her and made her face a shadow. He only heard her gentle voice speak his name, and the sound of the waves was quieted. The wind was stilled.

"Euphemia the Mer had returned from the water, and Elric was righted."

The pages droop toward my lap before Effie and I sigh in unison, bursting into laughter a moment later.

"I mean, it was aight," she says when we're calm again, then she nonchalantly fiddles with her eyelashes as though searching for a wayward one.

"I loved it." I reorder the pages and hold them a second before handing them to her.

"Me, too." She breathes deep again. "Two weeks till curtains up."

"Are you nervous? About being promoted?"

"Mm-mm." Effie isn't reading the story again, I can tell by how her eyes move over the page. She's thinking about something; finally she tells me what. "No, I'm ready. I'll be right there with the Hidden Scales, where I've always wanted to be."

The Hidden Scales are synonymous with Effie's mom, Minerva, at this point.

"Your mom would be so happy for you," I say, and now she looks up at me. At first there's no expression to read, and then her trademark smirk.

"I know. She would."

I don't know if that means she wants to talk more or less, so I vacate her bed just in case it's the latter, pretending I need to stretch. I'm back at my own bed before she says any more.

"This year feels different, Tav."

"How do you mean?" I sit with one leg underneath me, I guess because it doesn't look like I'm trying to get too comfortable. I don't know. I just don't want to put her off whatever it is she has to say.

60

I mean, I get it. I can see how much has changed with her just in the past few months. All of her symptoms have escalated pretty noticeably, but I thought she felt better in the water, and she's been swimming more than ever. Anyway, I can't imagine she'd let her skin stuff sour the best part of her year, so I really need her to tell me what's wrong.

But she doesn't say anything. Then, what I think is going to be another smirk crumbles all of a sudden, and I'm too taken aback to know how to respond until she starts to sign.

"I miss her."

I don't wait for more, I explode off my bed and meet her in the middle of my room, throwing my arms around her.

"Eff," I whisper into her twists.

I'm so stupid. Of course, she meant her mom. What else does a girl want when her world isn't making sense, and she's coming out of her skin? When things are going right, and she's moving to the sacred fairground she's been longing after since she first heard of the Hidden Scales?

"Love you," I tell Effie, and she nods back but says nothing, just cries into my shoulder.

She isn't like me; her voice isn't cursed. For her, signing is a second language, something lovely that makes her more Euphemia. She's never done it because she couldn't bear to speak.

Honestly, I think my sister just broke my heart.

VI

EFFIE

I love my sister, but it wasn't that big a deal. People get sad, and it's not just girls who've lost their mothers.

It's understandable that I'm thinking of my mom. Of all the questions she never got a chance to answer. All the things I'll never know about her life. She used to say to me there wasn't much to tell. Both her birth parents died before I came along and she had no pictures of herself as a child, no stuffed animals or sentimental things. She took a million of me because of it, and unlike everyone else, she didn't leave them on memory cards. She printed them out, old school, made painstaking collages and photo albums she sometimes carried with her even at Ren faire. I didn't get it then, but now I do. She had me, that's it, and Mama and Paw Paw. And she was all I had too. Whoever my dad was, the three of them told me nothing. And believe me, I asked.

"Everyone else has a dad except for me," I'd said one afternoon not long after Mom and I had moved in with my grandparents. I was almost eight, and I got the feeling Mom had put the move off as long as she could. But now she needed the everyday help. I thought we'd have all the help we needed if she'd just find my dad. "You really don't know where he is?"

"I'm sorry, baby," she told me for the millionth time. She

pushed my twists out of my face and cupped my cheek. "He isn't coming back."

I could see how much it hurt her to talk about it, so I just hugged her with everything I had. I wish I could say I stopped with the questions after that day, but I didn't. Sometimes she said more. That things would get better as I got older, like the ache and the itching would just go away. She told me his name (James), and once while she was staring off into space she told me he'd said he "couldn't live a lie." That part we both wished she hadn't shared. Mama Theo had less patience after that.

"You're not the first kid to have a single mom, honey." She'd lured me into her warm kitchen with a homemade lemon-blueberry muffin, but while I ate and while she untwisted and retwisted some of my hair, Mama Theo had said her piece.

I'd told her I knew that but nearly choked on the moist cake.

"So why do you keep bothering your mama? Especially now, when you know she needs her energy."

The guilt trip was cruel. If everything the doctor said was true, I didn't have much time left with my mom. I didn't have much time left to solve the mystery of my father.

"I know," is all I said, picking at the muffin and dropping bits onto my plate. But just when Mama Theo was about to get up from her seat, I blurted, "I just wanna know who he is."

"I'm doing this because I love you, Effie, and I love your mama." And then she bent down, her soft, knobby brown fingers lying over my much smaller hand. Mama has a wide mouth, but we always tease that she has thin lips for a Black woman, and just then they were slipping from a melancholy smile into something more fierce. "Your daddy made his choice. It's his fault he isn't here, nobody else's."

When my vision got blurry and wet, it wasn't because of any mirage.

"Effie, you've got your mama, you've got me, and you've got Paw. That's three people who love you and would die for you.

63

Don't give up on the real life you've got to go chasing after make-believe."

I couldn't very well answer when I was trying to hide behind my twists. I wasn't just crying out of sadness. I was pissed. Mama's always been good at the tough stuff, at being the bad guy, but she can't keep her poker face forever. I thought she was gonna leave me at the table with the ruined remains of my muffin, but instead she spun my chair toward her and hugged me so tight, she pulled me right out of the seat.

I wanted to hate her, and Mama Theo sure has positioned herself as the one to despise. I never noticed until much later that neither Mom nor Mama gave me answers, but Mama was the one who got all the blame. It's safer that way, I guess. She's still here.

So what if I'm sad. It isn't the end of the world, and anyway happiness is no better. Happiness makes you stupid. No one should ever be too happy, I say, and I guess that's the worst thing about elokos. Or having an eloko like you. It makes you happy. Which makes you agree to do very stupid things.

Let me explain.

Earlier today, a week after the moment that really wasn't that big a deal, Isabella Apatu was late to history. A tinkle of bells signaled her arrival. If it hadn't been the bells, the smiles from my classmates would've done it. Being charming is kind of the eloko thing, but I can't help but genuinely smile with the rest of the class. Isabella's nice.

"*Before* the bell, Ms. Apatu," Ms. Fisher offered without having to turn around and see who came in late. Her reprimand was understandably taken as a joke by the rest of the class and some corny mofo wondered aloud which bell Ms. Fisher meant. Groan.

Isabella hunched over as she scurried to her seat, like the board was the screen at the movies or something. She's too tall for that to make a difference, but she's also considerate. She's not the tallest person in our year, but her height gets pretty regularly mentioned by Ms. Fisher because giants supposedly run in the teacher's family. Like everything but elokos and sprites, giants are pretty rare, and they're reclusive, so Ms. Fisher takes any opportunity to remind us they're in her lineage.

"Sorry, Ms. Fish," Isabella said, invoking the nickname our cool teacher gave herself. "It won't happen again."

Not that it would mean war if it did; Isabella is easy to forgive.

Ms. Fisher turned to us, having scrawled the words "CIVIL LIBERTIES" in huge block letters on the chalkboard. Every other teacher uses whiteboards, but Ms. Fish isn't every other teacher. For one thing she'd never just jump straight into classwork, so while she dusted the chalk residue from her hands, she asked, "So how is everyone doing today?"

Her bright-red nail polish matched her noisy collection of bracelets, both of which pretty perfectly capture Ms. Fisher's personality. She's that teacher who's clearly not the youngest faculty anymore but won't accept it, who is convinced she commands attention with style and flair but actually demands it with annoying attempts at camaraderie. Take for example her unsolicited response to her own question:

"How am I, you ask? Well, my son refused to get out of bed this morning and I'm working at a caffeine deficiency, so that's fun."

All us students murmured at once, our lackluster responses a mix of actual words and polite sounds. She nodded like it was coherent, her shoulder-length black blunt cut sweeping her popped collar as she spun half around like she needed reminding what she'd just written on the board.

"We left off last time talking about the Civil Rights movement, civil liberties, blah blah blah." (See, she gets it.) "So let's get a list up here, what are some examples?"

Any time hands dart into the air I keep mine clutched in my lap just in case it's contagious.

One by one, Ms. Fisher called on people then parroted their answers like she'd otherwise forget them even while she scribbled them on the board.

Freedom of religion.

Right to bear arms.

A quiet kid named Corey bravely raised his hand and I could tell by the look on her face this was a personal victory for Ms. Fish. She'd finally brought him out of his shell. It's been a pet project of hers all year, and she finally did it.

Before Corey could seal the moment of triumph for her, Kyle yelled in his place.

"The right to remain silent!"

Only a popular kid could get away with such a middle-school burn with a few laughs, but even Ms. Fisher fought to hide a smile as she feigned confusion at Kyle responding to Corey's name. After three years, most teachers have learned the hard way not to encourage the class clown, but Ms. Fish likes to say she's not threatened when we express ourselves. Under her watch, Kyle regularly goes into total derailment.

"Last night on PDXPD, they were cuffing this banger and—"

"Haven't watched it yet, no spoilers," she said, looking away to mark the end of the interaction and asking Corey if he could think of another one.

I could see the boy's red ears from my desk. If it were me, I'd have scratched my scalp like a fiend. What can I say? It doesn't take much for me to retreat, but Corey surprised us all.

"Freedom of speech," he answered, but it was a question, like maybe he accidentally made that one up.

"Yes! Thank you."

There would be no reasoning with her after this. She'd changed Corey's life for the better, and all without stifling Kyle's enthusiasm.

"Freedom," she transcribed. "Of . . . speech. You're all familiar with that one I'm sure. My son tells me I'm infringing on his daily."

Our polite laughter was proof that we know her six-year-old son has a great vocabulary, but not that great.

"So what does freedom of speech mean?" she asked.

"You can say whatever you want?"

"Thank you again, Mr. Brooks." Ms. Fisher tilted her head. She'd graduated to using Kyle's last name, signaling it was time for him to shut up. "As helpful as you're being today, I'm gonna say no. Not quite. But that's a common misinterpretation. Freedom of speech protects you from government retaliation for expressing personal views or just generally dissenting opinions. It's a much more specific context than many people think. For example, it will not protect my son from my wrath when he's a back-talking teenager."

Someone started a disapproving hoot and when everyone laughed, a few people took the opportunity to ramp up the volume to unwieldy levels. As usual, Ms. Fisher rolled her eyes and let it play out a few minutes before swatting at the guys making the most noise.

Any other day, I would have paid at least a portion of attention, even when Ms. Fish turned what could have been a brief class discussion into a fifty-minute audition for some high-school sitcom only she's old enough to remember. Today I had more important things on my mind. Like the return of Euphemia.

For the past week I've been going to the pool every chance I get—after school, weekend mornings *and* evenings, and once during lunch period even though I only had time to get in and do one lap—and it seriously helps. A week and a half more and I won't just be Effie swimming at the community center; I'll be a mer. Life underwater, my scalp soothed, my dry patches made invisible. A glimmer added to my skin so that when Elric's gift of elixirs lets me walk on dry ground I'm still something more than human. Camps are great, and reading fanfic on the Hidden Tales or eavesdropping on the forums helps keep me sane throughout the year, but I've been ready to burst waiting for faire season to come back around. This is when I feel like myself. When I'm not afraid to speak, whether out loud or signing underwater. This is where I don't feel nervous looking people in the eye and having all their eyes on me. I'm not Effie, the weird girl who survived the park, whose mom died and who never knew her dad.

I'm Euphemia, daughter of Minerva the Chosen, love of Elric the Second Smith's life.

Who wouldn't prefer that. So sometimes in class I practice holding my breath. I tuck my chin toward my chest and let my twists fall around my face so no one notices that my eyes are closed. I count in my head, first to ten before I breathe, then to twenty, then to thirty. And I count slow. I want to scare the crowd a little more each year with how long I can stay beneath the surface.

This year I want to be Euphemia as long as I can. I'm closer than I've ever been to the Hidden Scales pavilion, to joining Mom's legacy inside the tent where major stories are decided and judgment is passed, and underwater is really the only place I feel . . . right. I want it to last, this season more than ever.

So today, while Ms. Fish yammered on, I counted. Meditated on the tent. Remembered standing outside of it with Tavia, hypnotized by the green and white stripes. The wafting, rolling carpet of smoke surrounding it. I envisioned myself passing through the flaps and finally seeing what's on the other side.

And then the class discussion lifted to the foreground again and I did something between releasing my breath and trying to swallow it, effectively choking myself till water rushed to my eyes. My skin prickled with embarrassment. It would've been worse if it had deterred the class at all, but somewhere along the way they'd segued from civil liberties to siren-bashing, and I had no idea what was going on.

Ms. Fisher gestured at her words on the chalkboard, like reading them would help everything make sense.

"We all know what power sirens can wield with their voices. If you think about it, their words are actual weapons. Right?" She extended her hand toward a girl who I guess had something to do with how the discussion got there.

And just like that, I wasn't Euphemia. I was plain old Effie again, and I'm pretty sure everyone could hear how loud my heart was beating. So I did what I do best; I gulped and slid lower in my seat, wringing my hands.

That's when Isabella Apatu raised her hand. "When has a siren ever hurt anyone?"

Ms. Fish didn't miss a beat.

"There was a group of people who were very hurt by the actions of a few well-meaning sirens. We've talked about the damage they did during the Civil Rights movement in the '60s and how it almost derailed progress meant for the entire nation."

What.

"Imagine what would have happened if not for the whistle-blower who turned them in? One or two sirens could've given the entire movement a bad name."

"That makes sense," someone said. "I guess people were dedicating their lives to a cause that might not have been their own to choose."

This is why I hate school.

It would've been a great time for me to jump out of my seat and school everyone on siren calls and how just because someone's a siren doesn't mean they're manipulating people all the time. I could have said something about how this really biased conversation was erasing Black people from a movement they started, or how when sirens happened in other communities too no one seemed to think they were dangerous. I could even talk about Rhoda Taylor and how no one even knew or really cared whether she was actually a siren or not. They just went along with her post-mortem character assassination because she was already the worst thing she could be: a Black woman.

I sort of wished Tavia was there signing it all so I could interpret. But I was also really glad she wasn't. If she wasn't safe from the media and the gossip and the constant anti-siren culture, at least she wasn't in my pathetic excuse for a class. At least in IB they studied supernatural-inclusive history as told by the people themselves. Being in unimpressive, regular-kid classes means we're expected to take Ms. Fisher's word for everything, whether she's so much as met a siren before or not.

But Isabella spoke up again.

"I don't know, it just sounds like we're comparing hurt feelings to actual danger and suffering. That whistle-blower started

69

a witch hunt," she said, easy as pie. I can't imagine looking like I do and having said that—let alone what she said next. "The sirens that were outed could've been killed, some of them *were*. What about the fact that to this day sirens have a shorter life expectancy once revealed? They're disproportionately represented in arrests, traffic stops—and they make up a *tiny* percent of the population. It doesn't make sense."

I stared at her. Not because she's an eloko, either. Unfortunately, it was like Ms. Fisher hadn't heard a word.

"Listen." She propped a hip on the edge of her desk. She was all in now. If ever a movie was made about her impact through teaching, this was gonna be the watershed moment where she really woke us up. "I'm not condoning that. No one is."

Except obviously *someone* was, all the time.

"You're sort of mixing apples with oranges, but as far as the witch hunt goes, that's serious. We're talking about something that has been compared to Salem. It was a dark moment in our history. But if we'd never gone through that we wouldn't have ended up here, creating solutions."

The room was a mix of agreement and uncomfortable silence. At least I hope someone besides me was uncomfortable. I knew what "solution" she was referring to, I just hoped she wouldn't say it. But this is Ms. Fish.

"There are sirens who agree with me, you know. What's her name?" She snapped her fingers. "She's on that reality show?"

Lexi.

A few people plus Ms. Fisher said the name at once before someone blurted out how hot the woman in question is.

"What's important is that she wears a dampening collar of her own free will, so her call doesn't give her any unfair advantage," Ms. Fisher said. "And you know what? That's something I respect. Let's make the playing field level."

When she scrawled the words "SPEAK SIREN" on the board, a jolt went through my body. The next few moments, everything she said sounded strange—and not just because it was hot garbage. It was like my ears were packed, or like I was underwater. Her voice pulsed so that I could almost . . . sense it. When other people spoke, their voices were the same, except the pulses were distinct. I could tell them apart.

This was a new level of anger, sound distortion. Add that to the list of strange hallucinations and "probably eczema."

"I've heard you kids saying, 'Speak, siren!' in these halls," Ms. Fisher was saying, even though she absolutely had not. It's one of those things attributed to teenagers that nary a real-life teen would say. But the truth didn't matter as much as being extra, so she kept going. "I get it. I totally get it. We should *all* speak like sirens. Use our voices to make a difference, because *all* of them matter."

Ms. Fish nodded, letting it all sink in. She could only hope we understood what she'd done today.

If I were brave, I'd have asked Ms. Fisher when siren voices had started mattering. I'd have clucked my tongue or grunted the way Mama Theo does when something's so foolish, anyone with sense doesn't need it pointed out.

Tavia's right. Everybody wants to be a siren, but nobody wants to be a siren.

But Ms. Fish moved right along. She announced final projects and when outcries erupted around the room, we went right back to class as usual. Everything she'd said was totally okay. Nothing to be offended by. No reason for my hands to be clenched so tight.

I held my breath and counted.

"Now, I usually give you kids free rein, let you choose your own partners, buuuut," and here she tapped her index finger against her lips. "I think this time around we're gonna mix it up."

Of course we were. I released my breath and started again.

Ms. Fisher announced that she'd be assigning our partners, in order, of course, to move us outside our comfort zones, which would obviously result in some really groundbreaking projects and end-of-the-year illuminations. None of which sounded at all interesting until she put me with Isabella Apatu.

Isabella gave me a timid wave, to which I grunted, before we both pored over Ms. Fish's handout. Aside from four options ranging from guesstimating the next extinction (for instance, she said, imagine sirens going the way of the oracles and defend the claim using what we now know were historical indicators) to spotlighting sprites, it was rife with exclamation points and Ms. Fish-isms.

Throw wide the gate!

Spin history on its ear!

"Wow," I said when I was done reading. "That was like having her *in* my head. How genuinely upsetting."

I didn't mean to say my snark out loud, but it was worth it when Isabella burst into the most beautiful laugh.

Which is where the real trouble started.

In my defense, I'm only accustomed to Tavia finding me at all amusing. When Isabella asked if I wanted to try number four, I garbled some response while endorphins overwhelmed my brain. It wasn't until after class that I realized it had to do with sprites. The assignment I'd agreed to was about presenting the historical consensus on sprite character and activity, and then an argument on how often consensuses are proven or dispelled. By then, we'd already set a lunch date, and a little secret about me: the only thing more anxiety-inducing than having made plans I don't want to keep is facing the person and telling them I'd rather not go. So at the end of fourth period, I was as ready as I was gonna be.

In the universe's defense, it gave me one last warning in the form of a boundary-deficient stranger. The lunch bell had just rung, the whole class was scrambling to evacuate, so of course the new girl chose right then to come for me. Her name's Sarah, I think; she hasn't been here more than a month or so. Pretty sure she's in my English class. I've never really noticed her that much, but apparently she's noticed me.

"You're the girl from the park, right? Right?" she insisted, like she couldn't tell how every muscle in my body locked up. "You're the girl with the sculpture."

Not this again. Not today. (Or ever.)

After three years at Beckett High most people have gotten over the novelty of going to school with "the girl from the park." All these years after my flesh-and-bone friends were turned to statues, I hardly ever see creeps hiding out in the shadows with absurdly huge cameras anymore. Yeah, there were a slew of articles written about me when it first happened, things I read years later when I had "perspective," a word that Dr. Randall (the perpetually mellow therapist that Mama Theo and Paw Paw sent me to after Mom died) liked to use constantly.

I don't Google myself anymore, but sometimes when I hear the snapping sound of a phone camera nearby, I wonder if it's trained on me. If someone's selfie is just a ruse to capture me in the background. It's probably just paranoia (I hope it's just paranoia), but I've always been worried that someone would wonder what happened to the kid who got away.

"Keep your head down," Paw Paw had told me when I started high school. The first one had been a hard year for me. He and Mama Theo had finally talked me into moving to the Philips house, I was starting a new school and overwhelmed didn't even begin.

"Don't let anyone distract you," he said. "They say something, you keep moving."

At the time it sounded like typical Paw Paw advice: general and applicable to any situation. My mom always said he would make a great fortune-teller.

"Was your mother an oracle?" she would tease him when he'd offer up a simple, bland solution to a complicated problem. "We could really use you at the faire! Do Libra now."

But I kept my head down like Paw Paw said. I ignored the questions and the lingering looks and, gradually, people began to leave me alone.

It wasn't long before I actually liked Beckett, and I *loved* Tavia, so. It wasn't like I lost my grandparents, either. I moved to the Philipses' house on the hill the summer before freshman year so

I could go to the good high school (that was Mama's idea) and I got a sister, plus play-parents already inside the community who wouldn't be spooked by claims that I'm part sprite or something. (Because that turned into a whole thing.)

It almost didn't bug me knowing Mama Theo had another motive. That she hoped watching Tavia close up would show me how hard (and horrible) being different can really be. She expected my Ren faire life to fade, and she expected Tavia's parents to help with that. But I wasn't mad. She was right. (About Tav and me being good for each other.) If there's one thing Mama Theo approves of, it's Tavia. When we became a package deal, she couldn't have been happier. To this day she doesn't let me come home to visit overnight without Tav by my side.

Things have been good. For years now—recent flare-ups notwithstanding. It honestly feels like a long time since I was Park Girl and forum commenters were debating whether or not the lone survivor of the incident must be part sprite herself. So of course some clueless transfer student had to come along and muck it up.

She hadn't magically disappeared, so when I got my bearings, I ducked my head and quickly brushed past the girl en route to my locker.

A throng of students moved through the walkway, but I couldn't hear anything except the footsteps behind me. The same sound distortion from Ms. Fish's class quieted everything but a really distinct and identifying sound. I knew which steps belonged to my stalker.

And lo. When I turned around there she was, shifting from foot to foot, smiling hesitantly.

"Hi." Like we're homies.

"Do I know you?" I asked. I gave her a quick disdainful look before glancing obviously at my watch.

"It's Sarah," she answered, but it sounded like you spell it some super unique way, maybe with two dots above the first "a."

"I have English with you?"

I just blinked at her. She had the decency to look embarrassed, but not to leave me alone.

"Listen, I know you probably get this a lot, but . . . that sculpture at the park? You were there, right?"

I never can hang on to the shade long enough; even when the other person's out of pocket, I always end up being the nervous one. How does my skin look, can they see my scalp shedding, do they know what's happening to me—and will they please tell *me*?

"Wow," she said softly. "You look exactly the same."

Great. She'd been studying pictures. Probably read all the old articles, too.

"So"—I gestured in the general direction of the parking lot— "I've got this thing."

On cue, Isabella jogged up. "There you are!"

"We were supposed to meet at the flagpole to get started on some sprite surveillance for our final project," I explained to Sarah. In unnecessary detail.

She was undeterred. "I'm so sorry if I'm being rude! Listen—"

Here it comes. Because it's never as simple as wanting confirmation that I'm Park Girl. If they actually come up and talk to me, there's something that they want. Sometimes it's harmless. They wanna know if I visit. If I've read the memorial plaque. It can be triggering, but they don't realize that when they ask. Other times, it's gross. People used to shout questions they knew would change my expression. They'd ask about the moment it happened, whether the kids knew what was happening to them, if it was fast or slow. If they cried while their bodies seized up and their breathing stopped. Right when I'd involuntarily turn (because that's what you do when someone says something super unacceptable; you check to see who would have the nerve), click. Another photo of Park Girl looking confused and frightened.

I wasn't interested in whatever Sarah with the weird pronunciation had to say.

"We've got that thing I mentioned, sorry." I gestured at Isabella this time, whose head swiveled between us.

"Really quick, though. I just wanted to know if I could inter-view you?"

"No."

"For my blog?"

"No."

She kept going, talking faster. "It's kind of a Keep Portland Weird type of thing, just highlighting what makes our city cool. It would take thirty minutes tops."

"No." It was weird how that word, my discomfort, my desire to be left alone meant nothing. If I were a siren I could've shut her down. Of course, there'd be consequences. . . .

"You're Sarah, right?" Isabella interrupted, catching both of us off-guard. "Welcome to Beckett."

While she talked, Isabella toyed with her necklace. Which Isabella never does. And like anyone would, Sarah bit.

"I *love* your necklace. My mom's friend is an eloko. She's actu-ally my godmother."

Wow. But Isabella didn't flinch. (Why would she.)

"Cool," she said, all smiles. "You want to hear it? My melody?"

The girl couldn't even say yes. She barely nodded. She'd forgotten about me and the park and the statues.

When Isabella was sure Sarah was paying attention, she held her charm between her fingers, took a breath and blew. As if on cue, the rain stopped. It actually stopped and the clouds parted, the sun almost blindingly bright.

If she's smart, Sarah with the weird pronunciation will squeeze more than a few blog posts out of that little exchange. In the mean-time, Isabella swept me away, getting me through the parking lot and to the passenger door of her truck before I even realized I couldn't drive.

I was suddenly incredibly exhausted, a side effect of unwanted attention and one I'd almost forgotten about.

"Thanks for that," I said as we buckled up. "The charm. And everything. I know you guys don't play your melody for just anyone."

76

"Seriously, no problem. It was mostly self-preservation, honestly. I had to get out of there before I cut her."

"Whaaat?" I couldn't stop smiling. "Elokos don't lose their tempers."

"No, never." We'd pulled out of the parking lot and Isabella's truck felt like some sort of warm and safe cocoon.

"We should go there, though," I said, and maybe I'm adding details after the fact, but I probably slurred my speech. I remember snuggling down into the leather-wrapped bench seat and grinning like a weirdo.

"Where?"

"To the park." I was still feeling really good about the decision, despite saying the words out loud. "Everybody and their mom has cashed in on my being Park Girl but me. The least I can do is cop an easy A out of it."

"You don't have to do that," Isabella contested, but I felt really happy and she'd just basically saved my life (or something) and it felt really good to think maybe I could have *two* friends. So I insisted.

"No, honestly. It's not even that big a deal." (I can't stop imagining myself drunk-slurring; it's the only way this makes any sense.) "Plus, can you imagine Ms. Fish's response? She'll think she empowered me to face my past or some nonsense."

To her credit, Isabella seemed really hesitant. She kept looking over at me, furrowing her brows, making thinking noises.

"It's got verified sprite activity," I said like I was dangling a treat in front of her.

"Are you sure?"

"Yep. Completely."

Or at least I was. Right up until we arrived.

Because now Isabella's parking, and as if to say, "Effie, you magnificent twit," the clouds have just opened up again.

I could say I don't wanna get my hair wet, except everyone knows I'm a swimmer. But I'm not a mermaid right now. I'm not fearless or confident. My twists aren't billowing out around me, moving in the water like they've got a mind of their own. I'm Effie on dry land, with dry skin.

What am I thinking?

Maybe if I take my time, we'll run out. Lunch period is only so long. But that'll only draw attention to myself. Isabella's the kind of friend who'll genuinely wanna know what's the matter, and as much as I like her, she's not Tavia. I don't want to try to explain something I know she won't understand, especially when being here is entirely my fault.

We won't see anything anyway. We're teenagers, it's super unlikely that we'll be catching any sprites in the act today. Then again . . . maybe we'll get "lucky."

I get out of the truck and so does she. After we flip our hoods over our heads, I take the lead for some reason. Like I can protect her because I did such a great job of that last time. I ball my fists while we crunch along the path.

There's no use trying to prepare myself. I haven't been back to the park since that last game of Red Rover, but at least I'm with Isabella. I feel guilty, but I'm trying to take some strength from the fact that I'm going there with an eloko. I'm no good-luck charm, but maybe she is.

Whatever you do, Effie, do. not. scratch.

Man, if Dr. Randall could see me now. He'd know I'm not ready, he'd read it all over my face and my posture and all the other "nonverbal cues" he used to point out when I refused to talk. I used to think I had him all figured out too but now I can't decide, if he were here, whether he'd tell me to keep going or take my time. I'm flip-flopping with every step.

It'll be fine.

This is a mistake.

It'll be fine.

This is a mistake.

The ground isn't paved or anything; it's as wonky as any forest floor, but right now it feels like I'm walking on uneven legs. Like wearing one of Mom's heels around the house because I knew I'd fall if I wore them both.

We pass the swings and the covered slides and the gated stretch of grass that dogs have trampled into mulch. I lead Isabella past a tree with these low-hanging branches perfect for climbing, and into the stretch of giant sequoias. It's instantly gloomier in the shade of the towering trees, which makes it like catnip to kids. And therefore to sprites.

It's more like the dream than I hoped.

When we hit the small clearing in the midst of all of the trees, I see it.

I mean, I see *them*. We both do, they're impossible to miss. Rain falls on their stone heads and rolls down their faces like tears.

Four kids frozen in time. They've become a popular stop for Portlanders and tourists alike, number six on the top ten "must see" list according to the *real* Keep Portland Weird site. How there are five weirder things I can't understand. Chalk that up to the hipster tendency to downplay things you want people to notice. It works. People come to Triton Park and take pictures with the statues, flashing peace signs while they pose with kids who won't grow up. (I'm sure there's a criticism in there that Tav would be able to explain. I just get sick.)

I guess it helps not knowing what it's like. Nobody gets turned to statues aside from these four kids, and no one's ever come back. So people imagine it however they want, whatever makes them feel the best.

It's like being asleep.

Suspended animation.

Nirvana.

But nobody knows. Over the years, I've managed to both avoid this place and stalk it online, and not a single theory makes sense. Not to me. I guess because I saw the life in their faces right before it happened.

The memory is swirling now, and the guilt. I was the one who wanted to play Red Rover even though we didn't have enough players. Everyone was fine with hide and seek, and then I'd gotten bored waiting to be found in the trunk of a tree. Ashleigh thought Red Rover was a dumb idea and I said she was dumb and the others told us to shut up and just start playing.

It was Ashleigh, Mere, and me against Wiley and Tabor; then it was me against the four of them. The last thing I remember is running toward Ashleigh and Tabor before everything went black. When I woke up I was at home, wearing my pajamas and tucked into my bed. It was almost like it had all been a dream until my grandparents came in with distraught faces.

They didn't say anything about sprites. That came later, but never from them. Paw Paw just broke the news of how my friends would never sleep in their beds again. After that everything's a blur.

I was asked a lot of questions by police officers about what happened. I was nine and scared and none of the answers I gave satisfied them (not even the watery blur mirage thing I told them about)—until I mentioned offhand how Ashleigh and I had seen a sprite that day. That's when they perked up. The questions suddenly became all about how often we had seen them, the sorts of mischievous things that they did and encouraged us to do. No one had ever heard of sprites turning people to statues (or "sculptures" if you're really insensitive and forget that kids don't start life in some art studio), but to be fair, there are a lot of things about sprites that we don't know. Maybe that's why I'm here with Isabella.

The memorial plaque is wearing a new wreath. (I cyber-stalk, remember?) Purple hyacinths this time, that's Ashleigh's mom. She must have been here recently, or else she sent Ashleigh's younger brother. Who's now her older brother, I guess.

When I step closer I can still see their shocked expressions, and that really cuts me. All of their eyes are wide and almost bulging, hands are gripping hands so tightly. I notice things that I hadn't before, that I can't really see in the pictures people take. Like how Tabor's toes are slightly off of the ground.

"Are you okay?" Even though Isabella says this in a hushed voice, I still jump a little.

"I'm fine." I pull back the hand I'd extended toward Ashleigh's floating ponytail and scratch my scalp. "It's just."

"Weird?"

"Yeah."

Isabella hangs back a bit and lets me look some more, and we both do a few laps around the perimeter looking for something that we can't name.

My breath catches a bit when I see one particular tree. The sequoia with a gaping trunk. It's split open like a tent. That's where I was hiding, before I got impatient and made everyone change the game. I make my way over to it and touch my hand to the crumbling bark. Isabella has followed me, and is rounding the other side when the rain comes down with more insistence.

"C'mon!" she says, waving me into the trunk for shelter.

I remember thinking it was big enough to house cookie-making elves, and I guess my kid brain didn't completely exaggerate. There's room for at least two more full grown people once we're inside. Isabella and I are standing on pine needles and cones and there's a spot on the inner bark that has the names of two people who think they'll be together forever. I turn in a small circle, look up, and blink as something flutters down from the black abyss above our heads and onto Isabella's thick mass of wavy hair.

"Hold on, you've got something." I gingerly dig between the thick black strands.

"What is it?"

I hold it out into the faint light from the outside world and then drop it immediately. "Oh."

"What?" Isabella flips her hair off of her shoulder. "What was it?"

"A butterfly wing."

Then Isabella yelps.

"What?"

"Just, be gentle, okay?" She's polite as always, but it creeps me out so I show her my hands.

"I'm not touching you."

"You are one of them." The words come whispered on the wind.

I can still see out the gaping trunk, so I know there's nobody there.

"There were five, not four."

We spin around, knocking against each other, looking for the owner of the voice.

Coming here was a bad idea.

"Red Rover, Red Rover, send Effie on over."

Nope. No, thank you. It's time to go.

"Red Rover, Red Rover, send Effie on over."

"Someone knows your name," Isabella whispers to me, and I know she's scared from the eloko trill in her voice. It's not a siren call, but it's indisputably charming and Isabella never puts it on. Not even to try to talk her way out of trouble, not even when she's late to someone's class other than corny Ms. Fish.

"A lot of people know my name." That's what it means to be Park Girl. I thought all that was over, the shutterbugs and people with questions and just plain creepers. But this is different. This is a sprite. It has to be.

"Send Effie on over!"

"I heard you," I say into the hollow. "We don't wanna play."

"Five came, four stayed." The voice is whisper-light and it swirls all around us. I haven't heard a sprite speak since I was so young that now I can't be sure it's even a real memory. For something that only talks to children, it's blood-chilling.

Next to me, Isabella pulls herself together and addresses it in a businesslike tone. "Please tell us what happened here the day she played the game."

"Do the trick." Whoever it is, they ignore an eloko entirely. That's something you don't see every day. *"We like the trick, do the trick."*

"What trick?" I ask. Then it comes to me. Maybe they weren't ignoring her after all. "Play your bell for them, Isabella."

She does, and her melody fills the trunk of the giant sequoia with beautiful sound.

Not good enough. *"Do the trick. Do the trick."*

"I don't think that's what they meant," Isabella tells me.

"Red Rover, Red Rover, send Effie on over."

"They want us to play with them," Isabella whispers like it's an option.

"Yeah, that doesn't go so well," I whisper back. "No, thanks."

"Do the trick. Two will come, and one will stay."

"What?" But instead of an answer, I hear a breath behind me and twirl around. It's a sighing sound, but really forced. Dramatic for no reason. This thing is like the Cheshire cat. I guess sprites can fly, or levitate, or I don't know, float. It's behind me, then above me, then somewhere out in front.

"That sounds like a threat." Isabella's understandably terrified. This was a bad idea.

"Do the trick again." It's a broken record. *"We like the trick."*

"What trick!" I feel a little bolder now, even taking a step toward where the voice seems to be now. If this is how everything ends, I'm gonna get an answer, at least one. At least this one, since I haven't cracked Mama Theo on any other mysteries in my life.

Nothing.

We wait for five minutes or so. Then five more. Just like that, the sprite's gone, and I'm itching so bad I can barely see straight.

Like always, I get nothing.

Isabella and I make a rush for the truck, driving back to school in bewildered silence.

"So, um. Good progress?" she asks before we go our separate ways.

"Yeah," I say. "Right."

Little do I know, I haven't even gotten to the worst part of my day.

VII

TAVIA

I'm always holding something back. Even in gospel choir, surrounded by the network, I've always been afraid of the power in my voice. I just didn't expect Naema to be my salvation. (Especially not since I found out she and Priam have been talking.)

The small ensemble choir competition was today, and we placed with distinction. We're good, but it also may have had something to do with our last selection, during which Naema laced her voice with her eloko trill. The trill—which sort of sounds like an eloko's melody is in their voice box instead of their bell charms—is illegal, and I wasn't even mad. Sure, I gave an Effie snort when the judges chose not to dock points the way they're supposed to (since it's a talent only elokos have). I might even have rolled my eyes when they included a special note about our choir's "diversity," and clearly weren't referring to Tracy. But even our own lead vocalist, Porsha, couldn't get over how lovely it sounded when Naema upstaged her, so whatever. It felt nice to unleash and know for certain that no one was listening to me.

So thank you, Naema. For once your showboating worked in my favor.

I also missed an entire day of school and social media to attend, so no talk of trials or hair tutorials. Just music and the beauty of technically illegal eloko trills. Overall, a pretty chill day.

I'm still humming the post-applause reprise of our closing number when I come into the bedroom.

Immediately something's off.

Effie's not a day-sleeper, for one, and she's passed out on my bed. The "my bed" part isn't normal either, because she's so self-conscious about her dry skin shedding on other people's things, but more than that, the balcony door across from my bed is open. And the gargoyle—who's usually on the roof and usually at night—is right there. Right outside the door.

The gargoyle is *on* the balcony, and I am staring at his back.

I'm standing frozen near the bed, almost to Effie but afraid to take another step. My heartbeat has leapt into my throat and I feel like a bullfrog. If he didn't hear me before, he has to know I'm here now.

After three years I didn't think I was actually afraid of him, but then he's usually much further away. Right now, he's facing the street, his massive back and wings taking up the entire door-frame so I can't see anything else.

I can't stop looking at the wings. I don't know what I was ex-pecting, feathers made of gray granite, I guess? That's not how they look. They're solid, except for what looks like veins spin-dling through them, like enormous bat wings. It's the first time I've seen them open like this. He's perching like always, squatting down and balancing on his fists and feet. Claws, I mean. But his wings are open.

Something is wrong with me because I'm coming up behind him. Not smart.

"Excuse me," I say because I'm not entirely sure what you're supposed to call your gargoyle bodyguard. Sir? Gargoyle? Gargy?

He shifts, his eyes still on the street but his chin turned in toward one of his shoulders. He's listening. Now would be a good time to decide what the heck I'm doing. Probably best not to keep approaching a beast made of muscular stone.

"Is something wrong?" I ask.

Nothing happens for a moment, and then his left wing goes

down, pulled back like a curtain. Like he's allowing me out onto the balcony. I hesitate for a moment, afraid of the damage it can do if, just as I step out, he snaps it back up. Because he's been waiting three years to tease me onto my own balcony so he can slice me in half with his wing. (Sometimes I make fun of myself so that, feeling sufficiently foolish, I can woman up and move on.)

I step out onto the balcony like it's made of hot lava. My back grazes the doorframe when I pass between it and the gargoyle, and then I'm outside in the dewy afternoon that already looks more like early evening.

If he stood upright, he would be almost twice my height. His left wing comes back up slowly, without a sound. So that I won't be afraid. Can gargoyles sense fear?

I'm studying the side of his face. It's actually chiseled, putting to shame all those dudes on my mom's romance novels who aren't literally made of stone, but it doesn't look human. His brow is an awning protruding over his deep-set eyes. His cheekbones are sharp peaks beneath which the rest of his face slopes into a narrow chin. I can't see his neck because his mountain of a shoulder is rolled forward, starting right below his chin, and the stone columns he thinks are arms are long enough that he's pressing his weight into his knuckles.

The attic balcony is not much more than a balconet, to be honest. Two steps and you're at the rail. Now that I'm out here with him, I doubt it can support both our weight. Except he seems so graceful, at once heavy and weightless, the way he looks when he's perched on the spire, balancing all of himself without destroying my roof.

"Is something wrong?" I ask again after I clear my throat. "It's just that you're not usually here so early. Or here. Outside my door."

He doesn't move or answer. Strong, silent type.

"And Effie's in my bed." I gesture toward the door and my fingers graze his wing. It's coarse, like the rim of the swimming pool

86

at the community center. It reminds me of the time I sat down to watch Effie swim only to get up and realize I'd snagged and ruined the seat of my favorite swimsuit. "Do you know why she's in my bed?"

More silence.

"Does it have anything to do with why you're not perching on the roof like normal?"

Nothing.

"Am I in danger?"

Nada.

"'Kay. Thanks a ton. Can you lower your wing so I can go back inside before my hair gets any bigger?"

His left wing slides down and behind him again.

"Awesome."

When I'm back inside, the wing is up and he's playing silent gargoyle shield again.

On my bed, Effie looks like she fell from the sky. One arm crosses her stomach and the other one's dangling over the edge. She's twisted at the waist, her legs against the comforter, both knees bent. Her head's turned toward her side of the bedroom, but I can't see her face. Her twists are a veil.

I don't know why something feels so off about all of this. I sit gingerly beside her and press her hair back, notice the darkness around her eyes. That's new. Like trying to remove smoky eyes with just one makeup remover cloth. Something's bound to get left behind. Only Effie doesn't wear makeup.

The hand on her stomach catches my attention, the way the tips of her fingers are swathed in silk. It's the same on the other hand, and I take that one into my lap and study it. When we were bored freshman year we used to drip Elmer's glue down our fingers and let it dry before peeling it off like we were removing a second skin. But this is something else.

I take the silk covering her middle fingertip and peel it off. Whatever it is, it shimmers. When the light catches it, it's not just white but an iridescent green and even a pale pink. There's something faintly imprinted on it, but it's too small a piece to tell what.

I catch another loose end of the silk and peel it slowly, trying to unwind more from around her finger this time. It's coming undone and staying intact, and I'm feeling pretty pleased with myself—until I realize it's not going to stop.

The white is gone from Effie's finger but whatever I'm peeling keeps right on coming, like it's a magician's scarf. It's Effie's skin, except that when it lifts it isn't brown, it's silky and translucent like the stuff I took off her fingertip. I pull and pull, but slowly, watching Effie's face to see whether she can feel this, to stop if this is hurting her.

This isn't eczema. It isn't flaking. It's coming off like a second skin and by now it's long and getting wider. I've peeled down the center of her palm and am following it up her forearm, watching the color glint in the light.

It finally stops. When I'm nearly to the inside of her elbow, the silky second skin separates and all that's left in its wake is a slightly lighter strip on Effie's arm that already seems to be disappearing.

What. Just. Happened.

What is going on?

Why am I sitting beside my sleeping sister with a lap full of her skin? I hold it up, try to straighten it so I can . . . what? Examine the skin I just ripped off of her body? And it's coiling now. The peeled skin is curling up in my lap.

I have no idea what to do with it. I just know I don't want Effie to see. Not immediately.

She groans and one of her knees connects with my hip. When I wince, she wakes up with a start and I sweep the collection of curling skin onto the floor.

"Hey," I say, squeezing the hand I just peeled. "Everything okay?"

Effie looks super confused.

"Hey," I say again, dropping my chin so I can follow her eyes with mine until she looks at me. Then I smile like there isn't a little pile of her beside the bed. "I didn't expect you to be home."

"Why not?" She presses the heel of her other palm into her eye and pushes back into my headboard. "Pool's closed for league stuff tonight."

"No, I mean because your car's not here."

"Wait." She stops, looks back and forth. "What? Then how'd I get home?"

"That's . . . a good question. I have no idea." I laugh. "I was wondering the same thing."

"Isabella drove, I think."

"Ah."

"No." She stops again, leans forward. "That was at lunch. We went back to school."

"Okay . . ."

She springs off the bed now, her twists flying wild, her feet narrowly missing the curly peel pile. She goes to her bed for some reason and then she turns back toward me. Her eyes are still roaming, but she's nodding, too.

"Oh," she says, calmly. And unconvincingly. "I went to see Mom."

A little moan escapes me. Effie hasn't brought it up since, but I can't stop thinking about her uncharacteristic breakdown last week. I feel stupid for thinking me and Eff and maybe even our weekly dinner with Mama Theo and Paw Paw were enough to keep her steady. Even though they've always seemed to. I can't ignore that something's different now. Now she's visiting her mom alone, at the cemetery. And maybe that explains the dark eyes and day-sleeping . . . but it doesn't even begin to make sense of the husk.

"Okay," I say again. "You drove there?"

"Yeah. But. I don't know if I drove back."

Something is up. I should get my parents. Or Mama Theo.

Paw Paw's probably a better call. He's always been quiet, like Effie, and maybe she wouldn't be pissed at me if I only told him.

He wouldn't say much, and he wouldn't expect her to, he'd just open his arms and let her climb in. He doesn't bake like Mama Theo, but I always think his hugs must feel like warm cookies taste, and I wonder if my Gramma would be good at either if she was still here. All I know is I'm not gonna take the chance of making things worse for Effie, even by telling Paw Paw what's scaring me. Not yet.

"It's okay," I say for some reason. "We can go get your car."

If I'm not gonna involve any adults, it would be totally reasonable for me to at least ask her why she drove to the cemetery but didn't drive back, but I just peeled half an arm's length of skin from her body, and I don't know what happened at her mom's grave or whether she goes there often now. So plan B is to just act like this is all fine.

"Come on," I chirp. "I'll borrow the sports car!"

~~~~~

Effie still looks a little ravaged around the eyes, but it's fading. I'm having a hard time deciding if that's a normal thing that happens, since at the moment everything is being compared to the silky skin pile beside my bed. That's the threshold for something's-wrong-here; next to that, everything else seems legit.

She doesn't seem at all excited that I've gotten permission to drive my dad's roadster even when I take the curve at the bottom of the hill a little quicker than I need to. We whip around it and stop just in time for the STOP sign and she just keeps twirling one twist around her finger, her head pulled toward her chest.

I'd planned on telling her what happened in our bedroom, the way I peeled the skin from her body, but looking at her now, this seems like a bad time.

"How was school?" I ask, and then grit my teeth. We're the same age. Why am I asking parent questions? "I mean, I missed the whole day. Anything good happen?"

She's not listening. Her eyes are moving like she's reading

something, and every so often her finger stops twirling the length of her hair and she does a sort of half shake of her head, like she almost agreed to something and then changed her mind.

Whenever I get lost in some thought, my mom starts saying purposely ridiculous things to see how long it takes me to notice. She thinks it'll lighten the mood, but that's never how it feels. It's more like the person who should know—who you really hoped would—thinks whatever's eating you alive is a joke. So I don't lighten the mood for Effie. I shut up. I don't even mention how the gargoyle she didn't notice on our balcony is now overhead. Every time we stop at a light or a stop sign, he gets a little ahead of us and I can see him through the windshield. Like he already knows where we're going.

When we get to the cemetery, I have to drive inside. I know the way to Minerva's plot, so I don't say anything to Effie, whose chin is trying to burrow into her chest completely now.

Faire season has never been hard before, but maybe I should've known getting promoted would send Eff into mourning. Maybe getting closer to the Hidden Scales is exciting, but maybe it's bittersweet. Maybe it's a reminder that her mom won't be there. I haven't asked because I never want to be the one who brings her down, but now I feel horrible. I've never lost a parent and I guess I should've been more supportive of her keeping in touch with Dr. Randall. He told her that grief can be cyclical. Years pass and you travel around the circle, thinking you've left the hard part behind, until you get back around and it knocks you down again. Time does not heal all wounds. I almost touch the keloid on my neck. I don't know if time heals any.

"There it is," I say, like Effie doesn't see her car up ahead. When I pull up behind it, she undoes her seat belt and I turn off the car and follow suit.

"What are you doing?" She's twisted in her seat, looking at me through the narrow part in her hair.

For a minute I just sit with my mouth gaping like a carp.

"I just . . . it doesn't feel right coming and not paying my respects."

"I already saw her today. I just wanna go home and go to bed."

"Eff." I grab her hand before she's out of the car. "If you're not okay . . . maybe we should talk to somebody."

"Who do you wanna talk to?"

"I don't know." I shrug and look around like I'm searching for the answer instead of trying to figure out how to say it without upsetting her. "Paw Paw. Or Dr. Randall?"

"Yeah, maybe *we* should see him, he was always really good about calling out joy bullies."

"I'm sorry," I say, shaking my head because I realize I'm about to make this worse. "I just. Have no idea what joy bully means."

"It means I'm not broken just because I'm not happy at the moment, Tavia. Gimme a break."

And she slams the door behind her and charges to her car without even glancing toward her mother's grave.

"Yeah, Tavia," I whisper to myself while I click my seat belt back on and start the car. "Gimme a break."

So much for being the savior sister who's gonna fix everybody's problems but her own.

Following Effie's boat of a car is no fun in my dad's roadster. He only lets me take it every couple of months or so and I've totally wasted the honor. Just wait till we get to the hill, that's when the real torture will begin. I'll be lucky if I get to drive the actual speed limit.

Turns out I get a stay of execution on creeping up the hill in a car that wants to burn the road. When we get there, lights appear in my rearview and a mangled warble of an abbreviated police siren makes sure I know they mean me.

I cross the intersection behind Effie and then pull to the side of the road while she starts her struggle up the hill. She's off in her own mind today. She probably doesn't even notice I'm not behind her anymore.

There's no reason for me to be nervous. I know sports cars get more police attention, but there's no way I was going too fast, not behind Effie. And I know the registration's current; my dad's not an idiot. But maybe a taillight burned out and he doesn't know. Anyway, if the officer would just get out of the patrol car, he could tell me what the problem is. But he doesn't. Not right away, anyway. He's leaning over, focusing on a screen.

Deep breaths. I haven't done anything wrong.

The driver's door opens. Finally. And the passenger side, too.

For some reason, this is a two-man job. They both approach the car, but the driver takes it slow, letting his partner get to the door Effie slammed when she got out of it. Knuckles rap on the window because it's Portland and my dad doesn't let me take his car without the hardtop being on.

I let the window down and crane my neck to talk to the officer whenever he bends down.

Crap. I know this guy.

It's Priam's dad.

"My partner's gonna help you on the other side, all right?" he says.

That seems ridiculously pointless, calling my attention to say, hey, look over there, like purposely trying to shake someone up, but whatever. I'm not a cop. The important thing is he doesn't seem to recognize me. Maybe he never saw me on a big hair day, or maybe Priam didn't talk about me. We were only together for three months. There aren't any homecoming pictures of us in their house, that's for sure, since we never ended up going. But my parents knew him. I must not have made an impression, because Officer Blake nods, covering the window track with both hands before giving it a squeeze and standing upright.

There's a rap on my window now and I let it down.

"Is this your car?"

"It's my dad's."

"And where's your dad?"

"He's . . . at home, I guess."

"You guess?"

"I mean, that's where he was when I left."

We just look at each other for a moment, but I lose the staring contest and tighten my sweating palms around the steering wheel.

"Something wrong, miss?" he asks me.

"I don't know." And then I glance over to the passenger window again, but Priam's dad has moved away.

"Are you nervous about something?" the officer asks.

"No."

"Why are you looking at the glove box?"

"I'm not, I was looking out the window, I just didn't know where the other officer was."

"Don't worry about him, you can just talk to me."

For some reason, now I'm remembering that viral picture of the Black boy tearfully hugging the police officer. It happened years ago, when I was still in Santa Cruz, but when we moved to Oregon, I heard about it even more. Portland loved that picture. Because that's what's gonna heal the world. If we're the only ones crying, offering unlimited love no matter what's done to us. No matter how obvious our distress and discomfort.

First that picture made me feel sick, and then it pissed me off. Not the boy. Not even the cop in the picture who wasn't crying. But that Portland claimed it. Would not shut up about it. Plastered it all over social media so I couldn't go anywhere without seeing it. Like that's the world we all live in up here, separate and different and artisanal. Self-congratulatory, like I'm not terrified right now because I've been pulled over and my ex-boyfriend's dad doesn't seem to recognize me and no one's asked for my license or the car's registration and there's hot flint where my voice box used to be and Effie isn't here to sign for me. Because if I refuse to speak or if I say even a single word whatever happens to me next is my own fault. It's always our fault. On some level, my dad must believe that, otherwise why am I always getting lectured on what I could have done differently? When I get home—if I get home— this is gonna be my fault.

Why didn't you show him the registration, Tavia? Not, why did he pull you over in the first place? Not, why didn't he ask to see it?

Why didn't you apologize, Tavia? Not, you didn't do anything wrong. Not, I've been there before.

Did you speak respectfully? Did you prostrate yourself, did you lie facedown and show submission, did you make them feel like they were overseers rather than civil servants?

Did you do something to make them afraid of you?

Did you have to be born a siren?

"Can you step out of the vehicle, miss?"

"Wait, what?"

"Step out of the vehicle." He stands upright and moves back to give me room. His hand is probably just used to resting on his holster but it makes my heart hiccup, and then it's thundering in my chest.

"Don't you want my information?" I ask, wary of the burn building in my throat. I've opened the door and am stepping out like it's my first time outdoors.

"My partner'll get it," he says, nodding to Priam's dad, who ducks into my dad's car and pops the glove box.

On the sidewalk beside us, someone's watching me out of the corner of their eye as they walk by, and they're taking their sweet time getting past.

I'm humiliated. I could describe it in some lyrical detail like it's an essay assigned by Mr. Monroe. Try to hone in on what it feels like internally, the way there's not enough air inside my lungs and my hair feels wild and unwieldy, like some sort of spectacle even though I loved this hairstyle this morning. I could talk about how hot my face feels, so much so that the heat vibrating in my throat is almost indistinguishable from it now. I could say the tears hanging on my eyelashes aren't just from embarrassment and fear.

I'm sure there's some sense to be made from the fact that I'm still thinking about Devonte Hart, too. How he went missing a couple years ago, presumed dead when his white adopted parents—the same ones who orchestrated pictures of their sobbing Black son holding on to that cop probably against his will—drove the family van over a cliff with Devonte and his five Black siblings inside.

There are thematic connections to be made, I'm sure.

But this is simple. One moment, I was driving home, worrying about my sister and the otherworldly nature of having watched her skin peel away from her body while leaving perfectly intact skin beneath, and the next I'm standing outside my car still completely clueless as to what I've done wrong. The passerby confirms it; I'm the problem. But I refuse to cry.

"I need to go," I say, softly, and the officer in front of me cocks his eyebrow, leans in the way I expected him to.

Now I lift my chin so that I'm speaking directly to him, so that there's no way the sound of my voice won't wash over him, sliding around the curves of his face, filling his head so that it's the only thing he hears.

I unfurl the heat in my throat and it shoots down the center of me, simultaneously pooling in my core and coursing through me like it's taken the place of my blood. This is the part I love, the part I rarely let myself feel before Naema made space for me this morning—when it plumes all the way back up. When I was little, I imagined it like a Victorian collar growing up my neck and folding open beneath my chin like flower petals. I didn't know about silencing collars then, so the one that I imagined made me feel beautiful.

The police officer is staring because, before the call, there's a breath that draws them in. They're always waiting by the time we speak, to see whether we will Appeal or Compel them.

But I don't want to be something else today, not even if he just thinks I am. No. He'll be the one to change, not me.

"You had no right to stop me."

There's a tremor in my call like there always is. Like sound and sonar blended. In front of me, the officer's brow breaks and we've traded places. His earlobes are flushing, red overtaking the former paleness of his skin.

He swallows and his Adam's apple bobs in his throat.

There are a million reasons I shouldn't be doing this.

We're out in the open, no choir voices to mask me, to make anyone unsure of the source if they hear my call at all.

I've been crying out to Gramma to teach me how to silence my siren voice, and between the choir competition and this, I've used it twice in one day.

But it feels so good, like I've been in a vise until now, like I've been walking on eggshells for the world and now I'm standing flat on my feet.

"It's time to let me go."

He blinks and I take it as agreement.

"I need my dad's registration," I remind him, the tremor gone but still reverberating around him. That'll take a few hours to dissipate, but by then I'll be long gone and he'll take credit for this.

"I'll get it." His hand's still on his holster, so I guess that's just where it rests. Maybe he's forgotten the gun beneath his fingers is a deadly weapon, but I won't. Not when (siren or not) Rhoda Taylor reminds all of us how real the threat of harm really is. Not when every Black person knows, cops face no consequences when they decide to pull the trigger.

Why should we be the only ones charged with taking care?

"Don't rest your hand on your gun. It's frightening."

His hand slides away from his holster before he goes back to the car. Officer Blake is sitting with the passenger door open, doing something with that monitor again. My officer puts out his hand while he's speaking to Priam's dad and then, when the seated officer hesitates, my guy makes an impatient gesture.

Hand it over.

He does, but then he looks at me. Even after my officer crosses between Officer Blake and me and hands me back the registration, wishing me a good night, Priam's dad doesn't blink.

He didn't hear my call. He doesn't know what I've done. What I am. He was in the patrol car. His partner just had a change of heart.

I'm back in the car when they pull out and pass me, but Officer Blake's still watching me and I can't look away.

He knows.

VIII

EFFIE

When I pull into the driveway it's like waking up from a daze. I put the car in park and set the brake, only to find I'm hazy on whether I really just did it and end up staring down at the parking brake for a while.

This is weird. All of my movements feel like I'm underwater, but not the way I'm accustomed to. I'm not in the euphoric, welcoming, safe embrace of water that soothes my skin on impact. No, this is the kind of water that weighs you down; it feels like shackles, keeping me from moving at the right speed, and it slows my brain too. I tighten my hands around the steering wheel, but it doesn't change the feeling, the tough leather cover just threatens to leave marks on my fingertips.

Better that than having my head snatched bald, as Mama Theo would say. (She's very evocative with her idle threats when she tells me to always keep my eyes on the road. Which, technically, I'm pretty sure I did.)

I open the door and put my left foot on the driveway, like I'm checking to make sure it's there before I commit to moving the rest of me. But I just sit. My hands are tingling and it's got nothing to do with the huge patterned steering wheel on Paw Paw's old cruising car. My skin feels like it's vibrating. I flex my fingers and stare at them until my eyes play tricks and it looks like I've got more than ten digits. It doesn't go watery, though.

No mirage. That's the good news.

The bad news is I'm sure now. Everything's starting up again. The questions and worries I've had since a sprite got more mischievous than they usually do and left me the only survivor in Triton Park . . . well, they're rushing back. It means all the anxiety I've felt between then and now has just been good old-fashioned puberty. The anxiety I feel *now*—the kind you feel when you magically get from a cemetery to your sister's bed—is something else. It's nausea inducing. Chest constricting. It's finally really believing I might be something else.

Something more than Effie.

Maybe something like Tavia. Maybe that's why Mama Theo wanted us to be together so badly.

Tav's the first thing I remember clearly after driving back to school with Isabella. The look on her face when I woke up in our room. It was the same basic look my grandparents gave me when they broke the news that Ashleigh, Tabor, Wiley, and Mere weren't coming home. And, if I'm honest, it's not a look that says "yay, sis, you're just like me."

It does, however, scream "something's wrong with you"; there's no question about that.

I'm losing time again. And the last time that happened I also lost four of my friends forever.

"What am I missing?" I ask out loud. No one's around to answer me, and I cannot for the life of me remember what happened today. How I ended up in Tav's bed. What happened at the cemetery.

I'm still in the car, one foot out on the driveway. Maybe time slipped again, because now I don't know how long I've been staring at the Philipses' garage door. However long it's been, I'm only just now recognizing the Fighting Duck in one of the small square windows.

That makes me smile a little. It belongs to Mr. Philips. (Or

CeeBeeAy, when it won't annoy Tav too much.) He may have left Portland for a while, but his U of O fandom is as rabid as anyone else in the neighborhood. I've gotten used to the football para-phernalia being everywhere—on luxury car bumpers, dangling from rearview mirrors. There's even a duck on a flag outside the neighbor's front door. If you'd asked me, I'd say it cheapens other-wise ritzy possessions but—

The duck handle.

I actually gasp, the memory hits me so fast. I'm at my mother's grave and a man in a three-piece suit holds a duck-handled umbrella.

But things are out of order.

Something else happened first, before I saw whoever the man is. I was alone in the cemetery when I put my hand on Mom's gravestone.

MINNIE CALHOUN

1973–2012

Mother, Daughter, Friend

"Minerva the Chosen," I'd said, like it was written right there with the rest of the engravings, the way it should have been. "Pi-rate Captain. Mother to Euphemia the Mer."

That's what she would've wanted, but Mama Theo had re-fused to budge. I shouldn't have been surprised; I used to hear the two of them arguing, usually in the days leading up to open season. She'd tell Mom it was make-believe. A dream. That we couldn't live there, and that it wasn't fair.

I know I was too young to understand "grown folks' business," but what she said didn't make sense. She despised the Ren faire (still does), and it had nothing to do with how unwelcoming it can be to nonwhite people, because she never once came along. I finally had to stop making sense of it and just chalk it up to a Mama Theo quirk. One I ignore just as quietly as Mom did.

"It's already stolen years away," she said to my back once when

I was heading for the door. It stopped me in my tracks, that time. I'd just lost my mother, and my grandma wouldn't let it go. It was a low blow. Like the faire had anything to do with Mom getting sick.

I know what the faire is, that it's something more than make-believe. Mom understood. She didn't give it up when Mama asked, and neither will I. It's the one thing I still have that was both of ours. I'm the daughter of Minerva the Chosen, and everyone on the grounds remembers her the way I do.

Mama Theo's lucky the faire only lasts two weeks a year.

On the hill, outside the Philipses' garage, I'm still sitting in my car, and I'm getting frustrated.

Something else happened at Mom's grave, but it's like my mind is refusing to tell me what. Like it's so used to people keeping me in the dark that it's turned on me, too. My memory's taking me everywhere but back to Mom's grave. Back to the man in the three-piece suit, with the duck-handled umbrella.

I'm squeezing my eyes shut, trying to remember something from the cemetery.

It was cold and damp, misting like the watering system in the produce section of the grocery store, so I couldn't tell whether it was raining or I was caught in a dewy fog.

I try to focus on Mom's epitaph, to feel my hand against it.

Instead I'm sidetracked. I think of the words I know by heart, but end up distracted by the knowledge that they're more than concise; they're brief. Like her life.

"Why didn't *you* tell me?" I'd asked Mom's headstone while the fog rolled through the cemetery. It had been thicker at my feet when I first arrived, but now it was all around me, making it hard to see even a few feet away. "Didn't I deserve to know?"

My scalp had started itching by then. One of my own twists leapt up like someone had flung it. The way Isabella's hair had moved at the park. When we spoke to the sprite.

"Is that why? Did you think it would scare me? If I knew he really was a sprite?"

I balled my fists at some point to keep from destroying my

102

scalp, but it was no use. I was surrounded by moisture and it still felt like it was on fire.

"You know that's been my fear all along, right?"

I pushed my hood back and went to town on my scalp, raking my fingers back and forth, not caring about the snags. I kept talking to Mom the whole time, even though it felt like it was getting worse. Even though there was no chance of her answering any of my questions now.

"I lost my period a few months back, Mom, is that a sprite thing? Did I get that from his side of the family, or is it stress-induced like my maybe-eczema?"

I didn't say the last possibility out loud. That maybe it's something like what she had. That after all these years thinking my skin and scalp and vision problems mean I'm supernatural, maybe I'm sick. Because losing my menstrual—that seems like something that could be ovarian, and cancerous.

By this point, I'd dropped to my knees in the damp grass. My twists felt like they were standing up at the roots, and it wasn't because I was tousling them.

That's when a voice came out of nowhere. Not a sprite hissy-whisper. A man. Just a normal professor-looking white dude in a three-piece suit, holding a duck-handled umbrella.

"Are you—"

"Yes!" I yelled from my knees. "I'm the girl from the park, it's me, can you leave me the hell alone?"

"You look like you're in trouble, and I wanted to make sure you're all right." He was quiet for a moment, but there was plenty of activity to fill the space. "I don't think I can just leave you alone here, dear. Should I call someone?"

I can't imagine how I looked. Scrubbing my scalp, my nails planted, my twists flying, and bent so far forward that I was curling into my torso. I wasn't going to stop anytime soon.

And then he touched me.

He must have. Something made me turn away from my mother's grave and stare at him.

He was still talking, or his mouth was moving at least, but I couldn't hear any sound. That's when I saw the umbrella with the wooden duck handle. The expensive suit covered by a trench coat. He was all put together, but he looked like he was gonna come undone.

He looked terrified. His eyes were on my hair at first, which only added embarrassment to the intensity I was already feeling. How bad did my skin look? Could he see the dry patches? The holes I must be making?

I untangled my fingers from my hair and he followed them with his eyes. Maybe the tips were covered in blood, I thought. It would explain the horror on his face. But when I looked down, I couldn't see my fingertips at all—and not just because my hair kept curling in front of my eyes.

They were covered in something silky white. All my brown skin was, and then the man was walking backward, away from me.

Whatever he was saying without a voice, it was obvious by the way he shook his head and stumbled that he didn't want to help me anymore.

But I was furious by then, so I didn't look away. We stared and stared and stared until I felt the anger draining out of me, starting at the crown of my head. It was draining, draining, pulling down like oil through a funnel.

And then, everything went black.

That's it. That's where the memory ends. A blackout, like the ones I used to have as a kid. The one I had in Triton Park the day my friends became statues.

In my car in the Philipses' driveway, the steering wheel has finally succeeded in dimpling my fingertips. But I can't let it go. And I can't ask any more questions. Because now I don't want to know.

The garage door opens in front of me, the Fighting Duck disappearing with it, and Mr. Philips's roadster drives past me to pull in. Which is the first time I realize Tavia should've been right behind me and wasn't.

Finally, I get out of the car. While Tav comes over, my breath catches and I pretend to be smelling the sweet, damp air. The gargoyle is above us, and when I look up, I realize he isn't perched. Just hovering. From there, he must've been able to see right through my windshield.

"Where've you been?" I ask Tavia, repeatedly glancing up at the monster floating above us because I can't help it. "Did you hit traffic or something?"

She's been crying. It's like dominos with us. I can't see tears in her eyes without getting them in mine. It pushes anything I was feeling before completely aside. I just want to take care of my sister.

"Tav," I whisper, stepping closer.

I got pulled over, she signs to me.

She doesn't make eye contact, which is usually my move, and I know she's shook if she's not able to talk. Freshman and sophomore year I got a lot of hall passes to come interpret for Tavia. (A lot.) I was summoned at least a couple times a week at first. Half the time I was pretty sure she was just doubling down on her dysphonia cover, but I understood. She needed me, even if she wasn't actually suppressing a call. Last year the summonses dropped to something like once a week and then a couple times per quarter. This year, I've been called from class just a handful of times, and I could tell they were all genuine requests. Until the time after she and Priam broke up. They were assigned a joint oral presentation and she lost her voice. But maybe she really did have to suppress. Believe me, she is not about that drama, and standing at the front of the room with Priam and me? She was pretty humiliated at the added attention my translating brought to her, and that was before he was seeing the eloko chick from her choir.

And now this. You don't have to be a siren to be shaken after a run-in with the cops, but it sure must make it worse. Black and female and a siren is just layers upon layers of trauma. Tav's so good at breaking it down, but she rarely does unless it's just her and me. One time I said she's too young to deal with this, and she said we don't get to be. I wish she had a blog or a YouTube channel or someplace all the people who need to be educated could go and shut up and listen . . . but of course I'm also glad she doesn't.

"Are you okay?" I ask, pulling her back in the garage so no one—and nothing—can see us. "What happened? What'd you do?"

"Nothing. I was driving while Black."

"Are you kidding me?" I don't doubt her, it's just the first thing out of my mouth. I'm surprised and I'm not, because even in what most people consider a liberal city, the small Black community always knows better. Portland is whiter than America, and that's a fact. But as jacked as it sounds, it's different when something like this happens to someone you care about.

Tavia doesn't sign anymore.

"Did you get a ticket?"

A shake of her head. Well, that's good, right? Especially if it means one less lecture from her dad. But instead of acting relieved, she's tense. What isn't she telling me?

There's a lot I'm not telling *her*, so I don't press it.

"I'm glad you're okay," I tell her, and wrap her in a hug. She stiffens for a moment, and then I feel the pressure of her head on my shoulder, my twists caught beneath it. If it were anyone else, I'd immediately want to pull back, but this is Tavia. She can touch my hair.

"You're okay, right?" I ask, pulling back to look at her. "Nothing else happened?"

"The cop . . ." She stops signing, falters with her hands still in the air.

"What?"

"Priam's dad," she whispers, before going back to ASL. *"He's the one who pulled me over."*

Yikes. What are the chances?

"Maybe it was personal then?" I ask. "He's probably way too involved in his kid's life." His precious eloko kid, I mean.

"Not personal," and she shakes her head. *"Trust me."*

I don't, because I have eyes and ears and I know how smug the parents of elokos can be.

"So he let you off with a warning?"

"Yeah. A warning."

We let out a weary exhale in unison and head into the house.

~~~~~

When the weekend finally comes, I'm out of bed and gathering my swim bag before I'm even fully awake. The last couple days I've decided it's best to just go on like normal, especially when I'm so close to Ren faire starting. If I can just make it one more week, just to opening day, everything'll be better. I'll be Euphemia again, and I'll have Elric. And everything'll be fine. Before I leave the house, I grab a necklace that reminds me of him.

Wallace's at the community center when I arrive. I spot him before he knows I'm there, so I take advantage. (He's fun to look at.) It's interesting, watching him watch people. He does more of that than swim, which is why I thought he was a lifeguard at first. That and he's always wearing the clothing that they sell at the front desk, and who but staff would do that? Maybe he just likes routine; I've known guys like that.

As usual, he's wearing a shirt and shorts with the pool's insignia, the white of the shirt stark against the golden brown of his skin. That's how Tavia describes my skin, but my golden is an undertone; Wallace's is a blend. If I had to guess I'd say he's probably of Mexican descent. Maybe mixed with a few things? We don't know each other all that well, and anyway, it's not the kind of thing you pop off and interrogate someone about.

He's crouched in front of the pool now, stretching out one arm, pushing onto the tips of his toes. His finger rests gently on the surface of the water, and then he lifts it, his tongue slightly peeking out between his teeth. Which makes my stomach do a little tumble. It's not particularly adorable, you wouldn't find it in a listicle about what hot guys do without knowing it's hot, but. It works.

I intentionally look away, play with the pearl ring at the end of my necklace and breathe.

When I pad quietly past Wallace to reach the pool steps, I can't help but steal a glance through my twists just to see what's got him so fixated. There's something tiny scooting around his index finger, and I have to pause to get a good look. Something tiny, red, and spotted. A ladybug, and it flies away when I brush by him. Wallace turns to me, and I feel like his eyes linger on the dry patches on my hips as they make their way up to mine. He smiles.

I feel off-kilter and find myself backing off toward the steps to the pool. "Whoops," I say as he slowly stands. "Sorry if I scared off your friend."

Was that smooth? I feel like it was, maybe.

"Effie." Wallace's dimples deepen. "Hi."

Tummy tumble number two.

For a moment I'm worried he'll try to shake my hand, but he simply slides his own into his shorts pockets and looks expectantly at me, like I have something important to say. His attention is direct and unwavering, and I feel like there are bright red arrows pointing at each crack in my skin. I wish I had my towel with me to wrap around the exposed parts; my hair can only cover so much. And when his eyes (the same golden brown as his skin) are on me I feel this pressure to be worth the attention, to be wittier than I actually am. All of which makes me long to be Euphemia the Mer. Which (of course) brings my mind back to Elric.

"Hi," I echo back inanely, long after the moment's over. That's the problem with being more comfortable in my head than in polite company; I fall behind.

"How are you?"

"Good, thanks." It's the only acceptable answer to that question, so I say it even though it's not remotely true. Then we stand there in silence for a moment before I stammer out, "And you?"

He ducks his head, rubbing his cheek. "Good, I'm good."

As usual, I have no trouble believing him; Wallace's face is an open book. But now that that's settled I'm not sure what to do. I turn away and ease into the water. I'm both pleased and alarmed when Wallace pulls off his shirt and follows me in. For someone who's here so often he's not much of a swimmer. Now, diving? That's another story. I've seen him do that once or twice and the way he leaps reminds me of a bird of prey, fall-coasting and then taking control.

I don't realize how tightly I've been holding my shoulders until they melt like butter down into the water, which shifts as Wallace surfaces cleanly alongside me, shaking drops from his head.

"Hey," he says.

I can't help but smile. "Hey."

"Wanna race?"

Now I can't help the incredulous look I give him and I'm rewarded with a soft laugh.

"What, you think I won't be able to keep up?" he asks.

"I know you won't be able to."

"On the count of three?" He raises a dark eyebrow.

We both take off immediately, and beneath the water I glance at him and the way he looks now that we're in my world, air bubbles hopping down the length of his body as they're released like a stream from his nostrils. Then I swim for real. And I beat him. (Duh.) He's fast, but not fast like me. It *is* kind of irritating that I'm the only one breathing heavy when we surface, and I smile placidly to distract from my chest heaving. I've done way too much conditioning to be out of breath like this.

He doesn't suggest we get out of the water once the race is over, and I'm relieved. After being repeatedly in the same place at the same time it's our first time actually hanging out, and there's nowhere I'd feel this comfortable.

That's not fair, I tell myself. When I'm Euphemia the Mer and Elric's potion lets me walk on land, I'm almost there.

Aaand I wish I'd stop thinking of Elric when I see Wallace. The faire's important, but it's a totally different world. What I do as Effie and whoever makes my stomach tumble doesn't count. At least it never has before.

A multitude of bells echoes off of the community-center walls. They blend together to make a sweet sound that sours when I see who's producing it.

Every eye is on the small group of teenagers that just entered, including my own. I can tell that Naema loves the attention. (For one thing, she always walks in front.) I'm just trying to keep my eye from twitching over the fact that this. never. happens. I have never seen her here before, and I'm here all the time. I get that this place doesn't belong to me; members of the eloko crew do show up from time to time. Just not her. And of all of Tavia's network, making polite conversation with Naema in particular is at the top of a very long list of things I hate to do. I don't know her that well, but I do know that she always has this low-key beef with my sister and it's annoying as all actual hell.

When I look back at Wallace, he's studying me. "Who's that?"

"Hm?"

"The eloko girl in the blue bathing suit."

I shrug and watch the submerged lower half of my twists weave around me for a moment before answering. "Just someone who goes to my school."

I don't think I've ever seen an eloko without their charm before, but I guess it isn't water resistant. Naema is always fidgeting with hers, so even without it on, when she's bobbing up and down laughing with her friends, her hand is clutched at her throat. When she glances my way, I steel myself. Don't come over don't come over don't come over.

She's coming over.

"Hey Effie!" Naema waves as she wades gracefully our way. Her texturized hair has gone more wavy than curly and it's glistening with tiny water droplets. It's her luminous, hydrated cherry-walnut-brown skin I envy. Not one dry patch; not a single crack.

Naema isn't taking the same attentive stock of me, but she does a quick double take when she looks at Wallace. Then she covers with an effortless, wide smile.

"Hey." She looks at him, then expectantly back at me.

"Oh, sorry. Naema, this is Wallace."

"Hi," he says politely.

"Nice to meet you," she says. "Do you go to Beckett?"

Wallace would be in high school in a show about high school. He's clearly at least a year out. It doesn't matter, because something plays out over Naema's face and I know whatever she's about to say is going to be much more painful.

"Oh, wait, is this Prince Lord Something-or-other?" she asks before Wallace can answer her initial question.

I'm glad she didn't call him my "imaginary boyfriend," which is her most common nickname for Elric. I don't know how anyone found out details about my Ren faire life. I don't talk about it that openly, and a lot of our cast is from the Washington side of the river. I'm not ashamed, I just don't have time to justify why I like the things I like, even when people make fun. I get it, fantasy wasn't created with me in mind. Move on. Anyway, if Naema knows anything about my other life, she knows that Elric's not royalty. She's just being a dick, but (as usual) in a way no one seems to notice.

"Nope, not him," I answer, even though she knows. After all, Wallace has more melanin than all of the guys at the fairegrounds, or isn't that how the joke goes.

"Aw." She's really disappointed. "I was hoping to finally meet your beloved. I'll have to wait till prom, I guess."

"What?" I say through an involuntary snort.

"Oh, right. You and your sister despise high-school functions," Naema says, and then sighs. She looks like she wants to roll her eyes, but doesn't. "Everybody goes to junior prom, Effie."

"Good to know," I mumble. Because first of all, I'm obviously not going. (C'mon.) And secondly, the idea of Elric and Euphemia crossing over into Beckett life is ludicrous. Isn't it?

Wallace's head swivels between us. I don't explain, just scratch my forehead to keep from scratching my scalp.

Naema's friends are talking among themselves and managing

to inch closer and closer to us as they do. I don't know them that well, but I recognize every single one. (Everybody at Beckett knows their lot by name, surprise surprise.) There always seems to be that kid who gets called by his first and last names, no exceptions, and at our school it's Gavin Shinn. He's the only Gavin we know, but he gets the honor because he manages to make the high-water pants he always wears look good. He's accompanied by a girl called Jamie. Jamie is indiscriminately chatty.

(A) I don't like indiscriminate chatter.

(B) The pool is where I go to *not* talk to people.

"Is that all your hair?" Jamie asks me when Naema's done telling Wallace and me all about the recent gospel competition. (Which is mildly entertaining, in that it differs wildly from Tavia's account.)

Naema shoots Jamie a look and calls her friend's name.

"What? What did I say?"

"Girl, no. Don't ask questions like that."

"What? She has a lot of hair!"

"Is *your* hair real? C'mon." Naema flicks some water at her to lighten the mood and I cover my face when a mini water fight results. I guess she's not *completely* insufferable. At least she knows to check her friend on Black girl stuff.

Wallace, Gavin Shinn, and I are moving slowly toward the stairs as things get out of hand. Shivering, I rush over to my towel and wrap it around myself.

"Effie, I swear I wasn't trying to be rude," Jamie says when she and Naema catch up to us. (Can't. Escape.) "I'm just super envious. Your hair's really cool."

Alarm shoots through me when her hand slowly reaches toward my head. I have to bend all the way to the side to avoid her touch.

"Hey. You want to get something to eat?" Wallace asks me, in a low voice. I always avoid the pool's overpriced snacks, but I'm more annoyed at the idea that he's trying to keep me calm, like I'm the one who's out of line.

"No, I'm good."

"You sure?"

"Yep!"

I freeze as my twists pull away slightly from my face. I'm overcome by the feeling I had in the cemetery, and that threatens to bring the whole episode back into focus. Jamie's playing in my hair, making it ripple like waves, and I shake as a twist shimmies across my cheek, determined not to overreact.

"Please," I snap. "Do not touch my hair. Why would I have to ask you twice?"

Everyone falls silent.

When I look up at them my twists are moving around my face like I'm a model in a Pantene Pro-V commercial. And Jamie's on the far side of Naema. She's well over an arm's length away.

"Your hair," she says slowly while they all stare. "How are you doing that?"

"What?" I'm in denial mode. "How am I doing what?"

"Effie," Wallace says.

There's another moment of silence where Naema and her friends are just gaping at me, and if the world's made of toy blocks, it's about to come crashing down.

"I knew it," Naema hisses. "I. Knew. It. I knew there was something wrong with you!" She snaps her fingers. "You really are a mermaid, aren't you?"

"No!" I shout, but my body is pinned in place. "I mean." I want to die. "I don't know."

"You swim like a fish," she says, counting off the evidence with her fingers like this is grade-school math. "You like to dress up like a Disney princess with a bunch of weirdos. C'mon. You're Ariel."

"Ariellll," Jamie and Gavin Shinn say, like it's actually a logical conclusion.

But Naema's face is completely serious. "I knew it. I thought your dad was a sprite, but I knew there was something."

I can't speak and I don't know how long it's been there but

Wallace's hand is on my arm. He's leading me out of the pool area and into the lobby and through the double-door entrance.

Finally, I yank my arm away and wrap it around myself as goosebumps erupt over my wet skin. "What are you doing? It's cold out here!"

He steps back a couple paces. "I'm sorry. I just thought . . . I thought you might need some air."

"No," I bark at him. "What I *need* is for strange dudes to keep their hands to themselves."

Crap. The look on his face almost breaks me. His eyebrows get tight and he stops looking at me for a second, like something stung him.

"We just, we don't know each other. So stop trying to save the day."

It's better I cut this off anyway, before I see Elric again and things get weird. The faire is where I snag hearts, not here.

"Effie," Wallace says, but he's looking off to the side again.

What does he want to say? Why doesn't he just say it?

He steps back toward me, and his fingertips barely graze my arm before I jerk away. If he knew me, he'd know better than to touch my skin. Or my hair. He'd know there's something about me that doesn't make sense, and he'd know it makes everyone but Tavia back all the way off. But he doesn't know me. He's a cute guy at the pool who likes the way I swim.

I whip around without saying goodbye.

IX

TAVIA

The last thing I want to do is ask Naema for help. I'm not a fan of waking up well before school starts and driving to a construction company in north Portland either, but that's the easy part. Asking Naema to meet me here—invoking the network credo that requires all those entrusted with my secret to shield me from discovery and respond to any distress call—is the part I'm afraid I'll regret.

I mean, no one's even said anything. So far. When I got home the day of the run-in with the cops, I waited. Thursday came, then Friday, and the weekend, and nothing happened. No mobs formed outside my house in the middle of the night, and maybe thank Gargy for that. But Priam's dad hasn't shown up with a siren collar either.

I saw his face, though. It's an unmistakable look. I can't pretend not to know what it means, not when the calls have been burning my throat ever since. Every time I think it's over, the heat flares up again, until it's almost painful. I'm so scared that for the most part I just haven't been speaking. I don't want anyone to know. Not even Effie. I never told her what I did, and somehow it seems like, in order to explain what's happening, I'd have to. So on top of everything else, I'm avoiding her. On Saturday I pretended to oversleep so she'd go to the pool without me . . . but this can't go on.

I have to do something.

Something more than listening for a Gramma who clearly isn't there.

Something smarter than what I tried before. Hopefully stealing (well, borrowing) Effie's car in the early morning and driving to a secret meet-up with Naema is that something.

I feel something in my throat, and when I touch my neck, I don't feel any heat. Just a keloid. Just a reminder of how badly things can go. How badly things went before I had a sister to sign with, and before I had a network giving me cover.

I was eleven years old when I decided that choking myself was a solid solution. I wasn't an anatomy geek or anything, but the fire was coming from my throat and that's where vocal cords are, so. One day I came home from school, closed my bedroom door, and put one of my dad's belts around my neck.

No one outside my family knew I was a siren; I'd never given myself away. But I was afraid it was only a matter of time. The way my dad talked, it was only a matter of time. The fact that I'd heard him break down into tears one night, talking to my mom about how he wished I was normal, like her . . . I couldn't just wait for my voice to ruin our lives even more. And once it was gone, once my siren voice was destroyed, maybe I wouldn't have to be alone anymore. It was suffocating, being surrounded by people and hiding from them at the same time.

I wanted it to end, but just that. Just my voice, and my sirenness, and my loneliness, and my fear.

My own strength wasn't gonna be enough, or else I was too hesitant to pull the belt hard enough, so I secured the belt around one of the bars of my iron bedframe and leaned all my weight in the opposite direction.

The keloid on my neck is because of how the belt strap and the buckle piece pinched the crap out of my skin. But it really didn't take long for me to pass out, which of course wasn't part of the plan. Neither was my mom finding me and calling the ambulance and my parents having to choose between telling the medical social worker that I was a siren, or that at eleven years old I'd tried to commit suicide.

They didn't ask for my input. And they didn't say I was a siren.

Anyway. That was Santa Cruz. This is Portland, and there's a network, and even if Naema and I don't really get along, she's on her way to meet me.

It's too late to change my mind now. I'm already breathing into my hands in the shadow of St. Johns, trying to keep my eyes on something. Anything. The industrial wasteland of the construction outfit where I'm waiting, the river that looks like glass today, or the park on the other side. That's where a normal person would be, not skulking on the wrong side of the bridge in what looks like a great place to dispose of a body. While across the river Cathedral Park looks lush and distant, not yet overflowing with the Portland half of Effie's Renaissance brethren, here I am standing in what may as well be a robot graveyard. Not shiny androids, either. Filthy, first-gen clunkers we'll eventually torture for entertainment when civilization falls into shambles. When the train rumbles along the tracks behind me, the dreary scene is complete.

I accidentally glance over my shoulder and the workman who let me in nods from beneath the overhang. He's network, too. He knows what I am, and he's going to watch out for me. That's the promise, and for the life of me I can't figure out why anyone makes it. If everyone felt the way my dad does, I'd be a pariah even among them.

Maybe *especially* there.

No Black man, woman, or child—no one who could be mistaken for a siren or her relation—would ever come within a square mile of me. They'd pretend I don't exist. Go out of their way to be disinterested. I'd be on my own.

As far as I can tell, that's how it is for Black women and girls most of the time. Outside the network—this tiny community that never has to explicitly organize because it operates inside another tiny community, passing information discreetly whenever the Black residents of Portland come together—the only ones who seem to stand for Black girls are Black girls.

I hope Naema knows that too. Even if she's not a siren, I hope she gets that had my traffic stop gone off the rails my protest would've gotten half the press it'd get if I'd been a boy.

That's if I got a protest in the first place.

It'd get half the turnout, too. Maybe being an eloko means she doesn't believe that. That members of my own might play devil's advocate because Black girls *do* have attitude. We *don't* know when to quit. We *never* back down. Which is a quality everybody benefits from when it comes time to organize or sit-in or climb a flagpole because it's past time for terror to come down. But when it's time to stand for us . . . it feels like it's just us. Maybe that's not true on an individual basis. But individual kindness or hate isn't what makes the world go round. When it matters, when a larger population or institution could make the difference, it seems they don't.

That's part of why I don't complain to anyone about how soul-crushing this secret can feel, not even to Effie. Because people *are* helping me. Last night, when I group-texted the gospel choir and asked if there was a secluded but safe place I could go to at six in the morning, someone knew someone with access to this all-but-abandoned garbage heap, and that second someone asked no questions before letting me in.

I have a small but complex web of people who want me to be safe, and they might not have the power or privilege to convince anyone else to feel the same, but they're still here. Fighting futility with me. I have a lot more help than a lot of people.

Which makes what I did even worse.

Forget that it completely contradicts my whole find-Gramma's-voice-and-be-normal pipe dream. Using my siren call in public—in front of an eloko parent!—was a giant mistake. And it means only someone with ties to the eloko *and* the siren communities can help me now.

No one but Naema would know whether I have anything to fear, so when her coffee bean pulls into this forsaken end of the lot, the sound of loose gravel crunching beneath it, I force myself to breathe and loosen my shoulders.

I was so jealous when she drove that espresso-brown Fiat to school for the first time sophomore year. Even Effie had her junker by then, but at least Effie was grateful. The same could not be said for Naema, and that's why I envied her. She'd expected it. She expected nice things to happen for her, for people to chirp and coo over things that just felt normal to her, so she didn't make a big show of taking care of it. Effie was a conscientious ninny by comparison, babying a hand-me-down land yacht like it was a prized possession. Meanwhile Naema let some dude drive her car within a week of getting it, and then scraped the bottom of the front bumper pulling the tiny thing needlessly far into a parking spot. Anyone else would've been embarrassed or, I don't know, terrified. Not Naema. She just snapped a picture of it, put some charmingly self-deprecating caption on it, and it went viral. Or anyway, it all turned out fine. Her parents got it taken care of and she went back to having a brand-new coffee bean to drive around in.

I can't have a car of my own. Might draw attention to myself somehow. It could alert people to the fact that I'm a siren. I don't know how; I didn't ask questions. What would've been the point?

When Naema gets out of the car, she's typing on her phone, so I let her come to me, slow as she pleases. Who could she possibly be texting at 6 a.m. But whatever. We're practically face to face when she stops, slips the device into the back pocket of her jeans, and squints beneath the droopy purple brim of her hat.

"What's up?" she asks.

My eyes dart around for a moment.

"I need your help," I say, every word stretched a little more than the previous because the answer is self-evident. I have never summoned Naema before. There is obviously a reason, and it's not for a casual chitchat. But I owe her a debt of gratitude so I rein in my confusion. "I might have a problem. I might have made a mistake."

"What'd you do?" Her hand instinctively lifts to fiddle with her bell.

For a moment, I don't want to tell her. I'm watching her look at me with what I can only assume is indifference while she plays with the only one of her possessions she fusses over, and I know she's in my network, but she's in one of her own, too. Which of course is why I need her. It's just that away from the gospel choir, she's much more standoffish. She doesn't like me and I know it.

"Tavia." She widens her eyes. "What did you do?"

But when I open my mouth I can't confess to being so stupid, not right away.

"You're really close with Priam, right?"

"I knew it," she says, breaking into a smile. "This is too good."

"It's not—" what you think, I would've said, if she hadn't cut me off.

"Okay, yes, I'm *with* Priam; no, you cannot summon me to try to get back on that. Yes, he asked me to prom, and no, I didn't ask if you were cool with it before saying yes because we're not down like *that* and you know it, Tavia. I think it's enough Priam and I've been ridiculously discreet to spare your feelings."

I'm about to tell her nobody asked for their discretion and that I have no idea why Priam thinks I can't handle seeing him with someone else—except that I do pretty much pretend he doesn't exist anytime we're in the same place. And anyway, Naema's not done.

"You and your sister, the drama. I can't."

"What does my sister have to do with— Forget it. No, Naema, this has nothing to do with wanting Priam back, please shut up."

She does, but it's not in the least bit subservient. She's looking at me calmly, blinking slowly. Languidly, if I were trying to impress Mr. Monroe. Her naturally curled eyelashes crisscross and then separate, and anybody else would fall into her dark-brown eyes.

"I'm sorry. I didn't mean that. I just need to figure out how to get this out."

"I don't speak sign language, so whatever you wanna tell me, you'll have to use your words."

I hate her. I mean, I don't, I have no reason to. I have no idea what it would feel like to be summoned, I have no idea what she was doing when I texted her, though if I had to guess she was probably in the shower; her hair is falling from beneath her hat in wet, wavy tendrils.

"I need to know if Priam's dad knows about me. And I guess I need to know if Priam knows and if he still hates me. Or if he might say anything when his dad asks him."

"Why would Priam's dad be asking about you?"

"Because I used a call in front of him."

"You used a call . . . on Priam's dad."

"Not on him, in his presence, and he was in the patrol car when it happened but I think he knows why his partner had a change of heart."

"Okay, no, this makes way more sense. So you're saying that while half of PDX is covering for you so you can do this whole sad-little-pretty-girl routine, you purposely unleash a call and basically out yourself to get out of a traffic violation."

"That's not what happened."

She digs her phone back out and starts typing again, shaking her head and the oversize brim of her hat.

"Naema," I say, but I don't know how to finish. I'm glancing between the back of her phone and the sliver of her face that isn't hidden, and my heart feels like it's trying to punch through my rib cage.

Her fingers are going a mile a minute.

"What are you doing?"

Shaking her head.

"Who are you talking to?"

Nothing.

"**Naema!**" I don't feel the heat in my throat until I've already spoken.

Right on the heels of my voice comes a lovely tinkling, like a careful breeze across dainty wind chimes. Her eloko melody.

When she speaks, there's a trill playing in her words, the way there was at the last choir competition.

"What the hell is your problem?" she barks, but the trill makes it beautiful. She can't have meant to do it. Which means I must've.

I just used a call. Again. And the fact that it wasn't Appeal or Compel—the fact that I don't know what it was—is the scariest part.

I don't realize I've taken Naema's phone from her hands until she snatches it back. I apologize, but even I barely hear it.

"You don't own me, Tavia! Grasp that." She flicks me hard in the forehead but I don't say a word.

I used a call. I know I did. The heat didn't plume like all the times before, but I did it. The heat didn't build, it just appeared, the way her melody did, without her blowing on her charm.

"I thought you were texting about me and what I'm telling you—"

"Do you get that I have my own life and world that has nothing to do with whether or not you're a siren? Does your family understand that we don't all wanna be wrapped up in this drama all the time? We don't all wanna be reduced! I don't!"

The workman is nearby and I don't dare look around for him or he might think I'm in distress. He might come over, get between us unnecessarily, and tell Naema to calm down. Which I can't imagine would go well.

"It's a difficult life, ViVi," my dad told me once. *"And not just for you.*

"It's hard to know a siren. It's hard to be part of the secret when you didn't have a choice in the matter, and it's hard to have to constantly assure the world you're not one of them."

I was getting released from my psych hold in Santa Cruz, and plans had already been made to move to Portland. He wanted me to know there was a network there, that it was the reason for the move—since my unabashed hatred for my hometown wasn't reason enough—but that I shouldn't be too imposing. I shouldn't ask too much when the community was already sacrificing for me. I shouldn't take advantage.

I'd tried my eleven-year-old best to make it a non-issue, to get rid of the thing that had caused him so much pain already, and because of that—because I'd tried and failed spectacularly and publicly—I was causing him even more. Because he was the son of a siren and he'd never intended to come back to Portland and the network that had served his mother.

I tried not to take offense at what my dad said, and in the years since he said it to me I've tried to skip over the part where he said it while I was still locked away.

I *knew* it was a difficult life. I *knew* it was difficult for people other than me. I also knew they were allowed to say so and I wasn't. Because he did. Constantly.

I didn't talk back to him, I just kept my eyes steady while my vision blurred. It was a little trick I came up with during the psych hold, but I really only needed it to get through conversations with my dad. I could keep my eyes on him like I was paying rapt attention but really I'd have blurred his face, and in my head (since I couldn't undo being what I was) I screamed with a throat on fire and pretended I knew every siren call there ever was. In my head, I told him I didn't have a choice either. That he'd known what happens when the son of a siren has a daughter. That he'd taken a chance, and my mom had taken a chance, and I was literally the only person involved who didn't get a say. And then he'd set up shop in a town without a network, one that was right on the ocean so that he'd always be nervous.

See, "nobody" believes mythos, but they never forget it either.

It's why once we moved to Portland, my dad took us up the hill where the breeze wouldn't carry a fallen siren's call. Because even though our mythos is just as silly as anyone else's, it matters.

Dad could stand to be by the water in California—just not in Portland, where his mother, the siren, died.

I've been trying for weeks, but I really wish I could hear

Gramma right now. I wish her siren call would lift from the sparkling Willamette River and drown out Naema's voice. I wish I could commune with the woman who passed this curse down to me, since my father kept us apart while she was alive.

I wish she could tell me if the call I heard inside my head when I was eleven was the same one I just used without meaning to.

"I don't care what anyone thinks, Tavia, you're on your own."

Naema is stomping back to her Fiat when I mentally come back to this side of the bridge.

"I need your help," I say as I follow after her. "It isn't just about me. Please!"

"Listen really carefully," she says, leaving the driver's side door open and whirling on me. "It *is* just about you. It sure as hell ain't about me." She leans in. "I'm not like you."

She makes sure every word is a sentence all its own.

"I'm not their enemy," she says. I feel the skin bunching between my eyebrows and she sees it. "I'm not. I'm not interested in being any kind of magic only Black girls can be. I don't want anything to do with you. I'm not a siren, or a siren's shield, or whatever the hell Effie really is."

That's the second time she's brought Effie up.

"I'm more. I'm eloko *first*."

"You have to tell me if Priam says anything, I mean it."

She gets in her car and slams the door without answering. I let my fingertips rest on the rubber trim below her window. When she side-eyes me, I hold her gaze.

"Naema," I say in my natural voice, but slow. "Don't cross me. Or my sister."

I don't use Compel or Appeal or whatever came out before, but she understands. I can tell by her hesitation.

Sorry, Dad. Sometimes shrinking just doesn't work.

~~~~~

Nothing says good morning like confrontation, but to be honest, I'm feeling pretty energized as I head to school. I've wanted to put

Naema in her place for a long time, and I finally did it. It feels . . . amazing. The constant turmoil in my stomach, the secretly unsafe way I feel around everyone but Effie—it's all miraculously gone. It's remarkable, and remarkably easy to breathe free; it's welcome, and takes no getting used to. It's like getting lost in a Camilla Fox video, only more potent, more hopeful, perhaps because I'm the reason I feel this way. Which means maybe I can feel this way from now on.

Shutting Naema up is a natural high. I feel like I can face anything, and with the start of the last quarter's schedule, Mr. Monroe's first-period IB Social and Cultural Anthropology is the perfect chaser. I love this class. Or I did before today.

The jury's in.

The jury in the trial of Rhoda Taylor's murderer has come back with a verdict, and every news outlet is standing by. The case that barely made the local news in southern Oregon where it happened is now on the national stage.

Mr. Monroe has the television on, and there are directions on the board to take our seats quietly, even though the last bell hasn't rung.

We're going to watch it live.

I don't want to watch this. I don't want to watch this *here*.

I don't even know what to hope. If the boyfriend is convicted, will anyone be pleased? If he's not, will people celebrate? Will people I know—people in this room—express relief that someone all physical evidence points to as the murderer gets to walk free? If he gets off, will they at least have the decency not to speak of the siren allegation in the same breath? And how long till someone asks if I'm a siren, too?

Everyone's in their seat now, and just as the field reporter who's been waiting patiently outside the courtroom starts to talk, the bell rings. Whatever she's saying, her finger pressed against her ear, her eyes are down like the news anchors she's responding to are on the ground instead of back at the studio.

Maybe she already announced it, and we couldn't hear it.

Maybe we missed it and now we never have to know. It's an entirely irrational hope, and it's dashed as soon as the ringing stops.

"Before the verdict is read, Tamantha, can you bring us up to speed on what it's been like the past few days?"

"Certainly, Joan," Tamantha replies from on the scene, and for a moment I'm thinking of how white girls in Portland seem to increasingly have names I'm pretty sure would be "ghetto" if they were Black. "The jury's been in deliberations for the past day and a half, but last week saw the defense presenting character witnesses for—" She says his name and in my head I replace it with "the defendant." "A close friend of the couple, who remembers Rhoda's impossible sway, not just over the defendant but over others, too."

Tamantha lets that information set a moment, her head cocked slightly to the side in a way that can't possibly be considered impartial, and I have to look away.

Down, at the faux wood grain of my desk. Surrounded by people hearing the same insinuations and thinking who knows what. Sensing my discomfort, I have to assume, because it's throbbing out of me, bleeding out into the air around me while Joan recalls the conflicting testimonies of expert witnesses on either side of the case.

"The defense closed by reminding us that this case from the beginning was about the question of justification," Tamantha reports, even though that's not at all true. In the beginning, he was denying it; I remember. She's talking like she's a member of the jury now, as if we all are, which I guess can only mean she's made a judgment. "Joan, there is such a thing as justifiable homicide, and according to the defendant's own testimony, for years now, he's been living in fear."

My guts churn. Audibly. I'm terrified that the next time I open my mouth, the contents of my stomach will leap to freedom.

Mr. Monroe rarely turns on the room lights, energy-conservationist that he is. It's morning, though, and the sun is bright, so despite how I'm trying to take refuge in the lack of syn-

126

thetic lighting, I'm not exactly in the shadows. If anyone glances over, they'll see my reaction.

IB students have a reputation for being thoughtful and informed and mature, but I can say, as one of them, that we are given far too much credit. We're always given the benefit of the doubt, whether it's over tardiness that would've sent any other student to in-school suspension, or whether someone's micro-aggression is generously interpreted as a tactless but benign miscommunication. That I'm surrounded by IB kids right now does nothing to stop me sweating as the moment of revelation gets closer. It does nothing to slow my galloping heartbeat.

But maybe it should, especially in this room, with this teacher.

Maybe he can keep this moment from getting worse.

But when Tamantha the reporter practically screams, "Not guilty!" and she leaps up onto her toes like it's the most wonderful news, no one can make it feel better.

Because killing sirens is not a crime.

~~~~~~~

Effie and I are sitting at a picnic table in the courtyard, eating in complete silence. She's eating. I've been chewing the same bite of cruelty-free chicken and alfalfa-sprout salad so long it's probably cud.

Eff didn't ask me anything when we finally met up, but I know she knows. If I listen hard enough, I can probably hear at least three separate verdict conversations happening in the vicinity.

Now she looks up at me.

"What?" I ask, and at first she just reaches across the table and frees a perfectly twisted-out strand of hair from the corner of my mouth. Camilla's last product endorsement may finally be the One for me. I feel like garbage, but my hair looks hydrated and amazing.

Effie retracts her hand and looks at me some more before asking.

"Do you still wanna give it up?"

I almost ask what she means but it's obvious. She's asking if

127

I still want to give up my voice—I just don't know why. I don't know why today of all days would change that. Why a man being acquitted of murder after saying his victim was a siren would make me want to keep the power in my voice.

Or maybe I do. Either way, I can't talk about it with Altruism and one of the Jennifers approaching our table.

"I told her you would already know," Allie says, rolling her eyes while Jennifer fiddles with her phone.

"I would already know what?" I ask, and Jennifer thrusts the device in my face.

"What?"

I can't answer Effie right away because I'm trying to make sense of what I'm seeing.

It's Camilla's channel, obviously, but I've never seen this video. It's new, but that's weird because today isn't a regular upload day for her.

"Wait," I say aloud but not to any of the three girls now huddling next to me.

"My voice is power," Camilla Fox is saying, even before her trademark intro. And as soon as she does, I know where this is going.

Heat explodes in my throat, but our calls aren't contagious. It isn't like a yawn. My vocal cords aren't going to burn just because I hear another siren speak or because someone speaks about us. It's just a tingle, like a nod of solidarity when you pass one of your own.

"I've dreamt of this day so many times."

Camilla . . . I want to tell her to stop, not to say what I know she's about to say. But I can't afford to speak aloud anymore, not with the way my throat is burning, not when Allie and Jennifer are right beside me.

The entire weight of today is bearing down on me. From the once-freeing confrontation with Naema to being trapped in a classroom for the Rhoda Taylor verdict, to what cannot be true of Camilla Fox. This is it. My bones are finally going to break.

I should get up and walk away. That's what my dad would say. Whenever anyone brings up sirens in public, I'm supposed to look the other way; ignore it, never engage with it, lest someone discover my secret.

Which, especially in moments when my body doesn't feel like my own, would be impossible and would just involve me being the solo person completely disinterested in sirens. Which feels like a flimsy cover.

"I knew something would be the breaking point. I knew someday I would have to stand up, even if I was scared." Camilla's septum piercing catches her perfect shoot lighting, and her matte maroon lips sit together frequently. She's taking her time. She didn't come to this decision lightly.

"Someday is today. Because today a man walked free despite overwhelming evidence and an implied confession of guilt, all because someone said his victim may have been a siren. And know, my first thought is to underscore that maybe was enough—but that means if she *was* a siren, this acquittal is okay," Camilla says, and it's startling and somehow warm to hear someone speak my thoughts so clearly. Like a hug, or burrowing into sunbaked sand. "It isn't okay."

And suddenly she's crying, and so am I. Effie's arm snakes around me and I don't even bother wiping my eyes. If sympathizing with a siren makes people suspect me, maybe it just proves how little people care.

"She's about to do it," Allie says, and then we hold our breaths.

"I was born a siren," Camilla says, her flawless brows bending. **"And I'm asking you to listen to the sound of my voice."**

She shrugs, still glassy-eyed.

"That's all," Camilla says. "I'm just asking you to hear us. The way no one heard Rhoda until it was too late. The way, by the time anyone asked about her story, she wasn't the one telling it."

"Did you feel that?" Allie asks, before whipping around to gape at Effie and me.

"Legiteral shivers," Jennifer says, "every time I watch it."

"We've watched it half a dozen times already, and I'm still amazed at her."

"How do you know Camilla Fox?" Effie asks.

"Tavia introduced us, but look." Jennifer hands us the phone. *"Everybody* knows her now."

Camilla's viewer count is astronomical. It's higher than her already impressive subscriber count, and while we watch, it ticks higher still.

I shouldn't, but I scroll toward the comments. I want to believe they'll be kind, that it'll be mostly her followers and maybe new fans, proud of her courage.

No such luck.

Shut her down! the top-rated comment demands. Camilla's a Black girl who dared to shine, and it only takes the second comment before that's what it's about.

How else do you think a nappy haired cow got such a huge following? Wake up, idiots!

I stare at that one, study the hundred-plus up-votes beneath it. Some days I'm actually numb to people like this, and what they say doesn't even register. Today's not a day like that.

And then there's the brilliant troll—one of the hundreds here today who've probably never watched a Camilla video before and certainly are not her audience—whose only contribution is to repeat Camilla's own confession a million times.

SIREN! SIREN! SIREN! SIREN!

In between the words, there are red-light emojis. Like someone's sounding the alarm, not just calling Camilla what she is.

SIREN! SIREN! SIREN! SIREN!

Jennifer and Altruism don't notice that I've said nothing. They're going on about how brilliant Camilla Fox is to use a call to demonstrate that she's a siren while not actually Compelling the viewer to do anything they aren't already doing. They're talking about a protest coming up in Vancouver this weekend, and how they're absolutely going now because Camilla is—but I didn't know she was, or what it has to do with her announcement.

"Wait, wait, wait." Altruism waves her hand to hush everyone, but I was already paying attention. "This is new."

There's an update made to Camilla's video, a black-and-white segment edited onto the end because of something going on in the comments.

"This isn't my march, y'all," Camilla says, her skin still glowing in grayscale. "It's not #CamillasVoiceIsPower, and I don't want anyone to get it twisted just because I'm attending. I care about us. I have to resist the breaking of Black bodies, no matter whose they are, but I'm not one of the organizers," she stresses, but I can tell by the fact that she needs to that she's gonna get caught up in this. They're gonna *get* her caught up. Even though she just today decided to out herself, and no one knows how the world will react. Even though nobody cared she was coming before.

I'm scared for her. My brain can't seem to keep ahold of the new fact that Camilla is like me, but every time that fact overwhelms me again, the fear I'm used to feeling for myself transfers to her. Because immediately, I think: someone's gonna use this. They're gonna use this double-edged celebrity and this courage and this confession without thinking about the danger Camilla might be in. Or worse, she'll think facing down danger is her duty.

Still. I can't help but think that Camilla's going to this march—this protesting of an unarmed Black boy's life being taken and then the officer not facing any consequences—might make it so someone's marching for Rhoda, too.

If only Camilla had a dad like mine, she'd know all the ways this can go wrong.

Before I know what I'm doing, my hand covers the tiny keloid high on the right side of my neck. While Altruism and Jennifer talk excitedly, Effie calmly reaches over and turns off the phone.

I can't move. I can still see Camilla's face, and then Rhoda Taylor's.

And then slowly they both fade to indigo. That deep, heavy

131

blue I saw before bleeds through Rhoda Taylor's mahogany-brown skin. I feel that floating sensation again, only this time there's something more. Something like an atmosphere to go along with the color and the feeling. It moves and glistens, and I can't look away.

But I don't think I'm in the courtyard at Beckett High anymore. And I know I'm not alone.

Gramma?

This feels like someplace else completely. Maybe this is the water, because I swear she's near. I swear she can hear me. She's been hearing me all along.

Gramma, I'm scared.

No one answers, no voice responds, but something asks what I'm afraid of.

There's no one in this deep-blue haze, and I can't hear my friends in the courtyard anymore, so maybe I'm really crazy this time. Maybe my dad was on to something, and it just took me a while to figure it out.

Or maybe I'm asking myself.

What am I really afraid of?

I'm afraid that someone knows what I am because I outed myself in front of a cop. I'm afraid people are going to be on high alert forever now, and they'll find me out eventually.

I'm afraid because as far as I know Rhoda Taylor wasn't a siren and that fact didn't save her. That fact didn't get her any more justice.

And then I remember Effie's question, and wonder: Do I really wanna give it up?

Why am I trying to get rid of something I'll be accused of anyway?

If I'm in trouble—if Priam's dad knows and Naema can't be trusted, if the world is on the hunt and everything's coming down—this power might be all the protection I have. After everything I've been through, that realization fills me with equal parts boldness and apprehension. I feel myself bouncing between fear and ferocity, my heart and my call fighting for space in my throat.

You don't have to take my voice, I tell my grandmother. *Just teach me how to use it.*

I blink, and it's like it seals a promise.

The blue is gone. I'm back at Beckett High.

EFFIE

It's been a couple days since Camilla Fox turned Tav's already hectic world upside down. Which means maybe now it's right side up. I don't know. She seems better. Maybe. Which strangely is making me think something seriously overwhelming can turn into calm for me, too. So since getting home from school, I've spent the better part of the past hour with my toes tucked inside my first mermaid tail—because that's as much of me that fits in it now.

When I found it in my cassone, I couldn't help but pull it out. Careful, though. The sequins Mom painstakingly stitched hang by a thread now. They still shimmer glassy blue and green and abalone even though it's falling apart, and I feel like Paw Paw when I ask about a black-and-white picture that's gone black-and-yellow. His eyes get misty and he mumbles something about it being "full of stories." Like the stories are deep inside the picture itself.

That must be why the tail felt so heavy in my hands.

"Is this why I love the faire so much?" I ask the old stuffed beagle I found alongside the tail. Minnie Dog shouldn't have been in the chest, having no relation to Ren faire, but she was a gift from Mom and keeping her close just felt right. I look at her big plastic eyes as though maybe she'll reply. "Is that why Mom brought me in? Because Euphemia's who I really am?"

Naema has me shook. It isn't a wild stretch having mermaids in my ancestry, having a recessive mer gene passed through my mother, even though she never transformed.

Maybe that's what's happening to me. Maybe that's why I haven't had my period in forever.

There's one person I trust to tell me the truth. Someone whose dad is deep enough in faire nobility that he might have let the truth slip to his son. Someone who's always just been a co-star, but who I can't stop thinking about this year. And maybe there's good reason.

Of the ten trillion social media apps, I just happened to triangulate Elric's local haunts using the one I don't totally understand. I hopscotched from the profile he used to get in touch with me last year to, like, four other apps, eventually finding one that basically tells me every time he leaves his house.

Trying a new burger joint? Check in.

Hitting a concert? Check in.

Playing pool? (Elric plays pool. A lot.) Check in.

If that hadn't worked, I was gonna head in the direction of his high school (which I figured out because he was wearing a letterman in his profile picture) and just . . . I don't even know. Luckily he decided to catch a movie.

I'm almost ready to go find Elric when I think I hear Mama Theo downstairs. At first I think it's just because I'm taking stock of the angry red welts I've left on my shoulders and the back of my neck. The ones Miss Gennie has been eyeing when she doesn't think I'm looking. The ones I can't help making lately every time my twists brush my skin.

In the bathroom I share with Tavia, I open a drawer and stare down at the scissors.

I'm not going to use them. What would I do if I didn't have the shelter of my twists? I'm already worried about Miss Gennie mentioning my scratch marks to Mama Theo, what would my grandmother say about me cutting my hair? (Whew.)

Black hair doesn't grow, so you don't cut it. That's what I knew as fact when I was a kid anyway, and it was common knowledge to all the kids, white or brown or otherwise. That and your hair's only long if you're mixed or if it's dreaded or if it's fake. Everybody must think twists are close enough to dreads because even when they ask if it's mine, at least I hardly ever get accused of lying. Weave accusations are reserved for Black girls who dare to wear their long hair straight, I guess. (And to shame the girls who wear units that somehow aren't ratchet on the runway.)

Tav's the one who changed all that, debunked those "facts." The same way living with her taught me things only people in the network know about sirens almost through osmosis, I've learned a ton about how society quietly tries to wreck us. Because it turns out buying products and adopting rituals designed for someone else is what wrecks our hair, not being Black.

Go figure.

Still, I don't have the nerve to cut them, so I'm just gonna cover my twists with a Dutch wax scarf—the only defense against what's becoming an uncontrollable need to inspect my scalp . . . and the self-moving phenomenon I can't really believe happened—but whatever I heard before, I hear again. And if Mama Theo really *is* downstairs, she'll notice the way even my baby hairs look parched and dull.

I grab the lavender olive oil Tav and I have been using and slather my exposed arms before I apply it to my twists. I squeeze oiled hands around several at a time, and then slide down the entire length of each.

It's the first time I've touched my twists since the community center. Since they moved on their own. They haven't moved since, and I'm not in the mood for Mama's interrogations ("Why don't you do your hair instead of just covering it?"), so I decide the scarf can go on in the privacy of my car.

I'm certain she's here now. What I've been sensing is more like

136

sonar than sound, and it's subtle but it's there. Like when you can't hear the music in Fred Meyer unless it's a song you already know. It's definitely Mama Theo's voice.

Maybe she's just here to chat with Miss Gennie and I can float right past them with quick kisses and a brief hello. Fingers crossed.

When I get to the middle landing of the staircase, I know my plan is shot.

Miss Gennie's standing closer to the entryway, like after coming through the door Mama rushed past her, and I can tell Tav's mom used to be a dancer because she's standing in what is apparently a variation of fourth position. Her hands are behind her back until she takes a graceful step forward and gestures toward me.

"Effie, your grandma's here to see you," Miss Gennie says, like maybe I can't see, and then she doesn't seem to know what to do with her mouth. It's slightly open for a second more before it settles into a soft smile. It's pretty, like she is—but it doesn't hide the fact that she looks a little confused.

I'm at the base of the stairs standing in front of Mama when I open my mouth to speak, but she beats me to it.

"When's the last time you went to see your mother, child?"

Okay. I can't even process the question before Tavia's mom excuses herself to the kitchen to get us something to drink. I almost tell her I'm heading out soon and not to bother, but that mess didn't fly at Theodosia Freeman's house and being under someone else's roof won't keep Mama Theo from putting me in my place. I'm here till I figure out why she is.

"I saw her a few days ago, I guess."

"When?" she insists, and instead of asking why it matters, I gnaw on my own lip like I'm trying to think of the date. It's not exactly fair that she's demanding answers, seeing as she never supplies them. Every time I've wanted to know something in the past, I've gone to Mama. It's never gone well (I mean, I've never gotten what I've been looking for), but she raised my mom. She knows things, even if she keeps it from me. If anybody knows what's inside me, I figure it's her.

Before I went looking through my cassone today, I sat with my cell phone, staring at her number for a long time. Every time I thought my finger was ready to press call, I hesitated. I couldn't handle it today if she derailed my questions. I couldn't hear about how "real life" was passing me by and how if living with Tavia should've taught me anything, she'd hoped it'd be that I was better off just being Effie. I couldn't pretend she made sense, not this time. I have eyes. I can see there's more to me than she wants me to believe. Now she just shows up at the house asking about visiting Mom's grave, and I'm expected to come right out with it.

So I do.

"Like a week ago, I guess."

I can't tell her it was exactly a week ago and I know that because it was the same day I went to see the stone kids I used to know. Or that I blacked out and since then everything's been hazy around the edges. If I tell her my hair started moving on its own at the pool, she'll tell me to stop talking nonsense. Or she'll ask me if going to the pool is part of wasting my life in the faire.

"You think? Or you know?"

"I don't— I can't be sure." I also can't stop chewing on my lip. She is making me all kinds of nervous, like I'm a tiny kid and I got into her perfume again.

"You can't be sure," she repeats, but it's a lot softer than the way she said everything else. Quieter, yeah, but less gruff, too. Maybe she's not angry at me after all.

She closes her eyes for a long exhale and I admire the soft, shiny skin of her eyelids. Mama Theo doesn't wear makeup anymore, but she has this glisten that always looks pretty. I'm not her blood, but when I decided I didn't wanna wear makeup either it was because I hoped I'd somehow inherit that glow.

I take a deep breath of my own and my gaze slips to the floor just by instinct. It's not allowed to when I talk to her because it's disrespectful, or so she says. I never figured out how my anxiety gets lumped in with defiance toward elders, but that's what it is.

Mama Theo opens her eyes and they're misty.

Crap. What the hell is going on?

"Tavia go with you, baby?" She can barely ask before she pulls her lips into her mouth the way she used to when a CeCe Winans song got her worked up.

"Mama," I coo like she and Mom used to do to me when I was on the verge of tears. "What's the matter?"

Now she's the one who won't make eye contact. She's running her eyes across the ceiling like she's reading. Or praying.

"You're not paying attention, Effie, I don't know why you can't see."

That shuts me up.

"I'm trying, Effie." She shakes her head like it's not true—or like it's not good enough. Whatever she's been doing hasn't worked. "You have to try too. You have to stop this if you can."

I don't get it. I'm so lost. I'm itching all over and I'm twisting my wrists and balling up my fists to keep from scratching everywhere. I just want to get to my car, but there's no getting past Mama when she's like this, and maybe I shouldn't leave her anyway. But I want answers for once, and I know her well enough to know she's purposely hiding things from me. Even now, when she's clearly so upset.

Miss Gennie never brought us those drinks, and now she only sneaks back into the room when there's a knock on the door. I'm grateful for the interruption until I see who's on the other side.

"Yes?" Tavia's mom says because she doesn't know Priam's dad and he isn't in uniform.

What is today *about*?

"Mrs. Philips?"

"Yes? Can I help you?"

I could've told him this is not how you show up to a Black woman's home. If it was Mama Theo's house (and she wasn't visibly "at the end of her rope"), she'd be demanding that he speak up. Out with it.

"I'm Officer Blake with the Portland PD, may I come in for a moment?"

"May I see your badge, please?"

She couldn't have asked more politely, but he looks completely surprised. I guess she was supposed to take him at his word. He fishes it out and hands it to her. She takes a good look before stepping aside to let him in.

"Good afternoon," he says to Mama Theo and me. She's still huffing and I'm letting my hair drape my face, so he turns right back to Tavia's mom. "Is your husband here, ma'am?"

"He's not, is everything all right? Oh God, is this about Rodney?" She reaches behind her but there's nothing there. Tavia does the same thing when she's overwhelmed and I've always wondered if it's learned or genetic. Now that I don't have anyone I'm biologically related to, I wonder if I have traits like that. Things I do that Mom used to do, I just don't know it. Things I do that I got from my dad.

I wonder if his hair moves . . .

"For heaven's sake, tell her why you're here and stop traumatizing folks in their own homes!"

"I'm just here to follow up," Priam's dad says to Mama Theo before turning back to Mrs. Philips. "I came as a courtesy because our kids go to school together."

You mean they used to date until your eloko prince of a son ghosted on her.

"Follow up with what?"

"A routine traffic stop involving your daughter, Tavia."

"She hasn't gotten home yet. What happened?"

"Oh, this was last week." He finally seems to get that none of us understand why he's here. "My partner pulled her over coming up the hill in your husband's luxury vehicle."

"Mm." Mama Theo might be distracted, but not enough to keep her from smelling something rotten, as she says. Her grunt comes with a jerk of her head, same as always, and she cuts her eyes at Priam's dad. Anyone else would know they're on thin ice.

"I don't think I'm understanding this," Geneva Philips says. "Did she get a ticket? Does she need to appear in court?"

"No, ma'am, she was let off with a warning—"

Mama Theo grunts again. Even when I was little and couldn't really understand grown-up conversation, I always knew who was winning by the grunts. They're like their own language. Once you figure out who they're directed at, you know just what to question and disbelieve. Right now it's Officer Blake.

"I just wanted to make sure you were aware of our interaction. Because she's a minor."

"As a courtesy," Mrs. Philips repeats it like it's a question.

Now *I* almost grunt. Tavia's mom might be polite, but she's not stupid.

"Yes, ma'am."

Everybody stops talking after that. If it's too quiet, they're gonna hear my hair moving. I can't be sure but I think one of my twists just swept slowly between my shoulder blades like a cat's tail. I go back to rolling my wrists. Anything to keep from reaching for my hair.

I almost gasp and then swallow it.

Tavia's coming. I hear her the way I heard Mama Theo from upstairs, in a sonar-sound distinctly hers, and it's coming down the hill from the spot she likes. She'll be here soon, and I doubt the gargoyle knows to protect her from going inside her own house.

"Well, I'm out," I say, and once it's in the air, it sounds as random as it felt. I stand still long enough to collect a blank stare from everyone and then shuffle quickly across the room, ducking when I cut between Miss Gennie and Officer Blake.

At the door, I turn back and give Mama Theo half of a smile.

"Love you."

Her eyebrows bunch together and she sort of pouts. Whatever's got her upset hasn't faded. Honestly, it's bumming me out now. I hate to think she's not okay, but I don't know what I can do.

I mumble out a quick goodbye and slip out the front door, stopping on the porch. Just like I thought, Tavia's almost home.

I should get the car started before anyone follows me out and both Tav and I get roped back inside, but I can still hear the adults talking on the other side of the door.

When Tavia waves at me from the neighbor's gate, I sign to her to stop. *Wait there. I'm eavesdropping.*

Inside the house, Priam's dad is still dancing around his suspicion, Miss Gennie and Mama Theo giving nothing away.

"If Tavia is what I think she is," he says without putting it into words, "I just want her to be careful. She put herself in a lot of danger."

"Excuse me, Officer Blake, but you did that when you pulled her over without cause."

That wasn't Mama. That was Miss Gennie. Tavia's watching my face, and when she sees my eyebrows spring up, she gestures to ask me what's going on and I aggressively wave her off. A moment later, the conversation inside seems to be winding toward a conclusion so I take off down the steps.

When I hop into my car and drive one house over to pick up Tavia, I can almost feel the gargoyle's confused stare. Little does he know he almost let his mistress walk into a trap. Well. What could've been a trap, for all he knows.

"What the heck was that about?" Tav asks when we're clear.

"Oh, hey, when were you gonna tell me you revealed yourself to two police officers?"

In the passenger seat, she gapes at me for a moment and then goes still as stone.

"Who's in the house?" she asks.

At some point, one of us has to actually answer a question, so I relent. "Priam's dad. One of two police officers who witnessed your call."

She's still not moving, maybe not breathing.

"Tav, it's okay. He came to warn us, not to rat you out."

Her breath comes out in a series of sputters.

142

"You're good," I tell her.

What I don't mention is Officer Blake's offer, if it's what she wants. And "it" is a silencing collar. "Just in case."

As heinous as it is, he thinks he's offering safety and solutions. Even though no other supernatural would get that offer, because cops have no other equipment specially made to control them.

But Officer Blake means well—Mama grunts—and the important thing is that her secret's safe with him. Anyway, Tavia's freaked enough processing her near-disaster, so I drive in silence.

I haven't told her where we're going, or why. I'm afraid if I explain it all, my nerve will escape on my breath. I can see myself deflating like a balloon, flying wildly around the car until my high-pitched death screams are whimpers and then squeaks.

But this is a good idea.

The cyclist I'm "sharing the road" with thinks 50/50 seems legit, so when another car comes up the road toward us, I have to brake and pull behind the bicycle. Dude's unpressed, keeping on his jolly way as I go ridiculously under the speed limit to keep from crushing him. I don't care. Not even a Portland cyclist can ruin my high.

I'm going to surprise Elric. I'm going to ask him if his dad, the Royal Blacksmith, has known my true story all along, and if he maybe told his son. If Elric can tell me if I really am Euphemia the Mer.

Every year we separate at season's end, pining for each other until the faire comes back around. The story stays alive online, on the Hidden Tales, and he leaves me gifts when prep time comes around, but the only time we've ever seen each other outside the faire was last year when Elric decided to stage betrothal pictures once he'd finished my pearl ring. Until now, neither of us had any interest in knowing the real stuff—but if I really *am* Euphemia, then faire stuff *is* real stuff.

While I drive, I slip the tip of my index finger through the pearl ring at the end of my necklace.

This is a good idea. And I'm not a stalker.

That's easier to claim before Tavia and I arrive at the theater in the boondocks of Vancouver.

"I don't think I'm in the mood for a movie," Tav says while I secure my headwrap over my twists, but when I tug her out of the car, she gives in.

"We don't have to see a movie to get movie popcorn, remember?"

Of course she does. I was only a few days into life at the Philipses' house when Miss Gennie came into our room and declared she had a craving for concession food. Which was totally not true because there is legiterally nothing there she would ever consume, but Tavia and I were delighted. She bundled us up (still in our pajamas) and took us to a theater for popcorn and drinks and nachos.

By the time we're ordering, Tav's actually smiling a little. My stomach's too excited to eat so I buy an ICEE to busy my hands while I wait for Elric's movie to end.

People pass our tiny table in the foyer, probably only glancing at me because I can't stop checking to see if they're looking in my direction. I've got my sister with me but I still hate that I can't trust my twists for shelter right now. Elric's movie'll let out in the next few minutes, though, and then maybe that'll change. Just because I can't really say *how* now that I've gone through all this trouble doesn't mean it won't.

A steady stream of people are turning the corner, making their way back through the concession area and toward the wall of glass doors broken up by the box office.

I don't wanna miss him, so I stand up.

"Eff?" Tav tries to follow my eyes. "Are you looking for someone?"

Now's a good time to tell her why we're here, or at least that Elric will be. I can't explain why I don't, except that I want it to be the way it is at the faire. I want her to be pleasantly surprised the way fairegoers always are when Elric and I have scripted but sudden interludes. When our fairytale comes to life and everyone gets swept up in it with us.

But I can't rely on the Elric I'm imagining. He won't be wearing a dingy white puffy shirt and brown trousers with a dusty canvas apron over them. His loose light brown curls might not be pulled back at the nape of his neck and he probably won't be wearing the goggles I always make sure to muss with my wet fingertips. Whoever he's with won't even be calling him Elric, which is the weirdest bit of all.

This is the first time I've worried about who he might be with. If I weren't already standing still, I'd freeze.

What if he's on a date?

My fingers instinctively go for a twist. Still none to be found.

If he were on a date, he would've tagged the mystery chick in his check-in, right?

He comes around the corner and I curse under my breath.

He's not alone.

It's like something out of a crappy high-school movie. A gaggle of white boys manhandling each other while they make way more noise than necessary, like they have to make sure everyone sees them living their best life.

He's definitely not Faire Elric in that striped tank top (which by the way is the same one he was wearing in at least two of his social media pictures, so it's clearly a favorite). He's got no apron or trousers, but he does have tight jeans under the loose hem of his shirt and he's paired them with flip-flops, which in any other situation would make me really sad for the guy (and which only newbies would ever wear to the faire).

Even his hair's unrecognizable. Instead of being bound at the base of his head, he's got his curls pulled back right at the middle and bunned.

I'm processing his transformation so slowly that he's at the door by the time I'm done. He's gone right by me, but I didn't exactly try to get his attention.

"Elric?" I say, and one foot steps forward for some reason.

"Wait . . ." Behind me, Tavia's figuring it out.

He doesn't even glance my way. I regret everything. But I'm

145

already here. Whatever magic abracadabra'd me home from the cemetery, I have no clue how to tap into it, so I may as well do what I came to do.

"Elric!" I have to say it louder because he's still got ahold of the door but he's outside now.

When it finally registers that someone's calling him—and by his faire name—he sweeps his eyes over the foyer. His eyes get wide when he finds me and I curse again.

He's surprised all right.

"Euphemia!" he calls. But the part I'm not expecting is when his friends throw their hands in the air and shout, "the Mer!" in unison.

He breaks into a casual jog and it's half the reason I like him in the first place. His approachable cuteness. Calmly adorable, which is my favorite kind. There aren't a ton of good-looking guys in the faire, I'll be honest, but there are one or two (always archers, and I'll give you three guesses why). Archers are known for their rakish charm and the fact that for them faire season is one big hook-up marathon. Yes, that's true of a ton of other people, but that's their storyline. It's more than half the reason they're there. It's not really my style and it isn't Elric's either. (He takes his craft seriously.) So when his friends know who I am, it surprises me—and then it calms me.

Even outside of our world, the people who know him know who I am. I'm starting to think I should've done this ages ago.

"Euphemia, on land, so far from water," he says, going down on his knee for a moment while he takes my hand where everyone can see. "By what power or potion?"

"Um"—even though my stomach's rumbling in a good way, I can't handle how naked I feel without my twists—"by yours, by one made of my betrothed's hand, to travel where waves may not."

I didn't really drink a potion, but I'll clear that up later.

"And brought near to me by some magic or happenstance? Or by love's direction," he says, which is one way of putting I-tracked-you-down-by-stalking-you-online. "Whatever, my heart is pleased."

One of his friends sighs a bit too whimsically, but otherwise they seem totally cool with this. It's confusing; Mama Theo loves me like crazy and has never been here for my faire life, but these high-school dudes are fine with it?

Behind me, I'm not sure Tavia's still breathing.

Elric cups my cheek and his thumb caresses my cheekbone the way he does when my waterproof makeup glimmers like tiny, iridescent gills. I can't help but press my face into his familiar hand and smile.

"This gift will keep me satisfied until we meet again."

And he's kissing my hand like this is farewell.

"Adieu, Euphemia," one of the boys says, flapping his arms slowly like an overgrown swan.

Now that he's rejoined them, they give him all the teasing he's likely to get, which is a few blown kisses and a pair of lips planted on the back of his hand. He's smiling like he's used to it, and it's more than mild as teasing goes, compared to what I got. Nobody's ever asked him if it's "historically accurate" to be in the faire. If he hadn't been a legacy—if he wasn't Second Smith to his father's legendary Blacksmith title—his backstory options would have been endless. His imagination could have run wild and no one (especially not someone who didn't even bother dressing up) would dare ask whether he'd "come to be there by laws of servitude." Like every explorer looked the same or like history is what's written in books. Tavia's people know better than anyone that's not true.

Right this moment, it's not Elric's white privilege that's throwing me off. It's the fact that my betrothed is just walking away.

"Wait, Rick." I step forward again, and he stops. He looks a different kind of surprised now and one of his eyebrows curls high.

I said Rick, not Elric. It's Richard, I'm sure, but online it always says Rick Morgan. He's not the Second Smith to the rest of the world, he's a varsity lacrosse player hoping to play in college. His faire life comes up in some of the Vancouver articles, because it's unique and he's well-rounded, and I guess because he's not ashamed of it. No one in his life is.

"Euphemia, are you well?" he asks, coming back halfway. "You spake a name like mine, but not. Is anything amiss?"

"It's just." I hook my finger through the ring at the end of my necklace, and wish I could disappear. There's a potion for that. There's one for reversing time, too, even though it only works in the storyline, not on a whim. "I just really need to talk to you."

When I speak in modern English, it gets real quiet. I can basically hear the wheels turning in Elric's head. And Tavia's. I can't bear to glance at her now.

"Did you know I'd be here?" The way he says it I can tell the right answer is no but they don't even give me a chance to lie. One of his friends whistles and everybody looks away from me.

Under my wrap, I swear my twists are tightening.

I don't know what I'm supposed to say here, how to get out of this moment. The guys I don't know are slowly splintering off, but not without what I'm very sure are mocking guffaws and snorts.

I finally turn and look to Tavia for support. All I find is confusion.

"Okay, it's not like you don't know where to find *me*," I say, mumbling most if not all of the words.

"What do you mean?"

I can't help but feel a little angry. I already feel unhinged enough for tracking him down. He doesn't have to act like he didn't do it first.

"I get the gifts you deliver," I say, rolling my eyes for effect.

But his eyebrows scrunch and now his eyes are roaming.

"At your home," he says slowly.

"Yeah!"

"In the cove."

What.

No.

No no no.

"Eff . . ." Tavia's soft voice comes from behind me, but I can't move.

This was a mistake.

I have gone out of my mind. Elric is lying . . . or else he thinks *I'm* making things up, and I'm not sure how to prove which of us is telling the truth. I just wish I hadn't come here.

"I don't get it, Euphemia," he says. "What's going on? You're not hurt, are you?"

"Effie," I say but not loud enough. I've pulled my chin to my chest, but without the twists to shelter me, it doesn't do any good. Would it make things worse if I reached up and tore the wrap away? Could I look any stupider if I dramatically unveiled my hair in the middle of the theater foyer and shook my head until all my twists felt free?

"What?" he asks. He's leaned in, but I notice he didn't take a step. When I answer, I may as well have marbles in my mouth for how garbled it sounds.

"My real name's Effie."

"Okay," and then I know what's coming, "but you're just Euphemia to me."

He's finally closing the space between us again, but now I wish he were made of stone.

That's sick. That's not what I mean.

I wish he'd stay away. All the fun he was having before I showed up is done, trailed away with the majority of his crew. He touches my arm when he's standing right in front of me but it sucks. We both wish I weren't here. And still, something in me crumbles when he leans in to kiss me—on the forehead.

"The faire opens soon, okay? I'll see you in a couple days."

I have no poker face. As much as I hope I give at least a weak smile, I know I don't pull it off by a mile. Not that it matters. He's already back out the door.

XI

TAVIA

I never drive Effie's car, but she's in no state. When I huddle next to her as we leave the theater—after giving Elric or Rick or whatever the hell that dick-face's name is plenty of time to get out of the parking lot—I take her keys.

Now we're sitting in her parked car, and she's staring at her hands in her lap. I don't want her to be embarrassed, but there's no escaping it. How could she not be? That POS just made a fool of her, even if nobody but the group of us know it.

I will dance on his grave.

When Effie moves, I whip my head to face her more fully, to hear whatever she has to say. But she's just untying her scarf and letting her twists cascade.

That makes sense. If I'd had a cloaking device after Priam dumped me right before homecoming, I for sure would've used it.

"Eff," I whisper, but she sinks lower in her seat and shakes her head once. I shut up.

On the dashboard her phone buzzes, and when it's obvious she couldn't care less, I reach for it.

"It's Isabella."

Have you been super paranoid since the park, or am I losing it?

And then there's a picture of what looks like a collection of butterfly wings. Cool.

"What's she say?" Effie must've heard me snort. She doesn't reach for her phone, but she almost looks at me.

"She thinks a sprite followed her home."

I wonder if I should've told her that. Effie's always had a hard time with sprites. A part of her has worried that she's been sprite-kin all along. The last thing she needs is some eloko princess getting her worked up.

That's not fair.

"Isabella's nice, huh?" I ask.

"Yeah." So quiet. "I like her."

And she tucks her chin back into her chest and disappears behind her hair.

I try to think of all the gentle prompts Dr. Randall might use to pry her open. The ones she hated because it felt like he was trying to trick or trap her, even though she knows better. Effie goes back and forth between being okay with needing outside help, and feeling forced; sometimes Dr. Randall was a trusted confidante and sometimes she hoped she never saw him again. I think maybe both were true, but she's got a right to process it however she wants, and for the last little while she hasn't wanted to see him. So rather than trying to be her therapist—especially in light of my own baggage—I decide to be her sister instead.

"Talk to me," I sign, but in the harsh light pouring in from the parking lot her eyes get glassy and I can't keep from speaking out loud. "Eff, what's the matter? Why did we come here?"

"Because I'm an idiot," she says, at last.

"You aren't," I insist. "Elric's the idiot if he didn't love you for real."

It's easy for me to leap all the way to hating his guts, but I should know better than to think calling him names will bring her any happiness right now. I've been where she is. Kind of. Priam and I were only together for a few months; Euphemia and Elric have been a fairytale for years already, even if they only play it out a few weeks at a time.

I study what I can see of my sister's face, and sigh.

That they see each other so briefly is probably what makes it intoxicating. It's like Elric comes to life anew every year, a fantasy bleeding into the real world all over again. He's declared his love in a dozen different ways—sending minstrels to sing below our balcony, or delivering small gifts to our doorstep without being seen. Only he's claiming some of that wasn't him. I don't know enough to guess whether he's lying, or why he would.

But that's when I get it. Effie called him Elric first. That's who she came to see. Rick is just the douche-y high-school jerk who plays Elric. Effie isn't in love with Rick, she just wanted the fairytale to be real for a moment. He should have been a good enough friend to wonder why. (Plus who the eff is named Rick anymore.)

"I'd love it, too," I say. I close my eyes because I'm about to get very honest. "I can't really imagine it now, but back when we were good, it would've given me my entire life if Priam knew me as Tavia the Siren. If he wooed me anyway."

She's looking now. She can't see the beads of sweat starting to appear on my skin because I'm so embarrassed to say this stuff out loud, but she's listening.

"Sometimes when Euphemia gets a little surprise delivery or when you're off at the pool preparing to transform for another Ren faire season, I . . . I imagine it's real for me, too." So stupid. "I imagine that at the fairegrounds, my secret could transform into something adored."

"Why didn't you say anything?" she asks so gently.

"I did. Not to Dad. There's not enough starry-eyed hope in the world for that."

"Miss Gennie."

"Freshman year." I nod.

"*Freshman year?*" She presses into my arm.

"I know. I've been creepin' on your world for straight years, my dude."

"So why didn't you join up?"

I can remember the conversation. The way, six months after Effie moved in, I nonchalantly mentioned to Mom that maybe Renaissance faires were like networks, too. That they could be, and wouldn't it be interesting to find out with Effie. That instead of visiting in plain clothes once or twice, I could build a character and a story and a wardrobe. (I didn't know much about the Hidden Scales then.)

I remember thinking Mom was gonna see the look in my eyes and believe that there was a place where I wouldn't have need of anonymity. Where people could fall in love with the whimsy of me and maybe a grassroots movement would topple "Lexi on a Leash" as the model minority, and it would all have started because I was brave.

Obviously that isn't how things went down.

"This is Effie's place," Mom had told me, gently. "Let's keep it for her okay, Vivi?"

In the car with Effie, I feel the cringe all over again.

"I would've been a distraction," I tell her, because it isn't the whole answer but it's still true. "I don't know the world like you do, and you would've lost time in your own story trying to show me how to learn mine."

Effie smirks the way she often does, but this time it's because she's wondering what might have been.

"Sure it sounds like a good idea tonight," I gesture toward the movie theater and smirk along with her. "But having a sister was still new to me then and I was being selfish. Back then, you would've hated me for horning in. It was your only constant."

"You're right. Miss Gennie was, whatever she said to change your mind."

"Wow. Thanks. 'No, T, I really wish you'd joined.'"

"My bad. No, T! I really wish you'd joined, you are my everything."

"I am!" I say, whimsically, like I've only just realized.

"You are. No, stop laughing, you are, though."

"I know." I can't undo my smile. "You are, too."

The light from outside the car doesn't feel as harsh now, and we sit surrounded, taking it in.

"I guess I thought he knew me," Effie says after a while. "The real me. The me who lives outside of Cathedral Park. Who might be a mermaid outside the faire."

"Wait." I can tell I'm making duck-face. "Who's a mermaid. You're a mermaid?"

Effie. My Effie.

Who might be having blackouts again, something that used to happen years before the incident in the cemetery.

The girl who swims like water's her natural habitat and even sees waves when she's on dry land.

Whose skin has always seemed dry but may be legit shedding now.

Who come to think of it hasn't snagged the last tampon in longer than I can remember. And that's saying something for girls living under the same roof, whose uteruses are more than occasionally in sync.

Crap. Is she a mer for real for real?

I'm waiting for the puzzle pieces to lock together, and I think so is she. Is that why . . . everything? Is that why Mama Theo hates the Renaissance faire? Is Effie's grandma more like my dad than I thought?

Except nobody despises their tail. Being a mermaid is the next best thing to being an eloko, but with a bit of additional drama. The eventual reveal toward the end of puberty, when the leg stiffness begins, right before they fuse.

That *would* explain the pastel glimmer on the skin I took off of Eff, except—

Nope. Something about this isn't adding up.

"You're not a mermaid."

"I don't know," she says, and it's clear she isn't sure. "At the pool, Naema said I was, in front of the elokos and Wallace, and now I'm thinking—"

There it is. That's why Naema kept bringing up Effie.

"And now you're thinking that Naema stays salty if you believe eloko mythos but also somehow mistakes cartoon representations of mermaids for truth? You should've told me she spoke sideways to you." I let my head fall to the side and cock my brow. Effie's not exactly looking at me, but she still smirks behind her twists. "Eff. Come on. Since when do mermaids spawn above the equator, for one thing? In the Pacific Northwest? In cold water? For real?"

"I mean . . ."

"Like why. Please."

I don't rhetorically ask her whether mermaids are known to shed (they're not) or whether anyone else loves the water (they do). I just sigh deep and shake my head, trying to keep her focus on mocking Naema so the obvious question doesn't arise.

"Okay, so I'm probably not a mermaid," Effie says, rolling her head against the seat to look at me. "But, Tav," and then the question comes out, because how could it not, "what am I then?"

The expression on her face is so soft and wide open that it almost breaks my heart. It deflates me so completely that I can't keep it from showing, but when I speak my voice doesn't crack like I worry it will. I don't know how I manage it, but I'm relieved when it comes out stronger than a whisper. When it comes out devoid of a siren call, but with authority all the same.

"I don't know." I roll toward her, too. "I feel like I should. Like a real sister would know how to help. I'm so sorry, Eff."

"Are you for real right now? Tavia. You *are* a real sister. Period." She inhales deep and then lets it out, and we fall back into silence.

"So Wallace was there, huh?" I nudge her. "The guy from the pool?"

"Yeah." She says it with an unmistakable reservation.

"Hm," two, three, four, "how exactly have you not caught feelings already?"

And right on cue, she flusters, tripping over my name and an assortment of abbreviated retorts.

"Say what now?" I tease her. "Come again?"

"You always think guys are into me."

"You always think they're not."

155

"Whatever," she says, sitting upright to signal that she's ready to go.

I start the car.

"I'm gonna go to the pool and meet him, that's all," I say calmly.

"No you're not."

"Okay." I'm looking straight ahead as I drive. "Watch when I do, though."

"Tavia!" She's got her seat belt on but she's stretching it out trying to get me to acknowledge her. "Tavia."

"Eff, please. I'm driving."

"Whatever." And then a moment later, "I'll tell."

I snort-laugh so hard, some snot wets the steering wheel.

"You're cleaning that."

~~~~~

I'm one to talk.

I've only ever caught feelings once. With Priam. And as distant a memory as it sometimes seems, it all happened at the start of this school year. We were something and then just as quickly, we weren't, and I couldn't even tell anyone why. And of course, neither has he.

I'd gone to the homecoming game with Priam even though in the two previous years at Beckett, I'd probably been to three sports events total. He'd already asked me to the formal, and I was settling into my new life of having a boyfriend and not buying my own ticket to dances, so I agreed to the game.

It was fun sitting bundled together in the stands, next to the marching band and all the off-field action. Effie had stayed home (which wasn't exactly shocking), so I was one of the elokos for the night.

Beckett High isn't just named for the first eloko president, it also boasts an unprecedented number of eloko students. Well above the average. At first it was a chicken/egg thing, where people weren't sure whether the number of students was because of the school's name change (until seven years ago it was called something corny and Oregonian, like Lewis and Clark High, or Willamette something-or-other) or whether the name change had been be*cause* of the higher percentage. Now all that matters is that it draws families.

As complicated as deciphering mythos can be, some things are admittedly demonstrably true. Expectant parents *do* hear a bell chime when their eloko child enters the world. Elokos *are* charming, and admired for their intellect—even though, according to what's been chalked up to fabrication, it's wisdom gleaned from being an ancestor spirit. Before Beckett became a beacon for hopeful families and Portland was thought to be some sort of hotbed for eloko generations, parents who hoped to bear one stayed near their ancestral homes. Because while the mythos can apparently be trusted when it comes to divining how to conceive an eloko child, it's the other part—the unsavory bit about elokos having originally been malevolent cannibals—that's a heinous untruth.

Which it obviously is, and I know that. But the night of the homecoming game, I didn't make that clear enough, or it didn't matter. All that mattered was that I saw the blood and Priam couldn't forgive that.

It was halftime and the marching band had already performed their four-song field show when Priam asked if I wanted to take a walk. There were other couples nonchalantly leaving the stands, walking the track to the end of the football field and leaving through the open gate beyond the concession stands. It wasn't the main exit, and for a little while I wasn't totally sure what was going on. The parents and assorted staff were still huddling in the stands and chatting or taking the opportunity to refill on snacks, so no one stopped the smattering of teens as we casually followed the band and color guard out the gates and toward the bus lot where the performers changed into jeans, band shirts, and jackets for the second half of the game. The rest of us wandered between them unnoticed, or else just immaterial, and I found myself on the far side of the opposing team's bus, with Priam.

As soon as we were out of view, he cornered me. I made an unappealing guffaw, which he muffled with a kiss.

It was basically the best moment of my life.

We were outside, scores of people and activity and energy just on the other side of a big yellow bus, floodlights lighting up the night, energy buzzing everywhere, and the smell of impending rain.

It was glorious. I felt so exceptionally normal. There was a burning in my throat but it was because I was trying to keep myself from crying, I was honestly that happy. Thankfully, when our lips parted slightly, what tumbled out was laughter.

"I don't even know what to make of that," Priam said, smiling at me while he cupped the back of my head. I could feel his freezing hand through my infinity-scarf-turned-headwrap, and when he pulled me into a new kiss, it couldn't smother my giggling. "What is your deal, am I tickling you or something?"

He decided to play along, I guess, and redirected his kisses to my neck. I was too sensitive by then and clamped my chin to my shoulder, forcing him to switch sides.

"That actually does tickle," I told him through my laughter, my ab muscles crunching mercilessly, one hand on his chest like I wanted to push him away, the other around his waist so he'd stay close.

"Fine." And he nibbled instead. When I scream-laughed, I heard a nearby couple snicker unseen. "What? Is that not better?"

Priam bit my neck, applying a little more pressure this time, and instead of just making me coil protectively, it felt nice. His breath was so much warmer than his hands, and I could smell his vague aroma, the way his long hair had recently been shampooed. We were embracing, my back pressed against the bus I could no longer feel, and then I winced.

I didn't scream the way I'd done when everything tickled. I hadn't pushed Priam away, even though he somehow ended up two full steps back. I just winced, and when his lips looked wet beneath the glow of the floodlights, I brought my fingers to my neck and felt the mark. Not my keloid. This was new.

There wasn't a ton of blood (duh, there's no such thing as vampires), my skin was just broken and my fingertips were a little wet when I looked at them. And slightly red. But I knew why he was looking at me like he could see through me. I've been that kind of scared before. Because if we went back into the stands, if we came back with all the other couples and their hickeys and everyone saw that I'd been bitten, maybe being an eloko wouldn't be such a charmed life anymore.

"Priam, it's okay. We can go. You can just take me home." When he didn't answer, I stepped into him and wiped his mouth, but he batted my hand away before I was done. Then when he licked his lips—which I didn't make him do—his eyes leapt back to me like it was my fault.

I tried to tell him it was fine. I wasn't going to make a big deal about it, and I don't even believe the mythos. No one does. I could understand his being embarrassed, but he didn't need to be, not in front of me. I kept hinting at the fact that I wasn't exactly proud of my own record, but he never bit. Which I realize now is an unfortunate choice of words, under the circumstances. I just mean, he never asked me what I meant. I would've told him how I got my scar if he'd asked.

Priam drove in silence, both hands on the steering wheel, while I nailed the coffin of our budding romance shut by repeatedly referring to the cannibalism I needed him to understand I *knew* wasn't true.

When we got to my street, he didn't park further up the hill like he usually did. He idled in front of my house and mumbled goodnight. By then, I'd flicked more than one tear off my cheek, and I'm pretty sure he was so far away, he didn't even notice.

Getting out of the car was the hardest thing I've ever had to do. Which sounds so trite and ridiculous for someone who's lived with a secret as big as mine. But I guess I'd really thought life was gonna be different from then on. I thought falling in love was gonna change the world, change me. Change the way my dad thought about me, and the way I felt about everything. And

159

yes, Priam being an eloko at Eloko President High School in eloko hotbed Portland was a big part of that.

Priam texted me that he was coming down with something and he didn't think he wanted to go to the formal, so we didn't.

And then he didn't text at all. It was over and I still have no idea whose fault it was. I guess it doesn't matter.

~~~~~

I wake up in the middle of the night and Effie's still there beside me. I smile. It's been forever since we fell asleep in the same bed, and I'm glad she stayed after what Elric put her through.

Effie's scarf is all askew, bunched up at the top of her head like she's been restless, and one of her twists is lying across her face. I gently rearrange it, twirling the end around my finger first. In reply her eyes squeeze tight and then they bat open.

"Hey," I whisper when she frowns.

"Hey. Go back to sleep."

"You're not the boss of me." I wait to see if she's awake enough for conversation. "Hey."

"You said that."

"I'm gonna go to the march this weekend. In Vancouver. Pretty sure there'll never be one for Rhoda Taylor, and at least Camilla'll be at this one."

She doesn't answer, but I know she heard me. She's thinking.

"You wanna come?"

"That's opening day," she says, and then she sighs and I know she's thinking of Elric. Of Rick, and the movie theater.

"It's okay. I didn't think about that; you don't have to choose."

"It's an easy choice. God, I'm glad Mama's not here to hear me." She rolls her eyes. "Of course I choose you. Now go back to sleep."

"I'm going," I say, then close my eyes, intending to fake like I'm drifting off. Only, something strange happens when I close my eyes again.

I'm floating. I feel it in my abdomen. It's like my eyelids are a

160

remote and closing them changed the channel, because not only does it feel like I'm floating but I'm somewhere else.

No more attic, no more Effie beside me. I'm not even lying down.

It's still dark, but I'm back in the lot outside the construction building. The first thing I notice is that there's no Naema. No coffee bean Fiat, no employee who's also part of my network.

Everything is stained indigo. Me, the construction lot—which, awash in dark, abyssal blues, now looks more like a scrap metal yard. The river is nightmarishly two-toned as well, and St. Johns is a behemoth of darkness. What should creep me out isn't the way the whole scene has been washed in an eerie blue-black light—I'm getting used to what I've begun thinking of as "the Indigo place." It's the stillness. I was beginning to hope this color is where Gramma will be, but here I am, all the way inside of it again, and seemingly alone.

Or am I?

No one else is in the construction yard, but I hear a voice, or something I know to be a voice despite the fact that it sounds more like water. Despite the fact that there are no words. It reminds me of dream logic, but this is not a dream.

"Gramma? Gramma, I'm here!"

I haven't moved since I arrived and I don't move now, because I don't know how this place works. I don't know what I'm here to do. Or hear. The voice that sounds like water is ever-present, but I still have no idea what it's saying. What I do know is that nothing has changed since I got here, and maybe that's because I haven't. Maybe speaking isn't enough and I need to *do* something.

The moment I take a step, Naema's there. She just manifests, and still it isn't jarring. Nothing is, not even the way that she, too, is bathed in shades of blue. I'm not even bothered by the fact that her eyes are closed.

I come close and Naema doesn't stir. Waving my hand in front of her eyes doesn't make her flinch, nor does lightly pulling her hair. That part was just for fun; Naema isn't really here. This isn't really her. Those aren't her thick eyelashes, laced shut over her big, deep-brown eyes. Those aren't her tiny, baby ears—the one thing she gets picked on for, if you can call it that. They're adorably small, and Priam was the first to notice. He's the one who bought her noise-canceling headphones on her last birthday, because she can't stand to have buds in her ears for more than a few minutes. Adorable.

She's the only other person (or illusion of a person) here, so this time when I speak, I say her name.

"**Naema.**"

Just like in the lot, there was no buildup, no heat, no flint in my throat to explain how this call manifested. Nothing had to unfurl, it just came out, the words almost beside the point. But it's a siren call, that much is certain. It isn't Appeal or Compel, but when I speak to her, the thing that is a stand-in for Naema opens her eyes and her mouth and her eloko melody swells into the space between us. She doesn't speak but a trill is in her throat and it comes crashing into me.

And I'm awake. I'm not gasping for breath or sitting upright like I've been chased out of a nightmare. Nothing like the movies. I just open my eyes and I'm home, lying in bed in the attic bedroom I share with Effie, who is sleeping beside me.

I have to go back to the construction yard.

I check the time on my phone and know that borrowing one of my parents' cars is out of the question. Borrowing Effie's boat of a clunker again is just asking to get caught; starting it up would wake the neighborhood.

I have to go back to the lot where I met Naema yesterday, it's just a question of how.

Stone talons scratch the roof above my head and my eyes roll in their direction.

I only stand when I've listened to Effie's low and constant breathing for a moment more, and then I tiptoe to the balcony door. It opens without a sound and the cold leaps into my chest even before I step outside.

He's there when instead of looking down at the street, I look to the roof. Good Ole Gargy, stoic and gray and stone and imposing. I do my best to pretend we're old pals, consider reminding him that I've stood next to him before. The truth is after three years I'm completely comfortable with the *thought* of him; it's when I actually *see* him that I remember how ridiculous it is to live beneath a gargoyle. To have a gargoyle bodyguard. To need one, and not know precisely why. What's different about me these past three years that I didn't need him before that? I assumed it had something to do with my choking myself out and ending up on lockdown, but he waited two more years to come keep watch. So that isn't it.

Gargy's granite eyes rolled down at me as soon as I came out the door, and the way he's leaning forward I think he's gonna break his pose and rush me. I can imagine it now, the way the roof tiles will shoot out of his way like throwing stars and how the last thing I'll see is one of the projectiles flipping toward my forehead. I'll wake up three days from now at OHSU, just in time for my dad to disapprovingly tell me how much it's gonna cost to repair the roof.

"Seriously, please don't break anything," I say to the mountain of gray muscle. "My dad is not a fan. I'm not trying to hurt your feelings, I'm just saying. He doesn't like you. Which has more to do with me than you, just. You know. Be careful up there."

He's been perching without incident for three years, but no harm in being careful. That and, three years ago, things were quiet. My dad was worried, but outside our house, it didn't feel quite so chaotic. Portland seemed like a world away from Santa Cruz, California, and since the drive was literally the longest of my life, it was easy to imagine that my troubles were a distant memory too. Things are different now. Rhoda Taylor's life didn't matter, Priam's dad might be as fickle as his son, I'm not sure I can trust everyone in my network, and the whole world knows about Lexi and Camilla. I asked Gramma to take my voice and instead I'm pretty sure she taught me a new siren call, and it's beginning to feel like maybe my dad was right. Maybe this gargoyle's arrival was a bad omen and it's only becoming apparent now.

"Anyway."

He does something that looks remarkably close to a sigh, his shoulders rising and falling before he lifts one massive fist from the roof and rests it on top of his granite knee. Is he listening?

"I know you're here for me, I mean that's what everyone thinks." I pause when he blinks. There's something so strange about it, like he's imitating human behavior. I can't imagine stone eyes need lubricating. "So . . . anyway, I need a favor. From you."

I wait, but he doesn't move.

"So. Yes? Can you do something for me?"

"Yes."

I jerk back like his voice was accompanied by some extraordinary force. Mostly it's shock that after all this time, I've just heard the gargoyle's voice for the first time; some of it is the fact that it was simultaneously deep and quiet. I would've guessed a gargoyle's voice was gravelly, like a rock tumbler in action. Instead it was regal and robust, and more like a sensation than a sound. It reminds me of the way my dad's roadster rumbles when it starts, and then it sort of quiets down and you forget that you heard it at all.

"Yes," I repeat back to him to confirm. Now that the sound is gone, I'm not sure I didn't imagine it. Maybe I can get him to speak again. "You will?"

"Tell me what it is."

Shut up. This is wild. I wanna run into the bedroom and shake Effie awake. Maybe I could make him start over so she can hear it from the beginning, but I'm afraid if I go inside now he'll never speak again.

He's waiting.

"Right. Everyone's asleep, but I need to go somewhere and I can't take one of the cars. I don't know if this is in your job description, but I need you to take me to a lot near St. Johns. I could ride on your back, I guess."

164

"No." This time it's his smooth, gray wings that seem to sigh. "You can't. But I will carry you where you need to go."

The gargoyle's going to carry me. In his arms, I assume, although maybe he means in his claws? As ridiculous as I'd feel being carried like a fainted princess, I feel like that'd be preferable to being clutched like a mouse on its way to hungry eagle babies. None of which I say to him because I'm not sure how to ask not to be carried like dinner.

"Quickly," he says, and lifts off without hesitation. His wings just bat the air once and he raises from the roof and unfurls himself so that he's standing in midair. "Before he knows you're gone."

I guess he knows my dad by now.

"Okay."

I feel my body tense as he lowers himself on the balcony in front of me, and then his massive hand is closing on my elbow. Again, it would make zero sense for him to suddenly fling me like a ragdoll from the balcony and watch me roll down the street, but I can't help imagining it. Instead I feel myself tremble and lift my chin so I can look at the monster slowly trying to get me to turn my back to him.

"What—"

When I've turned around, he puts his hands around my waist, his oversized fingers overlapping on my abdomen. The strangest part (of a gargoyle holding me by the waist like we're ballerinas and I'm preparing to leap into the air) is the way his hands aren't hot or cold. They're neither, no sweat or chill leaking into my clothes.

"Ready?" he asks, the deep husk of his voice rolling over my shoulder.

Mom. Dad . . . I'm in love with a gargoyle.

I'm kidding.

"Ready," and for some reason, I close my eyes. There's no tightening on my waist, no gust of wind in my face, but when I open my eyes again, we're airborne. We're gliding over the rooftops on the hill. The wind must be breaking against him before it gets to me, because it's perfectly lovely in the air. I don't know what I expected it to feel like suspended in a stone monster's grasp, but his grip doesn't feel coarse the way his wing did on my balcony. If I didn't know better, I'd swear he'd softened since the last time I touched him. If that's even possible.

I've lived in Portland since middle school, but I've never seen it like this. We coast as far as Nob Hill, the lights below failing to shine on us. It's strange to think how much ground we've covered. That no one knows we're overhead. Tucked close to the gargoyle's stone body, I fly above changing streetlights, people walking in loose and lively clusters. Couples strolling side by side, cars that look remote control from this unfamiliar vantage point. We're not airplane high, just far enough that the city looks like a model beneath us. Finally, Gargy swoops north and follows the river, a wide track of darkness peppered on both sides by reflected spots of light.

When the construction lot isn't far ahead, I pat the great stone claws around my waist and gesture that it's our destination. In the middle of the night, it's almost as eerie as it was in my not-dream, long hulking masses stacked on the end where Naema and I met. I know they're freight containers, but I'm not looking forward to standing among them until I remember who I'm bringing with me.

Gargy doesn't land, extending his arms I'm now certain are softer than solid stone to set me on my feet like a little boy arranging toy soldiers. It looks like he plans to keep watch just off the ground, ready to engage anything that might be in this deserted space.

But there's nothing here.

The otherworldly blue-scale filter is gone, replaced by pools of sharp security light, and deep shadows where the light doesn't reach. There is no Naema-stand-in. The only thing that looks the same is the river, dark and abyssal. It looked like a sheet of glass when we were flying overhead, and it does from the lot, too.

"What if sometimes stories are true?" I say aloud, like Gargy knows about sirens and water and the blue place where I just was.

I look high over my shoulder to find him surveying the lot, the river, and however far beyond them his stone eyes can see. He glances in my direction and makes a sort of noncommittal nod, the way my dad does when he's half listening, but I know what I know. At least I think I do.

My dad was right to fear the water and hide up on the hill.

My grandma's voice is here.

"Take me over the water," and I lift my hand toward him like I'm an old pro. In reply, he takes it, lifting me a little ways before wrapping a thick arm around my torso. In a moment he's holding me by the waist with both hands again and we're making the short flight to the river, over which we bob, dipping low before he bats his wings just enough to put us back in place.

The Willamette is like a black mirror, our reflection made almost entirely of shadow except where a nearby light manages to illuminate a portion of my face.

I am inky darkness except for my left eye and cheekbone and a sliver of what is still an obviously broad nose. For a moment, I turn my head slightly one way and then the other so that pieces of my face appear and disappear, now my jawline and ear are visible, now the full range of my nostrils.

Above and around me, the dark reflection of Gargy ripples slightly when a breeze catches on the water. And then, his reflection is gone.

He sees it too, letting us dip closer to the water, close enough that if I reach out, my fingertips can almost find the surface.

Suddenly I can see all of my face, both eyes, my nose, my mouth—but it doesn't gape the way I know it should. My mouth is wide open, but the one on the water is not.

And then it moves. The reflection mouths a single word.

"Awaken," I say aloud, and my reflection—the me that is not me—smiles. "The call I used is called Awaken."

The reflection knows me well enough to see my declarative statement for the question that it is, and she nods.

Mom always says I could be Gramma's twin, even if Dad

refuses to tell me so. Now I know for sure. Whatever part of her returned to the water is my spitting image, or I am hers.

If I use it now will she come back? Will she . . . awaken? Is it possible to bring a siren back from the water?

I draw in the cool air above the river and then I speak.

"**Awaken!**" I felt it lace the word as it escaped, but nothing changes. "**Awake!**"

My fingertips slip beneath the surface, but they find nothing but water.

This isn't the way it works. Siren calls don't work on sirens, and Awaken probably doesn't bring people back from the dead.

"You're really here," I tell my grandmother. "I was beginning to think 'the water' was, like, a special place in every siren's heart or something. But you're here."

The reflection smiles again. Gramma nods that, yes, she's here. And then she disappears. The reflection doesn't turn back into me and Gargy, just erases from the water and leaves the black behind.

I should have told her I was grateful to know the call's name, even if it didn't do what I hoped. That I'm glad to meet her, to know that she can hear me. That she's been nearby and listening.

Gargy lets us bob a moment more and then he takes me home. I watch Portland pass beneath us again, but I barely see. Minutes pass, neighborhoods reduced in my immediate memory to nothing more than dimly lit streaks. Only my second flight and it can't keep my attention.

When Gargy sets me back on my balcony and floats backward to perch on the spire, I'm not ready to go back inside. I'm too spread out to be contained right now. I'm too big to fit in my bed.

"So. Where are you from?" I ask the gargoyle, and he moves much less now, his skin (if you can call it that) looking impenetrable and bone-crunching again.

"Nearby."

"Cool."

His voice is still regal and deep, so that part of the night I didn't imagine. Already I'm not sure I was really floating over

Portland, or if I saw anything more than my own reflection in the water. If it feels like this right after landing, by morning any certainty I had will be gone. I need to keep talking.

I fix my gaze back on Gargy up on the spire. He's no doubt unimpressed with my conversation skills. Scores of oral presentations in IB and I'm dying out here.

"Is that where you are when you're not here?"

He blinks again, and this time it doesn't look so strange.

"I just mean, I know you're not *always* on guard. Because sometimes you're not around. Or I don't see you. Not that I'm questioning your work ethic, you probably know what you're doing. I mean, you do know what you're doing."

"You aren't my ward."

"Sorry?"

And then it makes sense.

"You aren't here for me. You're here because of Effie." It should be a question, but I'm sure. "You came because she's here. Why? Did you live at the Freemans' before? Why doesn't she know, then? Why does she need a guardian?"

I sound like a toddler, asking a thousand questions one after the other, but I can't stop.

"Wait, then who did you mean when you said, 'before he knows I'm gone'? And what's she becoming?"

The gargoyle relaxes on the spire, his feet loosening their grip without slipping even slightly. After the sound of his massive stone form adjusting, his voice sounds even more divine.

"Herself."

XII

EFFIE

"You were right," I tell Mama as soon as she opens the navy-blue door. Paw Paw and I painted it when I was eight and he wanted me to believe the house needed painting to honor my moving in instead of as a distraction while Mom was at the hospital. He transformed the modest yellow home with a bright coat of white, and he let me slather blue all over the door.

"Effie baby? What are you doing out here?"

Mama Theo pokes her head out of the threshold to look around me like she's never seen the Portland sun shine so brightly, or maybe like I've multiplied and she expects to find more of me. When she's satisfied, she puts her hands on my shoulders and looks me over.

"How long you been out here? Where's Tavia?"

"It's just me. I just wanted to see you."

"And tell me I was right about something," she says, tugging me into the house. She looks around one more time before closing the door.

"Are you okay?" I ask.

"Am I okay, you're the one crying on my porch. You didn't even ring the bell. If I hadn't seen you through the window, how long were you planning to stand out there? And what couldn't you tell me over the phone?"

"It's just. I'm taking a break from the faire. I wanted to tell you that; I didn't know I wasn't welcome at home anymore," I say, trying hard not to side-eye her. "I thought you'd be relieved."

"I am," she says. "But I hate to see you cry. Where's Tavia, anyway? Why isn't she with you?"

"We're not attached, Mama. We do *some* things on our own."

"Well. You shouldn't. It's good to be together."

"Okay." That was weird. "Wait, what?"

"Come sit down," she says as she leads me into the kitchen.

The sitting room may be the focal point of the Philipses' home, but at the Freemans', it's the kitchen. Everything happens around the table, and always with food. There's something so calming about the fact that Mama Theo always has something ready to serve. It means there's no such thing as an unexpected guest. Who could feel unwelcome when there's muffins, or pie, or baked macaroni and cheese? Except I do, a little.

Something feels off.

"Why are you so concerned with me and Tavia being together all the time, Mama? And what was the matter when you came by the house?"

"I thought you loved your sister, pardon me," she says with a dismissive wave. "And don't come interrogating me in my own house, you're the one upset today. Don't mess up your face, *some*thing had to happen for you to take a break from the faire. What was it?"

She's staring right at me and there's no way I'm gonna confess the whole "thought-Elric-was-really-my-bae" situation. Mostly because I'm realizing that might not be what it was.

I thought I was really Euphemia. I thought the truth was at the fairegrounds, that Mom left all the answers in the Hidden Scales. In a regular old tent with a ring of fog permanently wafting around the bottom. In a fantasy people pay to walk around in, I was hoping I'd found out who I really am.

Mama Theo's not eating her coffee cake and I haven't touched my slice. I started this conversation but I don't want to marinate in it, so I take a bite and try to shrug like nothing's that big a deal. If she doesn't have to answer my questions, I don't have to answer hers.

"Nothing happened. It just doesn't seem as exciting anymore." It's not a lie technically, but it's definitely a recent development. Mama eyes me. "I just thought you'd be happy."

"I wanna be," she says through a sigh. It's one of those things I can immediately tell she didn't mean to say out loud. Then she straightens up and lays down her fork. "Promise me something, Effie."

"Promise you what?"

"Don't tell anyone you went to see your mama." (I'm pretty sure I stop breathing.) "And don't go back."

There's no response for something like this. If it were a joke it would be super offensive, and the fact that it isn't . . .

It means something's wrong. Very wrong. Worse than being embarrassed in front of a clan of eloko, worse than making a fool of myself in front of Elric and his real-life friends, worse than maybe being sprite-kin or mermaid or not knowing what I really am.

I can't handle worse.

Theodosia Freeman has never tried to keep me away from my mom or her memory. And this is the last straw.

"You could've made my life so much easier, if you had— once!—told the truth."

"Effie—"

"Nobody ever figured out hiding things from kids isn't protecting them if they know something's wrong! It just makes me think I can't trust myself. I can't trust these feelings I have, these warnings I keep sensing. Like I never should have trusted you."

"Effie Calhoun Freeman."

"Don't you mean Effie Calhoun Freeman Philips?"

All of the air in the room is gone. Mama gasped and took it all.

"Maybe I'm a chameleon," I say quietly, because my air is gone, too. "Isn't that what orphans have to be?"

I don't know what I'm saying, or why. I don't know why I

would say it to Mama Theo except that she can take it. Paw Paw is so gentle, and Tav's got worries of her own. And what if lashing out at her dad meant I wouldn't be Effie-dee anymore, or that Miss Gennie wouldn't twist my hair?

I can be angry at Mama Theo. Only at Mama Theo. And she's earned it, at least a little.

I don't ask her anything about my father. I know better than to press my luck. If I was going to get any answers—about her recent behavior or mine—I've already ruined my chances.

I shove the rest of my coffee cake in my mouth. I'm too bitter and it's too sweet, so I hurt myself forcing it all down my throat at once.

"Tell Paw Paw I love him."

"Effie," and I turn back to the table, my eyes stupidly full of hope, "stay with Tavia. Keep your sister close."

"Yep," I mutter as I walk away. It takes everything in me not to say I hate her, and it's a good thing I don't because Paw Paw's on the porch. My face flushes warm with guilt anyway, and he pretends not to see it.

"Where you goin' in a hurry," he says, taking a seat on the porch step.

I don't answer, just sit down next to him because I know it's an invitation.

Paw Paw sighs heavy, his arms resting on his knees while he looks out into the yard.

"Waited too long, I guess." He says it softly, and just when I'm gonna ask what he means, he gestures at the newly overturned earth in the garden.

"Not too late for everything," I tell him, thinking about cucumbers and squash.

"Nah, not everything. Just shouldn't have taken my time."

Paw Paw and I sit still for a little while before I let my head fall onto his shoulder, let my person-sized hand slip into the huge palms I know so well. His face is dark and smooth, almost lineless, but Paw Paw's hands have deep grooves in them, wrinkled

173

skin so thick it looks like he's always wearing a pair of Elric's heavy work gloves. I'm admiring them, waiting, just in case we're talking about more than vegetables. In case he'll say something that'll make all the difference.

"You're gonna be all right," he says like there was a whole lot in between.

"How do you know?"

"'Cause it's all anybody wants. Even when we disagree."

I sigh, but it's not in relief. As usual, Paw Paw's on brand, his reasoning too simple to mean much.

I can't be okay just because that's what he and Mama and I want. There's more going on with me than that. This is more than puberty stuff.

I've always wished life were as easy as Paw Paw makes it sound; now I'm starting to think there's just a lot he doesn't know.

After I hug his arm and kiss his smooth forehead, we say goodbye, and I make a beeline for Southwest Community Center. It isn't just a weird way to spite Mama. I'm still skipping Ren faire this year (or at least the first day or two, however long it takes Elric to grovel so as not to lose his storyline), but that doesn't mean I have to give up the water. It's still my safe place, even if I'm taking time away from the fairegrounds.

I haven't gotten in the pool yet because I can't stop checking my phone. I texted Tavia during her after-school study group with a wide-eyed emoji and one of a cell phone, and I wanna be close to it when she calls. Her IB crew tends to take the whole phones-off-books-open thing more seriously than I do, but I'm crossing my fingers that today'll be the exception. My screen goes black and I unlock it again just in case something happened in that split second. I don't even notice Wallace until he's closing in on me, walking a wide circle like he's ready to abort the mission if I give the slightest hint of irritation.

"Hey, Effie," he says when I see him. He waves his hand like he's wiping steam off a mirror and it honestly takes me a minute to remember what he's got to be so shy about.

"Oh, hey." I put my phone back on the towel folded in the chair, but then I pick it up one more time and check for notifications. "Sorry. Waiting on my sister."

He nods and glances at the pool and then the floor and then my phone before his eyes make their way back to me.

"Hey," I point at him because now I remember where we left off and then I retract my finger because it's weird, "I'm sorry I snapped at you that day."

"No, that girl was gunning for you, I get it."

I don't know if Naema was *gunning* for me . . . or who says that.

"Anyway I'm not usually mean, so. Sorry about that."

"You weren't mean," he says in a hurry.

Geez, dude, can I apologize or nah?

I'm not sure what to say now. I'm more than a little surprised that he hasn't mentioned the whole "haunted hair" part of that situation, but maybe he's trying not to upset me. Which Tavia would say means he's into me. Man, if levitating hair is his thing, wait till he gets a load of my dry skin.

What sucks is how I still feel guilty talking to him, or wondering if he's interested. I don't want to, but my mind skips back to Elric. And then immediately to the way his friends whistled when they figured out I'd tracked him down on purpose.

("Stalked" makes me wanna peel my skin from my bones, so I'm going with "tracked.")

Everything inside me cringes. Because if Elric was being serious and he's really never dropped any gift off at my house, that means my finding him is several shades more embarrassing. And he could totally be telling the truth. For one, why wouldn't he be. And for two, there are plenty of Ren faire devotees who'd go out of their way to be part of the story.

The important thing is that I'm never going to live this down.

"So you're into the Ren faire, right?" Wallace asks right as my phone starts to vibrate.

I dive for it, but when I unlock it, the text isn't from Tavia. It's Isabella, wondering where I am again.

175

"Yeah." I'm reading and answering Wallace at the same time but then I snap my head back up. "Wait, how'd you know that?"

"That girl who was here last time mentioned it."

Naema? She did?

I can tell I'm mouthing Isabella's text (which is super rude of me) but it's the third time I've read it and I'm still not processing it. My brain is officially at capacity. I don't understand how Tavia's dealing with a siren-sized secret *and* choir *and* tiptoeing around her parents *and* IB. Like, why. I have exactly one friend and am basically on autopilot through the end of the year except in Ms. Fisher's class, and I'm clearly slacking there.

Isabella and I could be friends, if I weren't falling apart. She's so genuinely nice and consistent. For example, she's texting because we do actually have a final project we're responsible for and even though we haven't met up since that day at the park (and I haven't given her my half of the recorded-history component yet), she says:

I'm so sorry for being pushy—I'm officially a nag!—just wanted you to know I can totally help more if you need.

She even makes sure to relieve any pressure by being conversational at the end. She makes fun of herself for being a scaredy cat and thinking a sprite followed her home. She reports there've been no disembodied voices creepily inviting her to do tricks, and that the blur she saw out of the corner of her eye is just her imagination.

She's so rational and normal. I don't get why she likes me.

I'm supposed to text her if I wanna meet there, so I say I'll come by in about an hour.

She sends back an obese cat riding a scooter.

'Kay.

I don't know why I said I needed an hour. I could really just pack back up and go now. I don't need to do laps or breathing exercises and it's stupid to stay just to be around Wallace.

It feels like he's been standing in front of me forever while I ignore him in favor of my phone. That's sweet, right? If I ninja-style take a picture of him waiting patiently, maybe I can text it to Tavia or Isabella and they can help me decide.

"Anyway." I put the phone back on the chair. I'm totally not stealth enough to take his picture without giving myself away. "You know about the Renaissance faire?"

"No. I mean not really. I know it's about to start, though, right?"

"Yep." I sigh. "Tomorrow. Opening day's always a big deal."

I don't know I'm smiling until I see Wallace is too.

"But I'm not going this year. I think I've finally outgrown it."

"It doesn't seem like it."

"And you would know how?" I wish I'd rephrased it as soon as the words are free, but he doesn't flinch.

"By how wide the thought of it made you smile."

"Yeah . . ."

"It must be a lot of fun. Why don't you wanna go?"

Really wishing I hadn't found that stray hair tie in the car and bound my twists again. When my hand lifts to find nothing, I have to pretend the plan was always to massage my neck.

"It's complicated. It's not really the kind of thing I can explain—" I almost say "to a stranger" but catch myself just in time.

Wallace nods like I just shut down his advances or something, so I blurt out an excuse.

"Plus my sister wants to go to this protest in Vancouver and her—our—parents would kill her if they found out she went alone." And then there's Mama Theo's ominous and weird warning. "Anyway, it's the same day, so."

"Oh, that's too bad, I was thinking of giving the faire a try this year."

"I think it'll go on without me if you wanna go." Everything I'm saying sounds so much less flirtatious when it comes out of my mouth. Without a script, this romance game is difficult. I try to tack something on to soften it. "Worth a shot, right?"

"I was really only going to see you swim."

He is better at this than me.

"Do you think you'll be there another day?" he asks, and he starts to come toward me but he doesn't just walk. One of his shoulders is slung low, and the other one is higher, and is he a model on a photo shoot? When he's standing in front of me, he rubs his hand back and forth over his short hair. It's . . . delightful.

"I," am stammering, "I don't think so. I think I'm taking a break this year, to be honest."

But you can watch me swim whenever you want, I should say, right now, before the moment ends.

"Well, then," and his eyes slide around a bit before he suggests, "what if I come along?"

"To where?"

"To the protest."

"Um. Why?" Shouldn't have said that. *Come on, Effie.* "I mean, that'd be really cool, I'd love that, I just didn't know if you know what it's about."

That's his out if he wants to take the safe route and bypass what's considered a "controversial" subject for anyone who can afford to play devil's advocate. But just in case he's feeling adventurous, I steel myself for his answer. Tell myself not to hold it against him when he says one of those things Tavia calls "woke-adjacent."

Palatable, I call it. Something that sounds thoughtful without demanding action.

I promise myself to let it slide for the moment if he says "people" without specifying *which* people keep being killed by police officers who apparently stay scared but are allowed to unload weapons into us instead of finding new jobs.

And I vow to abruptly fade out and disappear if he says any variety of "but I take issue with the method."

Standards. A girl must have them. Whether all of her internal organs are in knots or not.

"It's about not letting being Black in America be an executionable offense," he says. Like he's had this type of conversation before. Like having a maybe crush on a Black girl isn't the first time he's watched the news and seen the problem. "Black Lives Matter. Everybody knows that."

I have to respond without sounding overly excited that he's a decent human being, so I blink a few times too many and settle on, "I mean. I don't know about 'everyone.'"

"Nah, they know." He nods and does a kind of shrug. "They just pretend they don't get it or they'd have to admit that they disagree."

He's just trying to impress me. Right? Like last year when some guy told me it was really important to him that he date a girl of every race. Except not like that at all because I didn't just involuntarily dry heave. Maybe it's because Wallace is brown himself, or because older guys are just more aware than the boys at Beckett High.

"So? Is that a yes?" he asks me, grinning like he can read my thoughts. "I can come, right?"

For once I'm glad there's nothing hanging in my face. This way he can see how hard I'm trying not to smile.

~~~~~

After we swim, I don't really feel like heading to the park. I know I told Isabella I'd go, but I don't wanna deal with high-school final projects or sprites or statues of kids I used to know. I don't wanna know whose mom came to refresh the wreaths this time or explain to Wallace that I've got more than run-of-the-mill Black-girl baggage. I feel calm for the first time in forever and I want to keep it.

I want to have fun, and I am. I don't think that makes me a bad person.

Across the booth, Wallace eats like it's his first meal in a week.

"Aren't you hungry?" he asks while holding half a burger in his hands and the other half in his cheek.

"I was."

His face drops and I snort out a laugh.

"I'm kidding! You're not the first guy I've watched scarf down Skyline, relax."

"Your boyfriend likes this place?"

I snort again. "For real?"

He shrugs but he's doing a mouth-full-of-burger, closed-lip grin like, "I tried."

"Yeah, you tried it."

"I was pretty sure you had a boyfriend," he says after washing down his monster-bite with a gulp of chocolate shake.

"I did . . ." And then I feel silly.

No I didn't, but a slideshow of Elric and Euphemia plays in my head anyway. Elric in his apron at his forge working on Euphemia's ring. Elric and Euphemia "kissing" through my tank. Her tank.

When did I start confusing my life with hers? Naema calling me a mermaid didn't help, but it also wasn't the start of it. This whole year, the weirder I feel, the more I've wanted Elric and the faire to be the answer. It just wasn't.

I guess I should've listened to Mama Theo years ago. And I should've gone to the park like I promised Isabella, because here comes Naema.

I took it as a good omen when Wallace and I got a booth with a view since I always seem to hit Skyline at peak traffic, but when Naema's car pulls into a miraculously free parking spot right outside of our window, I change my mind. And when Priam gets out of the passenger side of her dehydrated turd pebble of an overly expensive car, I really do lose my appetite.

"What's the matter?" Wallace must pick up on it quickly, because he straightens up. Like squares his shoulders and loses the flirtatious twinkle in his eye that even I can't miss. I guess it's fair to say he is not a fan . . . which is pretty cute.

"Please don't let her see me," I mumble.

"She saw you."

"Of course she did."

I prepare to give serious shade to Priam when they get to our table, but only Naema comes over. Smart.

"Ariel," she says in a singsong voice while she plays with her charm. "How you doin', kid?"

So this is gonna be a thing now.

"Are you stalking her?"

Both Naema and I whip our eyes to Wallace.

Um. What? (But also, hilarious.)

Like a true eloko princess, Naema doesn't clap back without thinking. Her smile spreads across her face with the zen of a baby who just unloaded into their diaper.

"You're the pool guy." She offers her hand like teenagers go around formally introducing ourselves and shaking. "I'm Naema."

Wallace has to submit and shake her hand if he doesn't wanna look like the douchebag. He does and she's smug in victory.

"I'm a fellow Portlander who requires sustenance to survive, so yes, I often frequent popular dining establishments on Friday evenings, but no. I'm not stalking our mermaid friend."

"I'm not a mermaid," I blurt.

God. Why do I bother.

"Oh? You sound pretty sure now, but at the pool . . ."

All I can see is my hair floating, climbing the breeze that couldn't have existed in the community center. It's an out-of-body view that's been replaying in my head ever since it happened. It makes my skin tingle just thinking about it, and with Naema hovering over me it's making my tightly secured twists throb. I can't afford to wait and see what they do next.

"What's your deal?" I whirl in my seat and lock eyes with her. It's not my strong suit, but I already flashed on Mama today so I might as well keep it up. The irritation throbbing in my temples helps. "Did I do something to you? Why do you keep bugging me? Are you embarrassed that you're thirsty for my sister's seconds or what?"

"It's weird how you and Tavia think I've got nothing better to do than worry about you two."

"It's weird how you're telling me that after coming straight to my booth."

Boom. I so rarely have comebacks in the moment. Usually I'm in bed hours after a confrontation when I think of the most awesome retort that no one will ever hear. It's one of the most frustrating things about being me, aside from literally everything else, so I'm drinking this moment in. I want to remember how Naema's eyes snapped wide like she'd been slapped and how Wallace's smirk makes him even cuter.

"Your sister warned me about you." There's an unmistakable trill in her voice. Even the people around us perk up at the sound, their smiles widening. "I just don't think the two of you are as dangerous as you think you are."

"What *are* you talking about, Naema? No one's trying to scare you. I just want to eat my dinner in peace."

She rolls her eyes like she's amused and makes a calming gesture to match the long breath she releases like she's cooling down from a workout.

"Nice to see you again, pool boy." And then from over her shoulder, trill lacing the words, "Bye, Ariel."

XIII

TAVIA

Today's the day.

I don't think I slept last night, and if I did it wasn't well. Every few moments, my eyes snapped open to find more light bleeding into my room. More of a fog that might not have been there, rolling between me and the ceiling. I'd close my eyes again and listen, strain to hear what seemed so intrusive back when I thought he was perched here because of me.

At some point in the night I wandered out to talk to Gargy. I've done it every night since our flight, sleeping and waking and then finding myself on the balcony with him. It hasn't been as adventurous as the night I saw my grandmother in the water. We haven't flown down the hill again, but he lifts me onto the roof so I can sit with him, and we have a conversation that comes out in short bursts that break up the silence.

The quiet is just fine, and perched on the roof of my house with a gray, winged giant, I figured out what I like about hanging out with him. Aside from his voice, I mean.

Gargy's the most like me of anyone I've met. He's not envied or admired like the elokos, and he hasn't faded into myth like an oracle. He's not a lovable menace like the sprites, given immunity because it's easier than admitting there's nothing we can do about them anyway.

Gargy's a hulking oddity, a chess piece on a checkerboard. He stands out like a sore thumb. It's impossible for him to go undetected for long and it's equally impossible for him to find his place. He hasn't said any of that, but whenever I'm close to him, his stone skin softens. So I know.

When I find myself standing in a diner parking lot in the nipping chill of early morning, I wish I knew where he was perched so I can roll my eyes in his direction. I guess I didn't understand that Effie and I were the only ones having to sneak to Vancouver.

When we meet up with Altruism, the Jennifers, and a few other IB kids, I'm startled to be greeted by a couple of their enthusiastic moms. I mean, I guess the whole meet-at-a-diner should've seemed pretty random, if you think about it. (Nothing screams "fight the power" like ordering two eggs over easy first.)

Now we're huddled outside again, Allie's mom and one belonging to a Jennifer preparing us for battle.

"You girls—and guy!—make sure to keep these on at all times." Allie's mom is speaking into her open trunk while she hands the other woman bright orange drawstring backpacks for distribution. Like any respectable flight attendant, the other mom keeps one to disassemble for our attention. "You've all got smartphones, I'm sure, but you never know what could happen, so I put disposable cameras in each bag."

I take the camera out like everyone else, but instead of looking at it, my eyes keep jumping around the small crowd. I feel like I'm missing something.

"Is this milk?" Allie holds the plastic water bottle by the cap like she might toss it in disgust.

I feel myself shrink.

"Everyone has two bottles of milk, in case of tear gas exposure," one of the moms is explaining. She goes on to describe the side effects of tear gas and that we are to remain calm, help each other pour the milk over our faces if need be.

I know exactly where she got this informative speech. I've seen the pictures for the last few years; we all have. Protest after protest torpedoed into chaos; protesters stained white to combat the gas but thereafter easily spotted by journalists and police alike; people at home not only believing in the milk myth but also apparently unfamiliar with any law protecting protesters and suddenly in favor of police states.

I've been asked more than a few times whether I agree with destruction of public property and—even if I don't psych myself out with what may or may not actually be the heat of a siren call pluming in my throat—I'm not sure I'm allowed to speak. The question's always framed so that bringing up destruction of human bodies sounds like a deflection even to my own ears. Which is scarier than anything else.

And then the T-shirts come out.

"I know this protest is about the whole community and I know not everyone will feel comfortable wearing these," the mom continues, and more than half the eyes sweep over Effie and me, "but we also know Camilla Fox is going to be there, and this is just a small step toward solidarity."

I AM SIREN in big, block letters. White against a black shirt so it's impossible to misread.

My shoulders buckle further.

"Okay, huddle in, girls!"

An excited scuffle as we tighten, squeals barely restrained. Like this is nationals, like we're some group of performers about to take the stage, glitter on our eyelashes, ponytails sky-high.

"You, too, Wallace!"

I almost forgot he was here. I almost forgot Effie was until a moment ago. The Ren faire's opening festivities are still our cover story—I couldn't very well leave Portland without telling my parents *something*—but Eff really did decide to come to the protest instead. No more getting life and fantasy confused, she said. I don't know if that's got more to do with forgetting Elric is really Rick Morgan, or that she isn't a mermaid after all, but I know how it feels to be exhausted with yourself.

What sucks is seeing her give up on the Hidden Scales. It's her

185

favorite part of the world, after her tank and betrothal, and I think she thought getting inside that tent would tell her more of her mom's story, or her own, or . . . honestly I don't know. I just hope she's not giving up on it for good.

I'm glad she's here today. Or I was, anyway. I'd hoped she'd be something of a fun distraction, especially once I found out she'd invited the dude from the pool, but it hasn't kicked in yet. My sister having a maybe boyfriend would be headline news any other day, but now I'm huddled tight with a cluster of IB mates, preparing to attend a protest at the intersection of celebrating Blackness and protesting police brutality. It's a hefty burden, but you can't do the latter until the former is done. That's what the half of the protest organizers who wanted to list Camilla as a headliner (like this is gonna be a concert) said in a recent social-media post. And that we can't afford to focus on them one at a time when lives are at stake. The other half said they agreed, but that the march isn't about celebrity, it's about justice. Specifically, in this case, for a young guy named Kenyon Jones. That his family had already been promised this day and space. I'm too new at this to know what to think. I just know I wish Rhoda Taylor deserved justice, too. And I know I'm scared for Camilla, even if I can't articulate why.

The girls've already pulled on their solidarity T-shirts, and the fabric makes me cringe when it brushes against my skin.

It's not just . . . all of this. It's something about the hugely approving moms that keeps my mouth clamped shut. Not because I'm afraid of unleashing a siren call; because I wish I could literally breathe fire. It takes a moment to totally grasp not just that this is rage I'm feeling, but at what: I didn't know this was something I could get IB credit for. I wouldn't have thought to ask whether attending a protest could go toward the community-service component of my academic program. I didn't catch where it fits—Creativity, Activity, or Service—but apparently it does.

I didn't know this matter of life and justice could also help get me into college—but only if I were a tourist.

Maybe if I'd presented it to my parents that way they wouldn't have seen it as potentially devastating to my future and well-being. Maybe they would have taken me and my friends to breakfast, packed us matching sacks, and waved excitedly while we headed off toward the possibility of tear gas.

Maybe if it were a once-in-a-lifetime opportunity, they'd consider it "character building," too.

It's not even a fifteen-minute drive from the diner to Vancouver, but it's enough time for the curdle in the pit of my stomach to settle into cold fear. If anyone else is nervous, it doesn't show. Altruism and Jennifer are chatting like mad in the driver's and passenger's seats. First they're talking about how Camilla Fox (whom they apparently follow regularly now) devoted an entire video to explaining how Black lives don't matter until siren lives do, and she must've used the word "intersectionality," because they can't stop.

I can't decide whether I'm glad they're listening or whether I'm annoyed that the conversation's gone unheard for so many years. I think I'm both.

A few moments later they're going over some sort of checklist, things they want to pay particular attention to and something they keep calling the "anatomy of a protest."

Beside me, Effie and Wallace don't make a peep.

I want to go home. I wanna turn to Effie and confess that I don't really feel emotionally equipped for this. That I'm not ready. Not to be a siren in the real world, to know a third call that my river-ghost Gramma had to name for me. Not to be a Black teen on my way to participate in what might become civil disobedience.

I don't really have a choice about some of it, but at the moment I can't remember why I chose the rest.

Why did this seem like a good idea? Because I saw my grandmother? Because everyone else could afford to be excited? Because I might see Camilla Fox in the flesh? Because I've been going back and forth between being sure and being almost sure I want to be like her?

Now that the moment's arrived, it just feels stupid. I feel trapped. My friends are wearing I AM SIREN shirts, like . . .

Come on.

My dad would have a heartache and die, and Awaken would not bring him back. He'll have lost both the sirens in his life, and whether or not our identity had anything to do with that, he'll always think it did. Gramma died of natural causes, but according to him, her life was a specific kind of tragedy. Her sirenness did what sirenness does: it tore a family apart. No matter that even Mom sometimes reminds him that it was his choice.

Even when she passed, we couldn't come to Gramma's homegoing because she wanted to be honored the way sirens are, with fire to symbolize the way it feels, and water to remember the mythos, and a collection of voices singing her name in the unmistakable three-part harmony of a masking gospel choir. It's a rare tribute nowadays, because it's how sirens are usually found out— after they're already gone, after a lifetime of hiding, and only if their families honor their wish.

My dad didn't have a choice; he hadn't been around and someone in the network was Gramma's executor, but he would have been known among the bereaved as the son of a siren, who had a daughter. Everyone would've known what that meant. More than her network. Her friends, the little family who'd maybe helped fill the gap we left, her colleagues who before the funeral thought she was just a lively old woman. Years later when we came into the network anyway, I was known. Just too late to know my grandmother.

"Tav?" Effie's whisper pulls the car back into focus.

She's here, her twists pulled into a top knot and hidden beneath a wrap. Her eyes are like wide saucers and she's waiting for me to fill her in. But she's supposed to be my distraction today, not my shoulder.

I smile, but not so broad that she won't believe it.

"Camilla's gonna be there, I can't wrap my head around it. I mean, she's probably gonna be fawning over you if she sees us, what with my flawless execution of her wrap technique," I say as I straighten the edges, making sure Effie's scarf tuck holds. I had to detangle my hand from hers to do it, and I have no idea who took whose hand or how long ago.

Effie snorts, her hands never lifting to preen with me. On her other side, Wallace is expressionless and silent. Must be what she likes about him. Boys should be seen and not heard, I always say. To myself, in my head.

Altruism can't drive forever. Eventually we're there.

Outside the car, it just looks like a slightly busier street than usual. When we pile out, I'm confused by the loud laughter and general merrymaking.

"This isn't it," Allie comes up beside me, "there's shuttles to take us closer."

"Okay," I answer because I have to say something. I've been too quiet and as far as I know, Eff's the only one who knows ASL so my choices are limited. Plus today Dad's right. Signing would just draw attention to myself.

When the shuttle arrives, it's just somebody's van with a rectangle of brown kraft paper from a roll like the ones we have in some classrooms at school. They wrote "Pop Up People Pusher" in obvious haste and have apparently just been driving back and forth, for free. The name they chose sucks, but it reminds me that people don't. Not all of them, anyway.

They let us off a block or so from what sounds like a choreographed roar. It swells and then pauses, leaving space for whatever we're too far away to hear. My schoolmates and I are given directions, but we don't need them. Parked police cars line both sides of the street and I glance into every single one as we walk down the middle.

There's something about walking down the center of a road not meant for pedestrian traffic. It's enlivening, even to me, even if the excitement is neutral. It isn't good and it isn't bad. Not yet. It means real life has been suspended here; the rules don't apply for now. For better or for worse.

Altruism and the reunited Jennifers are picking up speed because up ahead is "the heart of the protest." It's the spot where Kenyon Jones was shot and across from it is a wall of police officers with hard helmets and Plexiglas shields, like it was one of them struck down on this spot.

I drop my eyes in case there are any here from Portland. In case there's one in particular.

The crowd is telling the story of the deceased. School portrait in full color, the larger-than-life poster held over their heads could be a different kid than the one I saw in the paper and on the news. In the picture his mother points to while standing on a ladder held steady by the crowd, he looks like . . . someone. He looks like someone young enough for his murder to disrupt the national news. Someone whose death could not possibly go unanswered. And because we're here, it won't. Today the rules don't apply and the street belongs to him because we weren't dissuaded by the photo circulated on the TV screens. We don't think his low-slung jeans and shirtless brown skin cancel out his right to jaywalk without a death sentence. We don't think there is one kind of Black boy worthy of life, or that in the wake of his murder we need to prove him that one, elusive kind.

And still my dad's voice drowns out Kenyon's mother for a moment and I find myself wondering, would it have mattered if he'd pulled up his pants for that casual photo? If he'd gone to the crosswalk to cross the street would he be graduating high school next month? Is that why I am alive and he isn't? Is that the thing holding death at bay? Etiquette, and an ever-present fear of being shot? Because the fear is in all of us.

The crowd is responding to his mother's grief, her inability to get the words out leaving room for us to speak to her. To hold her up on the ladder with our love and encouragement, with tear-strewn faces to match her own.

There are smatterings of other people peppered throughout the street and block. Some are standing a little bit apart, recording or observing. It's impossible to tell whether they're part of us or not, or whether they're still undecided. But the core, the tightly packed crowd that can't be mistaken for passersby, is like water, a tide swelling us toward the mother and then rocking us back, and among them I'm wet with perspiration and tears.

It happened so quickly. I'm deep in the crowd now and I don't remember how I got here, I just keep pressing closer. The curdle in my stomach is gone, replaced by a kind of peace that startles me.

I don't understand it. The police are still nearby, I'm still lying to my parents, and if the news is to be believed, this place is a powder keg that could explode at any moment.

But it feels like therapy, not chaos. I've lost Allie and the others, Effie and Wallace are back where I started, and I'm in a throng of people so close I can't tell the difference between their sweat and mine.

But I can breathe. I've seen dozens more I AM SIREN shirts, but now that it's here among what feels like a concentration of every person of color in the Pacific Northwest, it makes sense. It doesn't feel like a disservice to Kenyon's memory, and it doesn't seem a distraction. Kenyon and Rhoda (and Camilla, if that's who the shirts are for) were from the same community, and so am I.

I don't just feel like I belong *here,* I feel like I *belong* here.

Until the tide swells to the side and I turn and look at why. Whoever's approaching from that side isn't on the ladder yet, but I hear her name.

"Camilla!" My voice might be among the ones filling the air, waiting for her to step above the crowd and reveal herself.

But when I turn all I see is the wall of police officers, one of them turned to the other, his helmet in one hand, the other fiddling with a com or something in his ear.

That's when I remember *Lexi on a Leash.* Footage of one of her public appearances that included a photo op with security.

Lexi wasn't offended by their plugs, she insisted! Whatever makes everyone comfortable! She wears the collar, they wear the plugs, and then we can see each other for who we really are, and our identity won't be divisive.

Only there's something really intentional about the officers having siren-canceling ear plugs as part of their gear. Camilla Fox is here, but she isn't *why* we're here. She's here to support her community, same as them—so what are they anticipating?

I think I hear my name and snap my head in both directions. A moment later, Effie's got ahold of my arm.

"Wallace thinks we should leave," she shouts after pulling my shoulder down to bring my ear close.

"What?"

She repeats herself but my question was more about why dude from the community center has an opinion at all. He hasn't said two words to me—or to her as far as I can tell—but he knows what we should do.

"Do you think we should?" she asks, her eyes big and concerned.

We've traded places since leaving the car. If she were signing or if I were the only one who'd hear, she'd say she's the one who wants to go.

She feels the buzz in the air. There's tension and it's building, the way a good gospel number does right before the powerful, sometimes arresting release. From the look on Effie's face, she feels it but not the way I do. I wanna be a part of the release. I wanna be here when we are loud and powerful and locked in harmony. All the things I've ever wanted to say, I want to say now, even though there's very real opposition. Even though I don't know how it will end. Even though the cops are wearing siren-canceling ear plugs. Because they're wearing body armor, too, like every protest before. They're always dressed for battle against us; now they've customized their gear.

It's dangerous because they are here, not because of Camilla.

I almost give Effie a message to relay to her boyfriend. That what we need isn't dissuading, or discouragement, or consoling. We don't need to be told we're all helpless. What we need is action.

"Allies act," I tell her instead, but she doesn't hear me and neither will he.

There isn't even space to shake my head, so I speak a little louder, careful with my tone, mindful of the heat that's already built outside my body and that might be getting in.

"I just want to see Camilla." I don't know if she hears that either, because the tide swells toward the ladder again and we get separated.

That's fine by me. I'm not ready to leave this crowd. I'm not ready to go back across the river, to go back to hiding. I'm not wearing my identity emblazoned on my chest, and there's no siren call warning signs in my throat, but I feel honest here. I feel like a battery being recharged. Like an orphan coming home. Even the officers making it clear they're not here for our protection can't undo that. Because, come to think of it, the danger's as much a part of "home" as community is. The fear gets quiet but it doesn't disappear, and that might be what sets us apart. When we smile or we dance or we march or we win, it isn't because we didn't have reason to be afraid. It isn't because the uncertainty is gone. It's because we did it anyway. Because we cannot be exterminated.

Effie's lost somewhere in the crowd, adrift between Wallace and me if he isn't already gone. She's getting shoved one way and then the other, roiling in a tide she's out of sync with. I wish I could tell her everything I'm thinking, all the reasons we're okay. I could say it in sign, but I don't. I won't.

Effie came by it honestly, speaking ASL. For her, it was a lovely second language, romantic like any other would have been, but more practical than most and the only one that could enrich her other self. It was the only one that'd let Euphemia speak to her betrothed from underwater. Sign language was the clear choice for her.

Our signing stories aren't the same.

For me, it's been a deception. I can admit that to myself, buoyed by this tide of people. I adopted it to sell a disability I don't have so I could escape anyone finding out about the liability I do. I'm not a monster because I live in a world that gives me impossible choices, but I've met my grandmother in the blue place. Camilla

Fox is on the ladder, standing out above the crowd by choice. She's facing down danger, and members of her own community who want to use her powerful voice or else think her existing in this space is making things worse. She's holding Kenyon's mother's hand because hers is the only approval needed today, taking to the ladder and becoming visible because, if anyone's going to use Camilla's voice, it's going to be Camilla.

What didn't feel like an option to me before does now.

I can do this.

"Today isn't about me," she says, her hair faux-locked to perfection, the silver hoop in her septum a glistening accent to her sheeny, ebony skin. "It's about us. Men *and* women *and* children. It's about all our parts, of which I am one. So if I can use my voice in service, I will."

She means her common voice, and all in the tide know it, but the buzz in the air intensifies. I lock my eyes to her. I know what's behind us; I don't need to look. No reason to glance back when I can hear heavy steps. I don't know why they'd be approaching when we've done nothing wrong. If we turn and acknowledge that they're coming, someone will say *we* confronted *them*. And I still don't understand why they're here at all.

"If it is our destiny as Black women to stand before crowds, before press and police and people enamored of our grief—if we are to give eulogy after eulogy and defend the dead"—and now she raises her voice and her eyes go from the tide of us to the wall closing in—"if all we have are our voices, then why are we so feared?"

The sun is shining but there's gonna be a storm. My skin is goose-pimpled, an unseen sharpness dancing in the air and pricking me everywhere I'm exposed.

The peace is fading. I feel it escaping through my pores with every dull thud of armored footfall.

"Speak, siren!" someone cries, and they're echoed over and over again.

We aren't Camilla's audience anymore; we're her barricade.

Someone links arms with me and without pause, I lock my free arm with the person on the other side.

There's no changing my mind now. No going home. I'm here. We are. If it's a choice between running or surrendering or standing together, I have to stand. Sweaty all over again and trembling, but I'm here—everyone is here—because we mean it. We have to make it better, and because Camilla's here and I'm here, that means for sirens, too.

Hands take hold of my shoulder and pull me out of the chain, and I close my eyes. I don't mean to; it just happens. One minute I see Camilla on the ladder and the next, Gramma in the water.

I let myself go limp.

I'm a minor. Better a record that can be sealed, one of the IB mothers said, than one that can destroy someone's life.

But I don't look like their daughters. I won't be escorted away from the protest like some gracious catch and release. I'll be booked, caged with the grown-ups. I don't know how to imagine what comes after that.

Court. Lawyers. My dad.

When they've turned me around, the hands shake me and I open my eyes to Altruism, armored men two steps behind her.

"We have to go!" Her hair is down for the first time in two years, the shaved parts of her head covered along with the collection of earrings that've been her calling card all that time. "We have to go now!"

"Allie," I say, careful not to sway or fall in my relief. "Calm down—"

"We're meeting back at the car, find Effie!"

She grimaces, coughs on her own breath in her hurry, and I see the small white square at the base of her throat. Small icons describe proper care. Wash with like colors. Tumble dry.

"You turned your T-shirt inside out."

Her mouth goes slack for a moment and then Allie recovers. "It isn't safe here."

"No one said it would be."

We're searching each other's eyes the way we used to when we were small, when I first moved to Portland and the hill and she was my first new friend. But we aren't kids anymore, and this is no staring contest.

Suddenly the world is spinning. Both of us get jostled, an elbow connecting with my spine and sending me down on one knee. I grab for Allie on my way to the pavement and even though she follows me, she's wriggling in my grasp.

"Altruism!" I call.

Someone's lying on the ground beside me, trying to curl themselves into a ball while a swarm of black armor pries them straight. They take no notice of me, the single protestor in every-day clothes and the three officers dressed for a warzone.

But Allie stops in her tracks.

Only Allie stays crouched, not so the battle around us will pass her by, but because she knows what I've done.

She's been Awakened, whatever that means. I've used the call again, the one that comes spontaneously, that needs no fire curling up and out of my chest. The one that seems more specific than the others, as though the target has to be called by name or else directly in the line of fire. As though it has to be meant for the receiver.

Whichever is true, this call I don't quite understand has done something to her. I can see it in her eyes. They're not frantic anymore and her mouth doesn't gape.

When I let her go, she doesn't run away; she stands as I do, the world, the protest, the tide collapsing and breaking in a dozen pieces around us.

Whatever my call has done, she's not trembling anymore—but she knows what I am. We're surrounded by cops who look more like special forces, and she knows that I'm a siren.

I'm only still because I need to know what happens next. Three calls in so short a time when for years I've only used my siren voice in a choir.

Calls don't work on sirens, but maybe Gramma did more than

teach me Awaken; maybe she used it on me. Maybe she chose to give it to me so that I would wake up. So that I would stop trying to mask my power.

In the turbulent sea that the protest has become, it's impossible to make sense of what's happening around me. People seem attached, riot gear and denim rolling on the asphalt like a dangerous undertow, black batons pressing necks to the ground, closed fists cracking against helmets in futility.

My other schoolmates are long gone, I hope. They're waiting for Altruism back at the car, and Wallace and Effie were the first to arrive.

I should run. One of these times I get knocked down, I should grab hold of Allie, crawl across the street, and hide. I just don't know the point.

Maybe I remember Camilla and maybe I hear her first, even though her call has no effect on me. Which is why it takes me a moment to understand what it does.

She's calling at the top of her lungs, no megaphone in her hands. Instead she frames her mouth like she's all the amplification she needs.

She's shouting, still atop a ladder that's only occasionally held. Kenyon's family has been whisked away to safety and Camilla remains, as though to make sure they slip away unbothered. As though now she's an intentional distraction. Thankfully, some of us have stayed with her. Every time an anchor is snatched from her platform, someone else rushes in to take their place, putting one more body between the police and Camilla while she shouts and chants and bellows. She stays visible even though their plugs prove they came here ready to confront her in particular.

Whatever happens to her is what my dad worries will happen to me. But she uses a siren call anyway.

At first nothing changes. The undertow grows in number while the tide broils. I see the people running away now, am shocked into fear by the sight of adults running at full speed like the bogeyman's come to life.

And then I see the broken glass at my feet. Up and down the street. The streetlight above my head cracks and then shatters, raining down on us just like the others must have. Altruism looks at me one more time, still steady, and then she leaves to find the others, passing see-through shields that ram into protestors and are splintering like they're made of glass too. The ground might even be shaking beneath my feet.

Camilla's voice is power.

I spin to find her again, to see the siren speak, and I find that there are no more human anchors. The tide has ebbed for good, broken and dispersed or driven back.

Camilla's in an airy tunic and leggings, but the officers pull her backward from the ladder like she's wearing the same protective armor. Like there's anything to cushion her fall.

This time the fire plumes. This time I unfurl it lightning fast and it nearly burns my tongue.

"Leave her alone!"

It would have Compelled them if I hadn't changed direction. If I weren't yanked so quickly from the street that it feels like something in my abdomen is tearing, like internal whiplash, I could've made them let her go. But I'm suddenly in the sky, a gargoyle's stone wings snapped one time to take us careening through the air.

No one even cranes their neck to see us, Gargy snatches me so fast. I was there and then I wasn't, but no one seems to know. No one knows that we're above them when the police wrestle a collar around Camilla's neck before she even catches her breath. No one knows the way her eyes bulge and her mouth stretches while dark armor crisscrosses her body.

I'm reaching for her when Gargy carries me away, and even though I know she sees me, Camilla Fox is silenced.

XIV

EFFIE

I blacked out again. I must have.

I closed my eyes at some point and when I open them, Vancouver's gone. The people and the police and the noise and the street are all replaced by wilderness. Everything's green and brown and wet. The seat and hip of my jeans have a lovely dark grime bleeding into my underwear and onto my skin. Nice.

"Where am I?" I ask out loud, and when I do my voice crashes into the quiet. This is so wrong.

Standing up doesn't make me feel any more in control, but it doesn't make me feel worse. Usually my head feels kinda thick after a blackout, but I feel fine. That's even more surprising since I distinctly remember feeling like my guts were being rearranged after everything went gray. One minute I was in a surging storm of protestors, pinned inside a chaotic swarm and trying to get my bearings, and then everything was gray. Well, not quite.

First there was the mirage. My eyes were playing tricks on me again, making big sections of anything in front of me seem to be melting. But this time it grew, like it was coming closer.

Then the gray.

It came in from both sides, eating up my vision from the peripherals so that my view of the protest and the mirage got more and more narrow before disappearing. Like a scene change in a crappy old movie. And it was quick, but not the way it's happened before. Not the sudden poof-and-I'm-out I felt last time.

Plus. Everything was *gray*. Not black.

Except for the part where I "wake up" somewhere else, this was something different.

After feeling the world flipping and twisting around me, it reappeared right side up when I hit the ground. Or if I was already on the ground, it was like when you're dreaming and you jump, and in your bed, your body kind of jolts and wakes you up.

Somehow I transported myself here . . . wherever "here" is. There's no one else around to ask unless you count the trees and the moss and the thick, woodsy musk of humid air.

I wipe my dirty palms on my jeans. Whatever. They're done anyway. But when I suddenly remember who I was with, I punch the air.

"Wallace!" His name is mostly a sigh. This is strike two. First I flashed on him at the community center and now he's gonna think I invited him out of town and then bailed. I'm *pretty* sure I didn't, but I can't bet on it; nothing makes sense.

"Tavia?" I holler into the woods. "Tav!"

Nothing.

Awesome. I left her, too. She could be arrested by now, or . . . I don't let myself think beyond that. Arrested is the worst that can happen, I tell myself. Bad things happen in the news, not to my sister. Not to me.

If the rando-woods around me could talk, they'd probably laugh. What do you call careening through the universe by some unknown magic and then waking up alone in the middle of nowhere?

What was that sound?

I whirl around and study the unchanging landscape. I catch sight of a gnat reunion hovering and colliding over what I can now see is a body of water, but that's not what I heard. It's that sonar deal again. I *felt* something.

Tavia. She's here somewhere.

"Tavia!" I close my eyes and let her name tear out of me in a bellow that gets louder before it ends. I'm not a siren, but I can yell when I have to.

Wherever she is, she doesn't call back. Looks like I'm gonna have to trek through this mysterious marshy forest. I don't know where I'm going, but that doesn't really matter since I also don't know where I'm starting. If I get lost, I won't even know it. It's brilliant.

I pick a narrow opening that looks like it might've been made by something tall and svelte (a deer, probably) and I set out, immediately rolling my ankle just to prove I was never a Girl Scout. I suck my teeth and walk it off.

"Two-legged travel is for the birds," as Mer Shirl once told me, but I don't have a choice. I skipped opening day at the faire, so I don't have my tail handy. Not that I'm about to dive into unknown (and possibly inhabited) water. Who knows what's out here?

I feel the pulse of Tavia's voice again and make a slight adjustment to my path. She must be looking for me, too.

Wait. I actually stop walking for a moment.

If Tavia's here too, then I didn't black out. I mean I didn't get here by blacking out or whatever. Even if it exists, blackout travel couldn't have brought Tavia along; she was nowhere near me when the gray closed in and she's nowhere near me now.

"As if I know the rules." I bat a flimsy branch out of my face and it snaps back and stings the skin of my cheek.

Tavia pulse. A tone signature that I recognize as distinctly hers, just like when Mama Theo came to the Philipses' house. If anything clinched my belief that I really was a mermaid, it was hearing and identifying my loved ones the way sea creatures do. It's still hard to believe I was wrong.

Pulse. It's stronger now, I can almost hear when Tavia speaks. A few more strides and her voice is there.

What the heck is she yelling?

I see her on the other side of a staggered line of trees. They're barely wider than she is, the bark on the top pale and dark on the bottom like the water here used to be higher.

I can't make out exactly what she's doing. Every time I take a step, so does she, and I have to step around another tree to get her back in my sights.

"Gargy!"

I guess I heard her right the first time. That's really what she's saying, but this time she keeps going.

"Come back! Please!" She's got both her hands around her throat and she bowls over like she's going to catch her hands on her knees and put her head between her legs, only she doesn't. She keeps her hands around her neck while she cries, and then she shoots back upright and screams, "Take me back!"

"Tavia," I call out as I rush between the trees to get to her.

"Effie." She's barely understandable now. She's out of breath, her face is drenched with tears, and she still hasn't taken her hands from around her neck. "Eff."

I catch her against me when she goes to bowl over again.

"He has to take me back."

"It's okay, Tav." I don't believe it either now that I'm close to her, but what else do you say when your sister looks like she's coming apart from the inside? I'm scared. I don't know what happened between the moment I saw her at the protest and now, but she's a completely different person. I didn't know her back in Santa Cruz, but after what I've been told, I don't like her hands where they are. "You're okay now, I promise."

She's kneading her forehead into my shoulder and I don't see how it isn't hurting her. I bite back a grimace and tell her, "You're okay. I'm here."

I stroke the back of her neck along the strip of skin where her fingers don't meet, but when I do touch them she doesn't adjust. I pet her hair and hug her, but her hands stay put.

"He has to take me back." It's a whisper this time and even if she weren't right next to my ear, I would've felt the pulse of her words.

Finally her hands loosen. I notice but I don't stop rubbing her back.

"What happened?" At a time like this I would normally sign with her, but I don't want to let her go. "Tell me what's wrong."

"They collared Camilla," she whispers into me.

Oh God. That's what she saw. Another siren (her heroine) collared against her will.

No wonder.

"I'm sorry, Tav. I'm so sorry."

"It's gonna happen to me, too," and she's crying. "I keep giving myself away. I was just so fed up, Eff. I'm so tired of shutting up."

"It's never gonna happen to you," I say, squeezing her tighter for a moment. "I promise."

"It is."

"Priam's dad came out of concern, Tav, he did. He's not going to change his mind, I swear."

"No, today, at the protest, in front of Allie." She only stops because her breath does. "I did it again. There's a new call now and I can't help it."

There's too many things about that admission I don't know. Altruism was close to Tavia and then she wasn't. How am I supposed to know whether she can be trusted?

"She was wearing a siren shirt," I say.

Tav rightly snorts. But that isn't what I mean, so I look her dead in the eye.

"I'm not saying you should trust her. I'm saying *they* won't." Sorry, not sorry. Tavia's all I care about.

Her hands slide down from her neck and onto her chest. I hug her tight and trap them there.

"We're okay," I tell her. "We're okay now."

But that isn't what it feels like. She's deflated, and I don't think what I said helped.

"I don't want to use their hate of me against someone else. I don't want to deny what I am, Eff."

"I know," I whisper, and even though a part of me envies her even knowing that, most of me just loves my sister. "That's what makes you everything."

When Tavia slumps, I lower us both to the loose, wet ground-cover. We end up side by side, our arms and legs tangled and her head back on my shoulder.

It's a long time before we speak again. I hear things I didn't notice before when I was "tracking" Tavia. Rustling leaves, a plopping sound like balls dropping into nearby water. I imagine ducks or some other type of bird plunking their heads into the water to search for food and then coming back up. There are so many types of sounds giving away just how many things are living unseen in this place.

"Do you know where we are?" I ask Tavia.

"The nature reserve." She's not whispering anymore, but there's no power in her voice. The fact that she's a siren makes it even more concerning.

"The nature reserve? In Portland?"

She nods against me.

"How'd we get here?"

"Gargy."

Right. Whoever she's been yelling for. "Wait, you mean your gargoyle?"

"He isn't mine."

That must explain the gray. And the topsy-turvy.

I didn't black out.

"Did he carry me?" I ask.

She lets out her breath, but no words come with it. I should stop asking questions. Just one more.

"Where'd he go?"

I shouldn't have asked. Tavia sits up. She doesn't detangle our limbs, but she turns her head away.

"I don't know."

"That's okay. Maybe we should just head home."

"Yeah, that's not gonna happen." Out of nowhere, she decides she's done sitting down, and before I can protest, she's going from tree to tree looking between them and up into their branches. "This place is like two thousand acres and I've been here all of three times for a class project. I have no idea where we are." Then she raises her voice. "We're imprisoned here until your guardian deigns to take us home."

"Mine?" Now I look around too. "Are you talking to me?"

"Yep." She slaps a tree. "Turns out you're the reason he's perched at our house, not me."

What.

"How do you know that? Who said?"

"The gargoyle, Effie. He's not here for my protection, he's here for yours."

I don't believe her for some reason. It's not like I think she's lying. She just must be mistaken. She tips her head to the side like she heard that.

"Okay," she says, *"you* call him. See for yourself. Tell him you need help, I don't know."

"Just . . ."

"Just call for him."

"Okay." I stand up. You have to be standing to beckon a gargoyle. "So just . . ."

"Effie! Call him!"

I swing my arms to get loose. Limber. I try not to look at Tavia, but we're both biting back smirks now. This is the weirdest thing I've done in a while and that's saying something.

"Okay," and then I speak up. "Gargy." That feels wrong. "Gargoyle? Stone guard."

Tavia's shaking her head, but at least she's smiling.

"Sentry?"

She snorts.

"Um. C'mere, please." I clear my throat. "I'd like a word."

She rolls her finger in the air and I remember.

"I need help. Help me!"

And then we listen. Bobbing in the water again, and snapping branches. Nothing else. But a cloud couldn't have moved across the sun that quickly even in Portland. When we look toward the source of the shadow, there he is. The gargoyle from the Philipses' roof. He's hovering in the sky, huge. Monstrous. And he's staring at me.

"Will you tell her, please?" Tav's impatient, but who talks to a hulking stone behemoth in that tone?

"Do you two know each other or something?" I ask without letting my eyes wander away from him.

"He was with me when I saw Gramma in the water."

Now I spin around to face her. "Excuse?"

"It's a long story. Well, not really. I used a call in front of Naema but it was one I'd never used before and I had a dreamlike thing and then Gargy and I flew to the river and my grandmother told me the call's name."

Basically all I can do is blink for a minute. My brain is trying to cobble together my thoughts so I can come up with something meaningful, but all I've got is, "Your grandma's really in the water?"

"Yeah," she says like it's more a space filler than an affirmative answer. She closes her mouth, opens it and then closes it again. "It's complicated."

"Her voice," a deep smoothness says, "is in the water."

My eyes creep back to find the gargoyle still hovering and still staring at me. When I shoot my gaze back to Tavia she widens her eyes at me real quick.

"I know, right?" she says.

"Good Lord."

"I know."

The funny part is the way the gargoyle glances between the two of us, like he's pretty sure we're talking about him but not totally sure. It's the most human I've ever seen him look.

"So he's my guardian, but you got to fly with him."

"So did you."

"Right, but I had no idea what was going on. I thought . . .

206

Never mind." I watch the gargoyle while I turn and tilt my head. He gives me nothing.

He's *my* bodyguard. Interesting. I guess that's why he followed me home that day instead of keeping Tav safe from the police. (However he would do that. I wonder if he's licensed to kill. . . .)

"So," I ask Tav, "does he talk to you or is this silent stone thing normal?"

"He talks some. Right, Gargy?"

It's cute how he looks over to Tavia and then back to me. A shy gargoyle, who'da thunk it.

"Well, maybe *you* can ask him what happened to Wallace." I think the gargoyle drops a bit in the air but maybe not. I direct the rest at him. "The guy I was with at the protest. Is he here in the reserve somewhere too? We need to find him before you take us home."

"I cannot take you home." The delicious voice aside, I'm confused and glance at Tavia.

"What does that mean?" I ask her.

"What do you mean what does that mean? He's speaking English." Then she steps toward him. "Why not?"

"I cannot."

"We heard that part," I say.

"Is Effie in danger?"

"Wait, why do *I* have to be the one in danger? You said Camilla got collared, maybe he was worried about you."

"He isn't here for me, remember? And I'm pretty sure you were already here when he dropped me off, so. He obviously brought you first." She turns back to him. "Thanks for dropping us off in different spots, by the way, that was an unnecessary bit of drama, I think."

"I was in a hurry," he explains.

"Because she was in danger."

"She is in no danger if we stay here. Just for a little while."

"You're not making sense," Tavia says through a sigh.

"Does he usually?"

207

"Can you at least come down here? Please. It's filthy and wet and I want to sit down."

To my surprise, the gargoyle lowers himself to the ground. I'm not sure what's supposed to happen, but Tavia approaches him and he lifts her onto his broad back. His wings are spread wide with their tips almost touching the ground so she can get comfortable. Which she obviously is. She's lying against his over-long back while he hunches forward with all his weight on one fist, his other hand reaching out to me.

Okay. I guess we're doing this.

I come close, trying not to trip on the way over to him. He lowers his large palm like I'm supposed to step on it. Which is what I'm supposed to do, I guess. It's definitely bigger than my foot, but I'm not exactly tiny by comparison. I'm also a teenage girl who's pretty constantly aware of my weight and whether it's what it "should" be, and putting all of it into someone's palm (even if that someone is made of stone) is just asking to be humiliated.

At my hesitation, he opens and closes his hand.

"Here we go," I say and then immediately wonder why I did. As soon as I'm standing in his hand, I kneel down so that I don't fall if the short trip to his shoulder is rocky. (Rocky, geddit? He's made of stone.)

The gargoyle lifts me, and when I pass in front of his face, there's something intense in his eyes. In the way he's been watching me. In a moment I'm sliding down his shoulder blade to lie next to Tavia.

She's quiet so I don't say anything as we lie together on a granite monster. I don't ask why she didn't tell me the gargoyle was my guardian or that they were buddies or that she knew another siren call. Or that she'd seen her grandmother. I know my sister, so I know it had more to do with putting herself aside than keeping things from me. She would've told me eventually, after everything stopped spinning.

Or when she was sure I could handle my *own* ridiculous mess . . .

Now we're together (apparently safe), and in an oasis that looks so different from the rest of Portland that it's easy to believe that world and its troubles are gone for good. So what else is there to talk about?

What do other girls talk about when they're not sirens or freaks?

"So junior prom, huh?"

"What?" Tav looks at me.

"It's next Saturday."

"It is." She's amused, at least. "You going?"

"What makes you ask that?"

"Well, you randomly brought up a school formal when neither of us has ever gone to one, so I just figured you had some personal investment in it. Plus Wallace." She sings his name.

"Shut up."

"What's the status of that? Are we avoiding labels or is he officially the boyfriend?"

"Okay, what makes it official?"

"If he asks you to go steady. Doy."

"I just don't think guys literally ask that anymore." I don't ask whether Priam ever did.

"Whatever. He came to a protest with you, Effie, I'm pretty sure that's serious."

Garg rolls his neck. What an annoying conversation this must be to overhear.

"So," Tavia continues. "Is Wallace taking you to prom?"

"I don't know." I adjust against the gargoyle's back. I just realized I can feel him breathing. "I was waiting to see if you asked me."

"Aw," Tavia nudges me with her elbow, "you wanna go with me?"

"It'd be fun, right?"

"Of course. Until Priam and Naema are crowned king and queen and I'm there with my sister."

"Oh. You know about them?"

"Yeah, it's pretty hard to miss."

On the gargoyle's back, I find her hand. "He sucks."

"No," she says through a sigh. "He bites."

And then she starts laughing. Almost hysterically. She buckles forward and holds her sides. I am so lost. I can't stop grinning because she is laughing so ridiculously hard. She's wiping tears now.

"Okay." I nod.

She pants through the last few tremors of laughter and lies flat again, kind of moaning.

"So. You wanna fill me in?"

"He bit me," she says, wiping her eyes. "For real. Not like deep or anything, we were making out. But that's why we broke up."

"That . . . makes no sense. He bit *you* . . ."

"And then he broke up with me. Because he's an eloko and the worst thing that could possibly happen to him is someone wondering whether their cannibal mythos is true."

"What, he thought someone would suddenly go against our love-elokos-forever programming over a nibble?"

"It's literally the worst thing he could imagine."

"How sad. He needs a better imagination."

"Well." She's watching the sky. "He doesn't know what he doesn't know."

I turn on my side, pretend the gargoyle beneath us is Tavia's bed and it's just me and her.

"You don't still like him, do you?"

"They're just feelings," she says, and the laughter is all gone now. "They won't last forever."

Sometimes I wish Tavia would crush on someone else. It seems like people go through crushes and boyfriends and girlfriends like Tav and I go through hair ties. She hasn't dated anyone since Priam, not even to get people to forget they were together. Not even to shut down the rumors that she can't move on because he was her first eloko.

"Processing feelings is for the birds," I croak like I'm Mer Shirl and there's a cigarette dangling between my fingers.

"No lie." She lets out a deep breath. "Speaking of mermaids. You're really done with the Ren faire, Eff?"

"I told Mama I was."

"What'd she say?"

"To stay near you."

"Aw?" Tavia scrunches her face.

"Something like that."

"Just. Not seeing how the topics are connected."

"But she said it in the same conversation. Don't visit your mom's grave. Glad you're out of the faire. Stick with Tavia." Neither of us know what to say. "And now I find out I have a gray guard of my own. To add to the list of traits I don't understand."

Moving hair. Water mirage. Crappy skin. Sprite bait. Blackouts.

"I think she's literally been afraid for me. All this time. With the faire and everything. I just don't know why."

"Me neither," Tav says, and then, "The good news is she approves of me."

"I mean, duh."

"It's the most important thing."

"That's a given."

She rolls into me obnoxiously. "Love you."

"Same."

"Can we go home yet?" She's talking to Gargy again, and flips onto her stomach, her fingers gripping a gray shoulder like she's rock climbing.

The gargoyle inclines his head and a sort of grumble comes out like he's been holding his breath all this time.

He's definitely an eavesdropper.

~~~~~

As soon as Tavia and I walk through the foyer, I wish the gargoyle had escorted us all the way to the attic instead of leaving us on the porch. Not that there's anything he could have done about Mama Theo standing with Tavia's parents in front of the TV.

"Mama?" I look from her to the Philipses and back again. "Is everything okay?"

She's a wreck again, but worse. The glisten on her skin is tears, or at least there are so many of those that I can't tell the difference.

She looks like she's been on edge for hours, probably cleaning and pacing the way she did while Mom was sick. She didn't eat toward the end. She made a lot of tea she forgot to drink. Paw Paw and I would find cups of it everywhere, cold. Forgotten. The house would be sparkling clean except for those sad, out-of-place teacups. Whatever's happened, she looks just like she did back then. I don't even notice right away that I've started my breathing exercises.

No one's spoken since we came in and the sound of the television news fills the space. Tavia and I turn to watch and everything stops.

It's Isabella. She looks tall even in pictures and her wavy hair looks thick and heavy, just like in real life. For some reason that means the reporter must be wrong.

Isabella Apatu isn't missing. We were just texting a couple of days ago.

They're saying there's concern that she's met the same fate as other recently missing persons.

There are other missing persons. All reported today.

And then they're in the cemetery and I can't breathe.

I know that spot. I know that headstone.

I know that duck handle and that umbrella—except the last time I saw them they weren't part of a granite statue.

"What's going on?" I ask in a way that only Tavia can understand. After I sign, my hands don't know what to do. They grip each other and then slide up the opposite arms until I'm cradling my elbows, my fingernails scratching at the skin.

The man at my mother's grave is still on the screen, still in his three-piece suit, and still reaching toward me. Except now I can

212

see how he tried to recoil at the last minute. He saw what was coming or he was just terrified. I can see it even though his eyes have turned to stone.

He's been in the cemetery all this time. He never left.

Not since he met me.

"What happened to him?" I ask aloud. "Why is this happening again?"

"Effie." Mama Theo puts her face in her hands.

"What! What aren't you telling me?"

I can't see her when she's covering her face like that.

"What do the sprites want from me? Why won't they leave me alone?" I ask, and she erupts.

"It's not the sprites, Effie! It's you!"

I start to say something, but it's nothing. I don't have an answer. My fingers keep scratching and scratching until—

"Eff." Tavia's voice is almost calm, and her hand on my arm is too. When I look down, I see the white film on my fingertips and the busted "skin" dangling from my elbows. It's white and maybe pink. It doesn't match my color. It can't be mine. But it's hanging like a torn curtain from both my elbows, tattered and shimmery.

"Oh God." And when I pull it, it just keeps coming, peeling up my arm and across my chest in a long, disgusting, curling strip. "What am I? Mama, what *am* I!"

Mama Theo is taking hold of me now, and Mr. Philips is standing too.

"Come on, Effie," Mama says, hustling me toward the door.

"Where are you taking me?"

"It didn't work!" She shakes me hard, one time. "I thought a siren would keep him away, but it didn't." Maybe she doesn't mean to, but she shakes me again. "I thought it would matter that you were with a real family. I thought you wouldn't change if I could keep you apart."

I keep opening my mouth, but she doesn't leave me space to speak, or to think, or to process the way the skin beneath the shimmery silk I pulled away is cold, and new.

"Minnie said he'd leave you be and it'd be up to you, but he kept coming for you. He keeps setting you off."

"Say it so it makes sense!" I finally erupt, and everything's silent but the reporter on the screen.

"It's too late," Mama says. "Now they'll fear you, too."

Suddenly I understand. "Now you want me and Tavia apart. After everything you said. You want me to leave here."

"I want you to hide. Before they find that girl and you *can't* hide."

Geneva is on her feet too, covering her mouth.

"I didn't do this," I tell them. "I swear."

"Yes, Effie. You did."

She corrals me toward the door, and when Tavia dives for me, her dad intervenes.

"Tav!" I'm being jostled away from her. "Tavia, Compel her!"

But when I get a clear view of her, Tavia's dad has his hand clamped over her mouth and she's crying. He's laying all his weight on her before she's even had a chance to resist. Like she's ever resisted him. She looks crushed between him and the stairs, caged in by the thin wooden beams of the rail.

As if she needed another reason to feel smothered or snuffed out.

I'll never forgive him. Or Mama. Or Geneva, for never speaking up.

They're really tearing us apart.

This is really happening. And if I don't stop fighting Mama Theo, I don't know what the gargoyle will do when we get outside. I don't know if he'll know not to hurt her. So for her own good, I calm down.

"I'll go," I tell her, throwing up my hands and falling in the direction of her shoving. "I'll go with you."

Her eyes are wild, but it's just because she's scared. Too scared to know the damage she's doing.

"Let me say goodbye. Please."

She's ashamed of herself. I know it by the way she drops her head and turns toward the wall so I can get past her and get back to Tavia. Her dad doesn't let her up until I get there, and then we collapse into each other.

"I don't know what you are," she whispers, "but don't be scared. No matter what. It's something wonderful."

That's what she says after everything she's been through today.

I don't answer her out loud, I just slide my right hand between our bodies and spell out one word.

Prom.

I'll get back to her. We'll find each other there and we'll figure out what's going on with me and with Isabella. I don't know how, but it doesn't matter.

Nothing's gonna keep us apart.

TAVIA

As soon as I was alone that night I tried to call Effie. Of course. It went straight to voice mail then, just like it did the next day, and today's no different. There's no outgoing message, just the automated one with a pause where she blurts out her own name like an awkward robot.

Lovely, consistent Effie.

Given what I saw in my living room, I'm fairly confident her phone was taken away as soon as she was hustled into the Freemans' car, if not before. I'm equally confident I wouldn't have seen her even if I had gone to school today. Which I didn't. (It would've been hard to do considering I still haven't gotten out of bed.)

I consider calling the landline at the Freemans', but I'm sure there won't be an answer. Or Paw Paw'll be on the other end or, worse, Mama Theo.

She said I was supposed to protect Effie, that she thought I could keep "him" away. Whoever "him" is. But I didn't, so it's my fault that I'm alone again.

I may as well be back in Santa Cruz, when it was clear nobody understood me, or was willing to try. I mean, it's been two days since they ripped Eff away from me and no one's said a word. When I didn't come down this morning, no one came to ask me why not. My dad left this morning at his usual time. No goodbye.

No apology. In bed, I looked myself over (on the triceps that were pinned against the corner of one of the steps and on my hip) to make sure there weren't any bruises. There weren't, but it didn't keep me from crying. It doesn't seem fair, that I have a scar from trying to save myself (and my parents) but not one to commemorate their betrayal.

There's a gentle knocking on the door and then it creaks open. Mom. (Who else was it gonna be?)

I turn over and face away from her.

On her way to my bed, she stops a few times and I know she's picking things up. Probably the clothes Effie left on her bed after deciding what to wear on Friday morning. I threw everything on the floor when I thought I was gonna collapse on her bed last night, but I couldn't do it and went to mine instead. Now Mom's putting them back where Eff left them.

Classic Geneva Philips, peacekeeper. It's not so endearing anymore. Not since I stood in the middle of a tide of people who convinced me it's better to make peace than to keep it. (My imaginary Mr. Monroe would understand the difference.)

"I've always been the odd man out," Mom says when she's sitting at my back. It surprises me, those words, and I've already half turned before I stop myself. "The magic's on your father's side, not mine. He got it from his mother, and he passed it on to you. I just get to be close to it."

I turn all the way over now. What is it about mothers and their ability to find the weak spot in our armor? I was never going to acknowledge her presence, never turn over, never let her know I heard a word. Now I'm on my back, eyes locked with hers, and she's tracing my eyebrows and cheekbones the way she used to when we pretended she was giving me a makeover. When I feel hot tears slide free, she stops perfecting my lip liner and wipes them away.

"I should've said something," she tells me. "I should've known your dad was more scared than anything else, and that it would end up hurting you. We want to keep you safe, but you don't belong to us, Vivi."

217

I'm waiting for two words and then I can stop holding back. I hate the feeling. I detest it, forcing myself to be something else, to be hard when I want to be soft. I'm no good at it. Maybe no one is, but it eats me up inside. It never makes me feel strong, just cold. Lonely.

Finally she says it.

"I'm sorry, Tavia."

And I'm free. I blink to release the tears struggling on my eyelashes, ignoring the way the back of my eyelids are indigo. If I close them a moment longer, I'll be in that secret place, near the river and Gramma's voice. There must be a reason she's reaching for me again, but I can't go just yet. Right now I want to lie still. I want to stay in this moment, with my mom, because I've waited for what seems like forever.

Her fingertip is on my keloid now, and she's torn between a smile and something sadder.

"People say that the reason oracles don't exist anymore is that people stopped believing them." Now her brows ribbon. "Isn't that awful? A part of me always worried what might happen to sirens if they're too afraid to speak. I don't *want* you to be afraid. It's crippling." The smile resurfaces and it seems more sincere. "Trust me."

And I do, so I tell her. "I went to see Camilla Fox."

Her gaze moves from my scar back to my eyes, but I don't wait for her to reply.

"Effie and I didn't go to the Renaissance faire, we went to the protest." I run out of words before I know it. My mouth hangs open for a moment and I remember all of it, the riot gear and the ear plugs. The ladder and Kenyon Jones's mother. The sweat and the explosion of chaos. And the collar. When my mother palms my cheek, she brings me back. "It was terrible," I say, "and . . . it was good. For a while."

"You're brave, Vivi," she tells me, and she may not be a siren but she's my mom; her words have power. My chest shudders as though the breath escaping it is the last of its kind, making space for something new.

This is like a dream. If the indigo place is some sort of siren alternate dimension, this conversation with my mom is further from reality than that—and I'm eager for it. If I have a choice between accepting an overdue apology the moment it's offered (without demanding some sort of compensation or period of penance) and basking in my rightful disappointment and loneliness, I choose the former. It's just too bad my dad doesn't know that.

My mom stays with me for a little while. She opens the balcony door and lets the fresh air in, and she comes back to sit beside me. I don't tell her about the time Gargy stood out there, or about the times he carried me through the sky. I don't even tell her about the majesty of his voice or why he won't be back tonight. Not because I can't anymore, just because I'm relieved. I just listen to her talk about Santa Cruz and all the things she misses. It's strange the way she describes it, and me. All her stories are about the ocean and tuxedo apples from Marini's and which taqueria was her favorite. She talks about jogging West Cliff Drive in the early morning and the look on my face when I watched the dolphins while she watched me. She reminds me of my first wet suit, and the way I hated tasting the salt when ocean water splashed into my mouth.

None of that matches my memory of the tiny town. I don't remember anything as much as the room inside Dominican Hospital, and that wasn't until the end. Nothing else comes to mind, though, except emotional memories that fit that locked room even though they came before it.

I like the Santa Cruz my mother describes. It flashes in my mind like sparks from a live wire, quick images and light. Joy and awe, not just over dolphins and whales migrating through Monterey Bay, but at the doe and her fawn grazing in the meadows on the local university campus. (The trash-eating raccoon up there and the honking sea lions at the wharf are a different story completely. They can go to hell.)

When she asks what I'd think about taking Effie to the boardwalk someday, I nod a half-dozen times.

"That'd be awesome," I say, and she smiles.

"I think so too."

I meditate on what feels like a sudden transformation—but maybe my mom's sneakier than I thought. It's impossible that she could change my mind about so many things so quickly. Right? Maybe she's been working at it all along and I couldn't tell because I'm not a mother. Or maybe I'm flush with optimism and endorphins because after everything that's happened, she said just what I needed to hear. Whichever, I'll take it.

She kisses my forehead and whispers that she loves me, before turning to leave the room.

"Mom?" I say, stopping her before she's gone. She's standing in front of Effie's bed again, and for a moment I just stare at my sister's empty space. "If I'd known I was supposed to be protecting her, maybe I wouldn't have failed."

"You didn't fail anyone, Vivi. Certainly not Effie." She comes back to my bed.

"What is she? Why did Mama Theo want her here?"

"If Theodosia knows, she didn't tell us." And then she tilts her head, like there's more to it than that. "She never said Effie was something else; she made it seem like something's been after her. Since always. And maybe she'd be safer near a siren. I just thought you girls would be good for each other."

"So I *was* supposed to keep her safe."

"Who says you haven't?"

"Mama Theo! She took Effie away!"

"She's scared, Vivi. Like I was. Like your dad is."

"If I knew what I should've done—"

"Maybe it's not something you were supposed to do."

"What?"

"It might not be a siren trait at all." When I gesture wildly, wondering what then it could be, Mom just shrugs. "Maybe it's not a 'you' power, it's a 'them' fear. Maybe that was supposed to keep them away. Whoever they are."

That feels different. Plausible . . . Familiar.

"I don't know," she says. "But all us grown folk seem to have fear in common."

This time when she kisses my forehead and turns to leave, I don't stop her. I can still feel Gramma reaching for me, but I need to think. I need to make sense of what Mom and Mama Theo have said.

Maybe it's a "them" fear—but it isn't a "them" Theodosia Freeman mentioned, it's a "he." *He* is afraid of me, or was supposed to be. And if this "he" is a grown-up the way Mom assumed, maybe he's the same one who's been missing from Effie's life all along.

Maybe it's Effie's dad who's afraid of sirens. Of me.

A bit of blue bleeds into view.

"Gramma, I swear to God, wait!"

Effie's dad is afraid of me.

That would mean he's here, that he's been here all along, and trying to get to Effie. And that Effie was placed near me so he couldn't.

If it's really him, then Mama Theo's been keeping them apart. She's been keeping Effie from the only blood family she has left. From the one person Effie's been asking for all this time, who could've answered her questions, told her if she was sprite-kin. Or at least why they spared her.

That's when I remember the images from the news. Effie and I only had a moment to take it in before the chaos of our families tearing us away from each other the same day her gargoyle protector airlifted us out of a protest that ended with Camilla Fox being collared.

Now the images come rushing back. The faces of the missing.

"Not sprites," I say as though Effie's there with me. "She said it was you."

But it doesn't make any sense. Effie was with me the entire day, first at the protest and then marooned in the middle of the reserve. However she would've hurt those people, I'm 100 percent certain she couldn't have.

Mama Theo's wrong, at least about that. (And about kidnapping teenage girls, granddaughter or not.)

What I have to take her word on is that *someone* is afraid of sirens. And maybe that someone is Effie's dad.

I stand up, one hand waving as though to quiet the empty room. Because I just realized how I can help my sister.

I pull out my phone. My first thought is to research sirens and histories and yes, even mythos, to see who or what has ever feared us. (Aside from everyone.) Maybe see what they think we can do aside from deceive them, which I already know about. But looking into sirenness and especially leaving a digital trail of said search has always been a no-no. I can't even blame my dad for that. It's not like he's wily enough to have a cloning program on my phone. It's my own fear that's kept me obedient to his rules. Ever since Santa Cruz, I've worried there's someone much stronger and scarier than my dad paying attention to what potential sirens do. And after the protest, I know I was right. So I research something else.

Because if "he" really is Eff's father, then whatever *he* is, *she* is.

I start typing in all of Effie's quirks.

Sensitive scalp.

Eczema. Scratch that. (Let's be real.) Shedding skin.

Blackouts.

Master swimmer.

I'm still typing in traits, and already there are images coming up and websites. They all have to do with serpents. Sea snakes, once I type in the bit about swimming. But what I'm really waiting for is some sort of mythos.

Oh, gargoyle protectors.

And mirages.

And when the next search results load, I nearly drop my phone.

The Hidden Scales.

Effie's Hidden Scales. The center of the Renaissance faire. The tent with the perma-fog. And the gray guard of cosplaying gargoyle protectors.

The first site is just a community-compiled profile, and it's clearly written by some very enthusiastic geeks attempting to entice the reader by withholding key pieces of information. There's something about the gray guard chiseled from stone by their master (okay, well, that part's not true, obviously, since those guys are humans in costume) to stand watch over his portal and protect it against mortals who might trespass.

I love Ren faire dorks as much as anyone, but come on. I'm looking for legitimate answers, not vagaries!

The next several links are for forums, and of course the most popular one is the Hidden Tales, the fan-fiction site I sometimes visit with Effie. Clearly she knows how to separate the chaff from the wheat, because without her filtering, much of it is . . . bad. But only from an IB English perspective. Which is the only one I have, so I skim.

This maiden's led inside the Hidden Scales in a trance. She turns out to be the master's betrothed and together they rule the twin fairegrounds.

This chambermaid discovers that she's the destined heir to the Hidden Scales, and in the end, she rules the twin fairegrounds.

There's a lot of poor, overlooked wenches finding out they're the prophesied somebody who was foretold to do the thing, and oh yeah, they end up ruling the twin fairegrounds.

Somebody's really into being captive to the gray guard. (A lot.)

My eyes are starting to cross, and Gramma's blue place hasn't stopped pulling at me, so I'm on the verge of giving in when I see it.

Someone's story mentions the "walking water" outside the Hidden Scales. They describe it as a moving blur, and it sounds like it could be what Effie's been seeing—

Everything goes blue.

I don't remember closing my eyes, but my bedroom is gone. My phone is gone, and the stories about the tent and the maybe-mirage with it.

I'm back in the construction lot and it's night, dark with the same wash of blues as before. There are differences, though. For one, instead of just the sensation of floating, I'm actually slightly off the ground, the way I was the moment before Gargy set me down. I'm levitating high enough to be impressive if this were some reality show about a street magician, but not so much that it counts as flying.

For two, I'm not over the river, but there's water all around. The air around me moves like I'm deep below the surface, light flowing through the layers like the tendrils of a jellyfish, slow and fluid. My stretched twist-out moves the same way, billowing and then curling back the way Effie's must when she's Euphemia.

If it's possible, the indigo place is eerier than the first time I visited. But, like, in a whimsical way.

"Gramma?"

The question moves the air-water in front of me, parting it like a curtain that was previously unseen, and another version of me appears on the other side. The me from the river. The me that is my grandmother's voice incarnate. Face to face it's easier to see the slight differences in our appearances, beginning with the curl pattern of her hair, the length of her eyelashes and girth of her nose. We are nearly twins, but my mother's genes got in there too.

You're beautiful, she mouths to me. I hear a sound like distant waves when she moves her lips. My skin won't blush, but the apples of my cheeks get round and high.

"You're sort of complimenting yourself, too, though."

I know.

Gramma's got jokes. And then she gets serious.

"I guess something's the matter if you kidnapped me." I mean for it to sound playful, but given what's gone down this weekend, I wish I'd chosen my words more wisely.

Effie.

Did I see that right?

"What about her?"

Before Gramma answers, Effie's there, beside her. It isn't really Effie, just like it wasn't really Naema. It's a strange stand-in who looks like an alternate in a way that I can't pin down. Her eyes are closed, her twists twirling and swaying and blue in the indigo light. She looks exactly like my sister, except for the way she doesn't.

I look back to Gramma and instead of speaking, she nods in Effie's direction.

"I don't understand."

Turns out Gramma's got eye-rolls, too.

"What," I ask through a laugh. "It's Effie."

Awaken.

"Awaken . . . Awaken Effie?"

When I was small and my dad thought I was purposely misunderstanding him or missing a point, he'd accuse me of "being cute." One glance at the smirk on my grandmother's face and I know he got that phrase from her.

"I really didn't know, I promise!"

Okay, Vivi, she mouths, and there's something really special about her using the same nickname my parents always do. **Now you know.**

But when I turn back to Not-Effie and open my mouth, she's gone. No such luck. If I want to see what my siren call reveals about my sister, I have to use it in the real world. The surge of curiosity is like a bolt of electricity through my limbs.

~~~~~~

Effie isn't at school on Tuesday when I muster the courage to go. Same on Wednesday, and Thursday, and I take the hint. She isn't coming. But whenever I call Effie's phone, I only get to hear her voice for a second while she awkwardly recites her own name. It's the same no matter how many times I call.

Five.

Seventeen.

Twenty-four.

Effie Calhoun Freeman. But at least I get to hear her at all.

225

I want to tell her I know what to do, that my siren call can end the mystery for her once and for all—which I'm just assuming is why my grandmother told me to use it. Of the two times I have, only once did I use it on someone with a special feature, so to speak. That must be why I heard Naema's melody and why there was a trill in her voice when she spoke. As for Altruism, she seemed to hear me. I mean really hear me. What I really meant, even though I only said (shouted) her name. I can't be sure what to expect when I "Awaken" Effie.

It'll have to wait till prom. I don't know how she'll manage to get there, but she will. She promised.

She'll want to know what's happened since she got taken away, probably locked inside her grandparents' house ever since the night of the protest. Whether there are more statues, and whether her friend Isabella has been found. What people are saying and who they think is responsible.

There are things I want to know too. Like what happened to Camilla Fox after I saw her lying on her back, the wind knocked out of her and her siren call trapped inside. I don't search it or visit her channel online, but there has to be something about it on the news. There has to. There were too many people, it was done in broad daylight and without provocation. Every news station in the Pacific Northwest (at least!) should have something to say. Questions that must be answered.

But when I turn on the news, it's worse than I thought. I don't have more than a moment to process the lack of reporting on the second-most-famous revealed siren in the country because there are more of them now.

More statues.

Gray and granite-looking figures appearing all over the city. People being found inanimate before their loved ones even know they're missing.

"Effie," I whisper like it's her picture on the screen. "What's going on?"

Something is very wrong in Portland.

The peace left over from my talk with Mom and all the time we've spent together since, and the excitement from what Gramma had to say, dry up.

If Mama Theo thinks Effie has something to do with this, it feels like only a matter of time before someone else has the same thought. Either way, there are statues sprouting up everywhere; eventually someone's gonna go looking for the only person to escape the first such phenomenon. Someone's gonna wanna know what happened to Park Girl.

For a moment my brain drowns out the TV. Maybe that's why there was no answer. Maybe Mama Theo ran away with her. Maybe she won't be at prom because she isn't even in Portland anymore.

Maybe I'm not getting my sister back.

"No." If anyone were watching it'd look like I'm arguing with the news. "She promised. She'll come back."

Effie would've found a way to let me know if they were taking her away. Gargy would've told me, flown fast to tell me before racing back. Maybe.

They're hiding in that house, that's all. That's all.

When I've decided, the local anchor raises her eyebrows like she has her doubts, but when I listen, she's not talking about Effie at all. She's describing recent efforts to investigate this new wave of troubling phenomena. There's a professor at University of Portland who wrote some paper on moon cycles and spikes in (alleged) sprite activity and she's poring over her data, updating it, promising to issue a statement soon. After her, there's a child who recently called 911 while being picked on by a sprite whose wind-whisper *might* be the first audio recording. When that story broke it was pretty lighthearted, so I'm surprised to see it resurrected in this context. The child, thank God, is safe and accounted for.

And then, bam. It's all our fault. It's the sirens.

227

I lose my grip on the remote and it clatters against the hard-wood floor.

Now there's footage from the protest. *Now* Camilla's on the screen—except she isn't on her back being wrestled into a collar. She's on the ladder, shouting over our heads. They're making it seem like there wasn't a wall of approaching riot police. They're making it look like the protest was about Camilla and sirens and our wanting to take apart the world.

Looking at the selective footage you don't see the barrier of protection we made with our own bodies, you don't see the people anchoring the ladder or the pictures of Kenyon Jones, and you don't hear the loving stories his mother told.

I'm watching someone give an account of me based on what they already thought, and there's nothing I can do about the fact that it's mostly lies.

They're showing individual images now, taken from people's social-media accounts because a week out this must all be old news online. I press pause to scour the scene for any sign of my-self or Effie. Nothing. I un-pause it and then think I accidentally double-tapped. But no, it's a new picture, a cell-phone still of something huge and gray, blurred in motion.

Gargy. He's standing flat on his feet and erect to his full height, his wings pulled up like a shield so that I can't see his face or which of us he had inside. I remember the tugging sensation in my abdomen, though. The suddenness of flight or, more accu-rately, of being ripped into the sky. He didn't land, he just yanked me off my feet before I could help Camilla.

He's protecting Effie in this picture, he must be. I feel the cor-ner of my mouth lift a little and I pause the program again to examine it.

Gargy's tree-trunk legs are the only part of him almost in fo-cus, his wings warped and welded together by the failed attempt to capture them snapping around his ward.

I'm searching for any sliver of Effie, but there's too much of the gargoyle, too many crystal-clear protestors with their backs to the camera, their arms sometimes wavy with movement.

Wavy but not warped.

I take a small step closer and now there's no space between the television screen and me. I squint because that's what you do when you don't trust your eyes. You mercilessly squeeze them in the hope that they'll submit.

There's something different about the motion in the protesters' arms and the motion in Gargy's body. I can see now that he's distorted, as though I'm seeing him through the old-school glass wall the Freemans have between their shower and the commode. Or like he's underwater.

Like Effie might see him when her eyes are playing tricks on her. When she sees the mirage, the watery stamp that makes her feel like she's back in the pool. That I said was from all the time she spends beneath the surface. What people on the Hidden Tales called "walking water."

"Wholly carp." I have to wipe my breath off the screen to prove that the distortion isn't coming from me.

It's not. And the mirage isn't a mirage at all. It's not Hidden Scales mythos.

It's real. It's something Effie can see. Something she's *been* seeing, for years.

I have to get a prom dress.

~~~~~

The night of the prom, the sun stays out forever. It must be so awkward, the limos and the pictures and the endless posing, and then going to dinner and it still feeling like the middle of a lazy Saturday.

I wouldn't know. I dress by myself at home, have my mom help me with an updo no online video will ever convince me can be achieved with only one set of hands, and then sit on the couch until it's time to go.

"You didn't want to go with anyone?" my dad asks when I'm fiddling with my mom's bracelet around my wrist. I'm studying the braided silver and gold like it's the first time I've ever seen it. My dad, I haven't seen for days.

"Nobody asked me."

"Mm."

He wants to give me some advice. Some hint about what I need to do to show guys I'm not shuttered off, that I'm available for romance. Maybe he wants to ask if I've tried to make up with Priam.

I'm ready. In my head, I'm replaying my conversations with Mom, and that'll bunt any unpleasantness right back out.

"Well. I'm glad you're going." Huh. "No shame in going on your own. Guys are pretty wack, especially at your age."

That's it . . . but it's kind of nice. (He didn't even put unnecessary emphasis on the word "wack," which he usually does when he tries to use inevitably out-of-date slang. So that's something.) Anyway, this is real life; my dad's not gonna suddenly be a different person, even if I am.

"Thanks," I say, and then fiddle with my mom's bracelet again. Maybe tomorrow we'll have another exchange like this, and maybe it'll be a tiny bit longer. I don't know. If we do, maybe somewhere down the road it won't be hard for him to say he's sorry.

I wonder if I'll ever tell him I've seen Gramma, and I wonder how he'd respond. For a split second I imagine him shutting down, wanting none of it, and then I imagine him doing the opposite. Asking if there's a way that he can go there, to the indigo place, and see her too. Wanting to know how she looks when we're there, and whether she asks about him. Maybe he'll want to know about all the years we didn't spend with her. Or maybe he wouldn't know what to think.

I guess we'll see.

It isn't long before I hold out my hand and he drops his car keys into it. Just because I'm only going to prom to secretly meet up with my sister doesn't mean I can't go in style.

~~~~~~

Junior prom is held at the school because the seniors need their "ball" to be the highlight of the year. (Petty.) I wasn't expecting much, but when I arrive in the parking lot it feels like I got super dressed up to go to class. The basketball courts are exactly how I left them, same with the tennis courts. At least the sun's finally gone down.

I round the corner and the quad takes my breath away. Garden lanterns pepper the courtyard and there are strings of lights decorating the trees and more strung up between them. They're wrapped around anything that isn't a seat.

In the middle of all that glitter is a sea of glitz. Members of my class (along with a few seniors and underclassmen dating or pretending for the night to date a junior) look like they spent a small fortune on blow-outs, ringlets, extensions, color, and just an environmentalist's nightmare of hair spray. There are dresses of every length, including a few mullet dresses, where the front is drastically shorter than the back. I'm so morally opposed to those things, but somehow the girls wearing them look nice. (It's the endorphins again.)

This is just the preamble before the cafeteria doors open, but it's pretty impressive. Even the chaperones are dressed in formal wear, including Mr. Monroe, who's got his hands in his pockets and is just nodding at random students.

Finally the doors open and everyone's rushing to see the way the cafeteria's been transformed for the evening—that is, until the elokos arrive.

I take a deep breath before turning toward the overflow of gapes and gasps.

There they are. Priam and Naema, with the rest of the crew. He's wearing his hair in a messy knot, strands meticulously displaced and framing his face. I don't suppose he did that himself. (My heart only aches a little.) It looks beyond hot, especially with the teal suit he's wearing, which was possibly tailored right onto his frame. It cost more than my uninspired ball gown, that's clear at a glance. But with her lavish mermaid gown (which *does* make her look suspiciously like a bride), he and Naema look like the perfect fit. Except . . .

Yeah.

Except for the collar Naema's wearing around her neck.

XVI

EFFIE

Other than the paint job, the Freeman house is identical to the one next to it, and that one's identical to the one next to *it*, and so on. The neighborhood went up fast, Paw Paw said, and after the first Black family could afford to get in and it made all the white families head for the literal hills, *then* he could afford one.

"It's a good little house," he says. "Keeps the rain out, just not the rabble."

He means you can hear people talking as they pass on the sidewalk.

That's how I know Gargy isn't out there. (For the record, it still sounds weird to use Tav's nickname for him.) If he were curling his talons the way he did on the hill, it'd be deafening here. But there's nothing.

I don't get it. Tavia said he was my guard. So what? Only as long as I was living at the Philipses'? Makes no sense. But I mean, I've been stuck in the house for a week, Mama Theo watching me every hour of the day no matter how many times Paw Paw suggested she leave me be. Yesterday she caught me going through the kitchen looking for my phone (she used to store money in the bread bin, so it was worth a shot), and ever since then, I've been locked in my room (which after three years in me and Tav's sprawling attic feels like a sardine can). So. Who am I to expect life to make sense, right?

I'm pacing, if you can call it that, walking a few steps from the dresser to the poof-chair in front of the vanity and then doing it a thousand times more. I'd get more range jumping on the bed. I'm not above it, it just feels a little strange, super seriously thinking while bouncing on my childhood mattress. I could steeple my fingers. That might help.

Jumping on the bed would also cover for the way my twists are moving. I took off the wrap, took out the hair tie (which snapped, surprise, surprise!), and my hair's been dancing ever since. I don't even know if it feels weird anymore. I give up. Plus I'm alone in a tiny room where no one else can see, so if they're gonna be haunted, this is the place.

I try the door handle. Still locked.

Still shocked. Still trying to decode everything Mama Theo said. It's the only way I'll ever figure out how long she plans to keep me in here. Bits of it have kept me from sleeping well, but I'm not totally sure I'm remembering it correctly anymore. It's been a week with no school or swimming to break up the boredom. No Tavia to keep me sane. And everything Mama said that night was . . . confusing.

I thought you wouldn't change if I could keep you apart.

The "change" is pretty obvious. I've been coming undone for a while now. It's the "kept you apart" that stumps me.

Minnie said he'd leave you be . . .

He . . . My eyes roll up toward the ceiling, toward the roof I can't see from inside the house and on which I know Garg isn't perched.

The gargoyle. This has something to do with him. *That's* why he's not here. *That's* why he's never been at Mama Theo's. She knows something about him.

Dude. (I actually gasp.) He's my dad.

That . . . doesn't make sense. Does it? His face is made of stone, it's not like I could guess how old he is. And I don't know much about gargoyles aside from them being big and brick, except that they don't have any history-affecting qualities or traits that the general population envies. Don't get me wrong, wings are cool and all, but not when you'd have to give up your skin to get them. Then there's the whole "gargoyles aren't born, they're sculpted" part of their mythos, and the belief that all the gargoyles that will exist already do. Not born, not very social, and fly so under the radar people forget they exist? They get about as much time in school lesson plans as reclusive giants. So I have no idea if it's possible for a gargoyle to . . . procreate with a person. Or what they'd spawn if they did. I'd look them up now if Mama Theo hadn't swiped my phone before pulling this Rapunzel stunt on me.

And then my brain jerks back to what she said.

I thought you wouldn't change . . .

"Whoa." *She* thought *I* wouldn't change . . . That means she expected it. She knew I was supposed to, that a change was even possible.

Then she must know what it is.

She knows what the change is doing to me.

What I'm becoming.

This is a new itch. It's not my scalp or my skin; it's underneath all that. When I'm awkward or embarrassed or wish I were invisible, I get that hot flush people describe, but this is beyond that. It's this molten heat riding through my body like a current of pure rage.

She knows. She's *known*. Probably for my whole life, and she hasn't said a thing. And it's not like I haven't asked, like I haven't been searching, pleading, desperate for answers, and she shut me down every time. Who does that? I wanted to know who my father was and she always flipped it into a character flaw, or something childish, something that disappointed her.

I slam my fist against the door before I even know I've made one.

"Mama!" I'm huffing now, like I've been underwater for too long. Like I've pushed my limit and now my chest feels creaky and fragile, like one extra-deep breath will crack me open. I don't think I've ever hit anything as hard as I am banging on my bedroom door right now. I scream for her again and then, "*You're* the monster!"

I hear someone rushing to the short hallway.

"You've known all this time! I asked for your help and you lied to me!"

"Effie Calhoun Freeman, get away from that door!" It's her. As usual her voice is stern, like she hasn't heard what I'm saying, just that I'm yelling. As usual her only concern is putting me in my place.

"Let me out!"

"I'll do no such thing."

"Theodosia, let her out already." I almost don't believe it when I hear Paw Paw from further down the hall.

"I'll do no such thing!" she hollers at both of us now. "That child being mad doesn't change that I have to keep her safe."

"You're evil," I say, and I bang the door to emphasize it. Like the sound of my fist beating the door is a period at the end of the sentence or a gavel a judge bangs when her decision is final.

"Effie!"

"You are." My forehead is pressed against the door and my twists are slapping against the wood grain like they want to get through too. "You're an evil, conniving, selfish old woman who has tried my whole life to keep me from knowing who I really am, and knowing who my father is."

I squeeze my eyes shut. Wherever Garg is, I hope he can hear me. I hope he's on his way.

"I don't know what made my mom trust you . . . but I don't. You're not my family. This isn't my home."

With my head still pressed to the door, I kick it with everything I have, hurting us both.

"I'm not staying here!"

"Do you know what's happening out there, Effie?" Mama's yelling now. "Do you have any idea what's going on? I can't protect you if you won't—"

"I don't care! Do you hear me? Whatever's out there, it's better than being with you! I'd rather be a statue in Triton Park than this! I'd rather be chased by photographers or be living stone!"

That shuts her up. At least until she gets back to the end of the hall where Paw Paw must be. I can hear them exchanging words, but I can't make out what they're saying. And then the front door opens and closes, and I don't know who left and who stayed, or if either of them did. For all I know, I'm on my own.

I raise my fist to pummel the door off its hinges, but the knocking sounds before I connect.

I didn't do that.

Twirling around barely registers on my hair since it's in constant motion now, but behind me is what passes for my bedroom window. It's the right width but it's small, the kind you'd put high in a bathroom so you can get sunlight and maybe some ventilation but people can't watch you pee. I used to love that window after the nightmare in the park and people came looking for me. I got to see a sliver of sky without feeling like the world could get in. Now I wonder who puts it in a kid's bedroom.

Someone knocks again and now I do jump onto my bed, just to see who's there.

"Tav?" I call out as my fingers curl around the sill. But those aren't her eyes. It's not her golden brown skin and buzz-cut hair. "Wallace."

"Hey. Are we still going to prom?"

I can't see his mouth, but his eyes crinkle and I know he's grinning. I can't believe he's here. If this were the Ren faire, he'd be one of the archers, with one of those befeathered caps. He's not dastardly the way they are, but he's got the charisma. And he's outside my window, ready to bust me out for a high-school formal. Tavia must've sent him, thank God.

"Yeah," I say. "We're still going." Like the door behind me isn't still locked.

And then I hear a click and maybe it isn't. I look away from Wallace's framed eyes and back toward the door like I might see through it to Mama Theo on the other side. Or maybe Paw Paw, finally fed up. I don't know why I give him more credit, I just do. Maybe because I never asked him, so the secret gets pinned on Mama. Maybe because she's the one who had whisper-meetings with Mom once she got sick, who decided she'd make a habit of dumping on my Ren faire life even if it was my favorite place to be. Who sat in front of me over and over again and lied to my face.

Whoever it is, they're not standing there when I open the door.

Wow, Mama. Even I'm braver than that. So much for the "I have to protect you" lie.

I hop back onto the bed and tell Wallace to come around to the front.

"You kids need a ride somewhere?" Paw Paw asks me when I step into the hall outside my room.

~~~~~

We ride toward Beckett High in silence, me and Wallace both in the back seat.

Paw Paw glances at my date a few times in the rearview, but he never says anything. Not even about the fact that we're holding hands.

I look down at our fingers laced through each other's and try to take a mental picture. Someday when things settle down (because they have to, don't they?) the memory of it might give me butterflies. It's too much to ask right this minute, given what's going on outside the car.

First there's just yellow police tape around someone's front yard. No way to tell why or what happened inside, and no reason to speculate. Things happen all the time. It sucks, but it's not exactly unique.

We pass three patrol cars before I give in.

Okay. Something's different.

I don't wanna hear Mama Theo's warning in my head, but I do. Something's going on outside, in the city. There are cars around and people walking down the streets, but the light is gone. Portland has this energetic way of carrying itself; it can be really annoying, to be honest. Sometimes it seems smug in an organic-er-than-thou kind of way. But I've never felt how strange the air would be without it, until now. When a city has a character, it can't just be replaced. If it loses its weird, you just feel the void. I don't like it.

Paw Paw has to slow down because up ahead the road is down to one lane and oncoming traffic is being allowed through first.

I'm a weird contradiction of wanting to know why and wanting to avoid knowing at all costs. I just won't look.

It could be anything. A burst pipe or something. Construction. Maybe they just replaced the asphalt on the other side of the street and they're giving it a chance to set.

Things aren't always sensational. Nine times out of ten, it's just the natural order of things. It's just the way things go. Things happen, whether you're an eloko or a siren or a giant or there was an oracle in your bloodline or not. People without "additional attributes" fall sick all the time, and even if you find out they had a love affair with a gargoyle, there's no proof that the one has anything to do with the other. Even if they have a daughter who everyone thought was sprite-kin. Even if maybe there was more to their love of pirate festivals and Renaissance faires.

I can't count the number of times I heard, "Effie, sometimes things just happen."

Nothing special. Nothing supernatural.

There isn't always a reason.

I don't know why that became about Mom. It feels like everything is coming to a head, and the void in the city isn't helping.

The cop in the neon vest has stopped oncoming traffic. It's our turn now. And I wasn't gonna look but Wallace is. He's craning his neck to see whatever it is before we've even gotten to the front of the line, and beneath my wrap my twists are tightening themselves again.

So I look. I look out my window and take it in. I look in the lane that's been taped off and it's like they're running toward me.

One of them's glancing back over her shoulder, but both of the statues are trying to cross the street. That's what they were doing when their skin changed to gray.

My twists flex and I wish I'd cut them off when I had the chance.

We're passed the congestion and Paw Paw picks up speed. I can't bring myself to look up at the rearview mirror and see if he's thinking what I'm thinking. I pin my chin to my chest and take my hand from Wallace's. In my head, I start counting my breaths. I think of my tank and the parents and the pictures and the kids who at least for a few minutes wish that they were me.

When I'm Euphemia, I can't be the girl who escaped from Triton Park.

But I had nothing to do with this. Those gray teenagers we just passed weren't on the news. When Tav and I came home from the protest and everyone was watching the report, it didn't show this street. They didn't mention a teen boy and girl or the look of terror on their faces. I don't know, if I had to guess I'd say whatever they were running from was nothing they'd seen before. And it certainly wasn't a critically self-conscious sixteen-year-old who's been shut up in her grandparents' house for a week. It couldn't have been.

I don't know what Mama Theo meant when she said I was causing all of this.

"You okay, Effie?" Paw Paw asks without looking away from the road. His voice is calm and steady like it always is. Like it was when he told me Mom had passed.

Mama Theo had sent him to my room because of that voice, and probably because I'd been falling asleep in the crook of his arm for over a week while Mom was in the hospital. They'd made me go home to sleep in my own bed, and that's when she left. I really felt like I left her first, like I should never have gone home, and only Paw Paw could have comforted me. Mama Theo knew at least that much.

"You still wanna go, don't you?"

I look up now. "Yeah," I tell him, "I still wanna go."

Garg isn't coming to Mama Theo's house. If I want to see him, find out who he really is to me, I've gotta be somewhere else. And being with Tavia feels like my best bet. I just wish I'd bought a dress.

When we get to Beckett, Paw Paw is the great de-escalator as usual. If I thought the world was about to implode, I must've been mistaken, because he stays in the driver's seat with his arm casually resting on the car door's windowsill.

"What's gonna happen is gonna happen," he says. It's one of his catchphrases, and it always ruffles Mama's feathers. It never really meant too much to me, as a kid, but I get it now.

Paw Paw knows, too.

He knows what I am and that I want to know, and that Mama's been trying to keep me from changing.

"You unlocked the door, didn't you?" I ask him.

He looks up at me and that's when I notice that his eyes are glassy. It makes something pinch in my chest.

"You don't mean those things you told your grandma." And then he glances away. "At least I hope you don't. If you did, you're gonna have to feel the same way about me."

I can't answer that without crying, so I just lower my head in shame.

"I made a promise to Minerva," and my head snaps up again. "A long time ago, and I took a long time fulfilling it. Too long. 'Cause I wanted to keep you too."

"Paw Paw," is all I can mumble.

"Anyway. It'll work itself out," he says, and it's so disconnected from the weight of all this that it's perfectly on brand for him.

"I don't suppose you kids'll need a ride back?" he asks with a smile, and while he watches Wallace, I rub the white hair on his arm like I used to when I was small.

"No, Tavia'll have the car." I don't hesitate to tell him I'm gonna see her here, if keeping us apart is part of why Mama locked me in my room. I *do* fail to mention that I'm holding out for gargoyle transit. Hoping Garg and I get a chance to talk—and maybe fly properly, the way he did with Tavia. Who knows. Everything could change by the end of the night. I'm hoping it does.

When Wallace and I get to the courtyard, we're holding hands again. But more importantly, we are royally underdressed.

Because this is prom, Effie.

I didn't have a lot to choose from since I took all my favorite clothes to the Philipses' and only left a few things in my old bedroom for the very rare nights Tav and I stay over. So no, on reflection, high-top Doc Martens and a thrifted wrap dress is *not* what I would have chosen for a formal, even if I'm not taking pictures. I have *some* decorum. And I'm not a people-pleaser, but I also don't go out of my way to shirk the norm. I am not looking forward to the attention this outfit is going to draw.

Wallace, on the other hand, could pass for intentional. He's got a white V-neck T-shirt on (I'm guessing I'm not the first person to notice the loveliness of his athletic arms), with a pair of dark-blue shorts and loafers. It looks like he had a choice between sailing and prom, and he needed his outfit to be passable for both.

It's only the second time I've seen him outside of community center duds, and I'm still getting used to it. Somehow his change in uniform makes it feel real. Like we're really "something" outside the pool. Like I haven't been imagining it. Like when everything is okay again, maybe I'll be a normal girl with a normal, quiet boyfriend. I'm down for that.

In the courtyard, Wallace's eyes light up. The lights are reflecting in them, yes, but he really looks impressed. It's cute. He doesn't seem to notice the raised eyebrows I'm getting, but of course when people see who I'm with (and maybe *that* I'm with *anyone*), the look changes. They're not just confused by my outfit, they're intrigued by my companion. People wave to me, say hello. People who rarely do. I've got my arms crossed by this point, walking aimlessly behind Wallace (who's just really taken with the lights and lanterns), so I just lift my fingers in reply.

"Effie!"

I spin around at the sound of Tavia's voice and see her rushing toward me in a Cinderella dress. The ball gown ripples and she's gripping some of the skirt in her hands so she doesn't trip on her way to me. She looks like a princess. Exactly how I'd imagine Tavia at prom, with her gorgeous hair in an elaborate updo.

She crash-lands in my arms.

"You came," she says, but it's more like a groan. "I looked inside for you and I was afraid you couldn't get here, how did you get here?"

"Paw Paw brought us."

She pulls back but we keep our arms around each other. "Just like that?"

"Just like that." I shrug.

"And Mama Theo just—"

"Look, if you want me to go home—"

"Shut up!" She yanks me back into the hug. "Does that mean things are okay?"

I remember the statues we passed on our way here. Tavia must have seen them too. She must know things aren't okay. She just wants me to tell her so.

Over Tavia's shoulder, I see Priam come out of the cafeteria. He looks like he's just wandering, but a few moments behind him comes Naema. When she finds him, she drops her head at an angle like a mom whose kid keeps toddling off.

I really don't want her to notice me, so I get still. Maybe she's a *T. rex* and she won't see me if I don't move.

"You okay?" Tav asks.

"Yeah. Just . . . a little out of place." I glance down at my outfit like that's the problem, and we both grin.

"Well, let's get out of here. I'd love to miss the coronation if you don't mind."

"You know I couldn't care less, but—" I don't know how it'll sound once I say it out loud. "I'm waiting for Gargy. I need to ask

243

him something." That part I'll keep under wraps until he finds us. I notice the way her face settles. She really doesn't wanna be here and I can't blame her. "We'll leave as soon as he comes."

Which reminds me, I'd better warn Wallace to stay close this time. I spot him under the big tree, the one with the most intricate light-stringing, and Tav and I start that way.

"Pool boy cleans up nice," Naema says from behind us.

Great.

"His name is Wallace." So much for avoiding her. "And I think it's pretty obvious why you shouldn't refer to Latinx guys that way."

"Relax," she answers while she rolls her eyes. And then I see it. I tighten my hand around Tavia's, notice the way she isn't making eye contact with Naema.

"What the hell is wrong with you?" She sort of jumps at my suddenly raised voice. "Why would you wear a fake collar to prom? To anywhere?" I lower my voice a little. "You're supposed to be on her side."

"I'm dating a cop's son, remember?" For a minute I have no idea what that's supposed to mean. If it's supposed to be some sort of threat, (a) it's sick, coming from another Black girl, and (b) Priam's dad already knows about Tavia. But then it gets worse. "What makes you think it's fake?"

Silence. We get so quiet so quickly that the music throbbing through the walls of the cafeteria has to fill the space.

She did not just say that. She did not *do* that. Who wears an actual siren-silencing collar in front of a secret siren, knowing she can't say anything? That's not even a micro-aggression. It's violent, after what Tavia saw. If there's any justice in the network, I hope it comes down on Naema and hard, eloko princess or not.

"I'm done," Tavia says through a sigh, more to me than to Naema, but I see the look on Naema's face.

She wants Tav to play along. She wants Tavia to be scared or angry or something she doesn't care to realize my sister already is most of the time. Because she wants it to con*sume* Tavia. She wants her to lose control. What she doesn't want is for Tavia to woman up and make peace with Priam, that much is obvious by how her whole face goes big when Tavia heads off in his direction. Naema's eyes go saucer-sized and her jaw dangles.

"What's the matter?" I ask through a smirk. "Did that not go the way you hoped?"

"Nice dress, Effie, did the Philipses finally cut you off?"

I laugh out loud. Wallace sidles up to me and threads his fingers through mine. He's been hanging back a bit, but I'm glad he's here now.

"Enjoy the rest of your night," I tell Naema as we're turning away.

"Hey, Effie, where's Isabella?"

She shouted it. Everyone heard. Most of the juniors might be in the cafeteria but the ones in the courtyard, including Tavia and Priam, are looking this way.

Wallace squeezes my hand so hard it almost hurts and then he loosens up again. Any other time I'd take my hand away, ask him what the hell that was—but this isn't any other time. Something very bad is about to go down, all because Naema has some weird fixation on my sister.

"I know it's you, Effie." She's making sure everybody hears. Especially Tavia, who she's looking at when I turn back toward her. "I know you did something to Isabella. She was nice to you, and you went after her. Just like you did to those people on the news."

"I didn't do anything," I say, but it's basically a whisper. And it isn't going to stop her.

"You did. Just like when we were kids and you changed those kids in the park. Just like that man in the cemetery."

I'd been looking at the ground but now my eyes shoot up.

"He was standing at your mom's grave."

Now there's whispering in the courtyard.

"It always comes back to you. Did you think we wouldn't notice? You're always the common factor when something horrible happens in this town."

245

I wanna say that I'm not, but I'm freaking out a little. It was bad enough when I thought that, when Tavia had to tell me it wasn't true, when she reminded me that I was the only person to ever think so. But then Mama Theo blamed me. Then she locked me in a room, maybe to protect everyone from me. Maybe because it isn't normal when your hair moves on its own and your skin peels off your body like you're a lizard or a snake. Maybe seeing water mirages on dry land isn't something that happens to normal teens.

I need to count my breaths, slow down my breathing before I get too worked up. I don't care what Naema thinks, but Wallace is standing next to me and Tavia's behind me. What's my sister gonna say when she finds out that what I am isn't wonderful after all.

"I know what you are," Naema says to me and then starts talking to everyone else. "I know what she is! Because I've been helping keep her secret!"

Wait. What is she talking about? I want to say that that isn't true, but once my mouth is open, nothing comes out.

The crowd is closing in, everybody coming closer. It isn't just that Naema's an eloko and that she purposely put the trill into her voice; they're gathering around because they know that something's wrong, in the city and with me. They'll trust whatever she tells them, and that part *is* because she's an eloko.

"Effie's a siren!" she yells.

I freeze. What is she doing . . .

"She's dangerous, she's been using her voice to turn innocent people to stone and I won't keep her secret anymore!"

The whispering is more than that now. People are shrieking, rushing back to the cafeteria, pulling phones out of their clutches and pockets. I'm looking around, yanking my hand from Wallace's before his iron grip can hurt me, so I hurt myself instead. I'm scratching my forehead right at the hairline because it's the only place I can get to my scalp with this wrap on.

And then it's yanked off. I feel the wrap slide back but it catches on my top knot and if Naema didn't yank a second time, harder, it would've stayed caught. I go down to the courtyard ground at the force, catching myself on my palms and one of my hipbones.

There were no hair ties in my bedroom at the Freeman's house. I twirled my twists around themselves and tucked the ends in just long enough to get the headwrap on. Now Naema's freed them and I can feel them flying in all directions like they're trying to leave my scalp altogether.

A camera phone clicks. Someone took a picture, or else they started a video.

Wallace is on the ground beside me, wrapping his arms around me and trying to cover my hair. He's trying to shield my entire body with his, but it's not possible. He's looking at me but I can't look back.

I can't believe this is really happening. I can't believe I came. I can't believe Naema did this to me.

"Do you want me to protect you?" Wallace whispers to me, but I don't answer. I know he's asking because of the way I reacted when he tried to help me at the pool. But this is different. There's nothing he can do.

Naema is saying something, narrating my public shaming over the chaos of my classmates' reactions. Turns out the people running into the cafeteria weren't trying to get away; they were going to get the others. If anyone's afraid of me, it doesn't show. It looks like everyone's trying to get a good look.

Wallace asks his question again, squeezing this time.

All I can think is that I wish my dad were here. I wish he'd show up, swoop out of the sky and carry me off. I don't understand why Naema's doing this—until I hear Tavia behind me. She can't hold it in anymore and Naema's about to get exactly what she wants.

I guess it's just too bad I got between them.

247

XVII

TAVIA

That wasn't supposed to happen.

That's not the call I meant to use.

I didn't mean to use a call at all. That's what Naema wanted, but that's not why I've been holding back. Priam is standing right next to me for the first time since we broke up, but that's not the only reason either.

After my run-in with Priam's dad, and everything that happened to Camilla, after watching Effie struggle with something she can't control, and finally talking to my mom, I wanted to choose for myself.

I wanted to be the one to decide.

Effie was on the ground before I could force myself to move, and then people were crowding, trying to record everything the way they always do. Nobody moved to help her except for Wallace, and I had to push my way through all of them to get a clear view of Naema.

All I said was her name, to prove I'm the siren and not Effie. There was no heat or buildup but I didn't give a command just in case Compel came out without warning.

It didn't. The call I blasted across the courtyard was Awaken, and immediately they began to change.

Wallace's arms were around Effie when I yelled, and he was

trying to shield as much of her as his body could. Once I spoke, he covered her completely.

His light brown skin turned gray.

His white shirt tore against the broadening of his back and the unfurling of his wings. He grew before our eyes, ripping out of his clothes and forcing everyone back. They'd never seen a gargoyle this close up; they didn't expect him to expand in every direction, to become massive in a matter of seconds.

Wallace—the boy who watched Effie swim—is her guardian, Gargy.

Gargy—the stone behemoth who's been perched on my roof for three years—is the guy my sister's falling for.

Now he's looking over his shoulder at me.

He's the gargoyle who carried me over Portland that night, who was there when I saw Gramma the first time.

I'm so embarrassed at the way my belly ached for a moment. If I had a crush on him (a tiny one) it was barely strong enough to put into words; I swallow it. Nod at him.

I wish I could have seen Naema's face. I wish I'd been on the other side of Gargy's massive wall of a body, standing next to her when he "awakened" into his natural form.

That's when I hear Effie moaning. I can't see her between Gargy's legs and knees and wings, and then her moans become a scream and I'm running to her, rushing around the gargoyle fortress that's keeping her out of sight.

"Gargy!" I slap his wing. "Let me in!"

He doesn't move it up or down, just out, and I rush inside.

There isn't much light. The sun has set and there are no lanterns trapped inside Gargy's protective huddle. I have to let my eyes adjust a little. I drop to my knees and reach for her, but—

I recoil, and then regret it.

"Tav." Her voice is so small and weak.

It's a little bit brighter now, but I can't believe what I'm seeing. There's a glimmer to her cheekbones, like the way her makeup looks when she's playing Euphemia; her skin has the same glimmer, and when she moves her arm, I see the subtle pink light in the skin that doesn't feel the way it did when we hugged. There's something rough about it; it's why I pulled away. Now I can see the faintest outline, like tiny scales clustered here and there. They haven't replaced all of her skin—at least not above the waist.

She's wearing a dress and it isn't until I look beyond the hem that I realize the greatest change is beneath it.

Her legs are gone. Replaced by a tail, but not like the ones she's always worn.

Effie's not a mermaid. She's a serpent. A gorgon.

They aren't supposed to be real; they're like fairies or unicorns, mythical things that came about when people saw a sprite or a horse in a strange light or from the wrong angle. They show up in stories, exaggerations of things that really do exist. They're things painted on walls in ancient places, with no basis in the reality we know.

But here she is, right in front of me. This isn't a trick of light.

My sister's a gorgon, I'm sure of it.

For one, her tail doesn't taper the way a mermaid's does. Instead it's thick and long, coiling around itself so it looks endless. For two, her big eyes have changed. Their shape isn't immediately noticeable (except to someone who sees her close up every single day) but the scales at the corners are. Everything inside is different, too. Her pupil is a long vertical slit through what looks like golden sand.

I reach my hand toward her again and Effie squeaks, her tail flexing, the scales clamping tighter, or so it appears.

"It's okay," I tell her, and lay my hand on her new form. "I told you you'd be something wonderful."

She shakes her head, and that's when I notice her hair. Her twists aren't twists anymore; now they've got scales of their own. They writhe and curl in the air around her head. I don't tell her so right this minute, but they're hypnotic.

I'm jealous right out of the gate, but I want to know how *Effie* feels. I don't remember what the moment of discovery is like;

I can't remember a time when I didn't know what I was—just a million nights spent wishing I wasn't.

I don't know why (and maybe it's just my siren baggage talking), but I'm happy for Eff. She's something extraordinary. Maybe something the world has never seen, or at least not for a very long time. And if they don't know her, maybe they won't hate her. Maybe she won't have to hide the way some of us do.

She obviously doesn't feel the same way.

"Don't let them see," she says, but it's a moment too late.

There's that click again.

Someone's lying flat on their stomach to get a look inside our stone fortress, and they're not the only one.

Gargy stands to his full height to frighten them, and it works. I hear a choir of gasps as a handful of well-dressed couples fall back. Some aren't sticking around to see what happens next, and the chaperones (who I'm sure now realize how few of them there are and how useless their presence has been) are trying to convince the others to leave. This prom won't last much longer. In a moment, someone will see Effie completely.

When I'm the next to stand, Eff does too. In a way. She glides up through the air until she's the height she's always been, except instead of standing on two feet, she's balancing on her tail. She's like a cobra lifting from inside a basket and just like the motion of her used-to-be-twists, her rise is hypnotic too.

"Stay here," I tell her.

"What're you gonna do?" When they grab me, her hands feel the way they always have, but there's no time to be fascinated by what has changed about her and what's stayed the same.

"I'm gonna Compel them—"

"Tav, don't, they'll know about you."

"They probably already do. I did this to you. I'll send them all away so we can get out of here before the adults come."

"You don't have to do that," she says, "just change me back!" And my heart sinks.

"I don't know how. This . . . I think this must be your natural form."

It's like someone pulls the air out of Gargy's self-made shelter.

"This is me?" she asks, her serpent eyes more beautiful than I've ever seen. Even the TV shows and the movies don't compare, the fantasies brought to life in theaters and in homes around the world. They always imagine gorgons as having either hideous faces or else sexualized reptilian ones, a fact I've never heard anyone dispute or call ridiculous, since no one has any stake in how a mythical creature is represented. "Tav," Effie says, sliding a bit closer to me. She sort of sways, exactly as a snake would. "Is this who I really am?"

When I nod, I don't have to try to smile; I can't help it.

"You're amazing," I tell her. "I wouldn't lie to you, Effie, you are. And you might be the only one of your kind."

"I don't know if I want to be."

"Eff," I'm almost whispering, "don't say that."

I look up for the first time, try to find Gargy's stone eyes, silently ask him for help. His eyes are on the courtyard, his head swiveling when his gaze has reached its peripheral limit. His job is her physical protection, it seems, and he doesn't appear concerned with the Beckett high-schoolers. They aren't the kind of threat he's been keeping at bay. They haven't warranted scooping us up and flying us to the middle of the nature reserve, for one. It's good to know we aren't in any gargoyle-activating danger, but it looks like anything short of that is up to me.

I'm about to tell her we'll figure this out together, that everything's gonna be different from now on—except she's gone. Almost too quickly for my eyes to register, she's swooped beneath Gargy's wing and zipped away.

I'm standing there stunned for a moment and Gargy doesn't even seem to know she's out. I'm alone behind his body and his wings, and suddenly there's screaming . . . and something worse.

A sound I can't place.

It isn't like a wall breaking apart. Or it starts that way and then sounds like the whole process is happening in reverse. Like boulders coming together, fast. So quickly there's no crumbling, no echo of them settling; when they find their place the noise just stops.

"Let me out!" I'm slapping Gargy's wings again, ducking to follow Effie through the space beneath them just as he's opening them wide. And what we see is terrifying.

Because I was wrong; Effie's gonna have to hide just like me. They will never forgive her for this.

There's a gray statue beneath the big tree, and he's wearing a tux. His arm is stretched out in front of him, but he's not trying to shield himself. He was trying to get a picture. Even while she was coming, he was holding his phone to capture the moment. That's why she did it. She's been at the mercy of photographers before.

I hear the stomach-turning sound again and I only turn in time to see the light devoured. That's what it looks like. The person's skin gets eaten up by gray, like a Portland sky being swallowed by overcast in a split second.

I'm looking around, whirling from one direction to the other, trying to see more of Effie than an aqua-green blur in a dress. Everyone's screaming, running, but never in the right direction. It's the kind of chaos that erupted at the protest, people running in opposite directions, looking for an escape, and too freaked out to know who to ask for help.

Except Naema. She's just standing where she was before Gargy changed, holding her phone.

She's not afraid. Not for herself and obviously not for her classmates, or for what'll happen to Effie when whatever Naema's been filming gets released.

"Effie!" I scream her name, run as fast as anyone can in a fairy-tale gown, stop in front of a stone pair of embracing teens, one trying to shield the other though both their phones are out. I stop myself before I accidentally touch them. (I don't know why.) "Effie!"

I don't want to do it, but I have to get her to stop. I need her to hear me.

"Effie, come here!"

I barely have time to see the blur and then my sister's there in front of me, swaying on her tail. This time it looks more drunk than hypnotic, as though whatever came over her took her out of her right mind. Her eyes are encircled with a smoky darkness, just like the day I found her asleep in my bed. It's not makeup; it's what happens when she changes someone with her eyes.

I take my sister by the shoulders, but all she does is sway. Finally her eye color fades from a pale white streak through deep gray sand back to the original black slit against gold. Maybe it's like a fugue state. Maybe that's why she's never remembered what she's done.

The park. Her friends. The statues we all thought the sprites made.

I shake my head, tell myself to stop. This isn't the time. I have to get her out of here. But first I have to finish what she started. I have to stop the pictures and the recordings. I have to keep anyone from seeing what she did, that it was her. I don't even know if it makes sense at this point. I don't know how many people who've seen Effie's transformation have already gotten away. I don't know what they'll make to put around her neck, or whether it'll be a shackle for her tail.

Pulling Effie into my arms completely, I look at Naema.

"It's time to stop this," I say. "You got what you wanted. I'm out. I'm a siren and everybody knows it."

She's still holding her phone level. Which means she's still recording.

"I'll never talk to Priam again. I swear."

She keeps going.

"Naema!" I yell in my common voice. No more calls. I can't let this get any worse. "The network's gonna find out about this."

That does it. Now she'll talk.

"Should that scare me? I'm done, I'm not one of your lackeys anymore. I don't care."

"They will. I can talk to everyone, I'll take your side if you give me your phone."

"You're amazing, Tavia. You're threatening me? In a few hours this video's gonna be viral and you won't even live here anymore. You'll have to go underground in some other town, if they'll let you. They have collars for people like you, remember? You might as well take mine. But what's the 'network' gonna do to *me*?"

In my arms, Effie's starting to come around. She's groggy, off-balance, her tail bowing where before it was sturdy. I have to get her out of here.

"Naema, please." I'll maintain eye contact even if it kills me. If she wants to see me beg, fine. I'll grovel on camera. Maybe that'll be enough for her to keep it to herself. "I'm nobody. Neither of us are. We're not like you, we're not elokos. Without that video, no one will ever say our names."

The courtyard looks empty now. Besides the statues that once were junior classmen, the hulking gargoyle on patrol, and the kids who are stuck here because in their fear they hid instead of running, it's just Effie, Naema, and me.

"If we become famous, it'll be your fault. Is that what you really want?"

Oh, thank God. Her arm falls to her side. She taps the button on the corner of her device and it's over.

But she's smiling.

"Too late for regrets, though," she says. "I was livestreaming. Guess both your secrets are out."

I can't move like a blur to throttle Naema; she's beyond my reach. I have no calls to hurt her like I'm hurting right now, not Compel or Appeal or Awaken. I'm just a siren, at her mercy, and now a sister who knows too well what Effie's life is going to be like from here on out. The magic Mom never told me she always loved is going to ruin us, just like Dad knew it would. The change Mama Theo tried to avoid has immediately destroyed Effie's life.

The world—our world—has fallen apart.

So should hers.

"**Effie,**" I say so calmly it doesn't even sound like a command. "**Stone her.**"

Effie's tail is steady again. It flexes and her wobble is gone. If I were looking, I'm sure her eyes would be terrifying. If not them, then her dancing, serpent twists. If not those, then the way she leans in. Nothing passes between her and Naema, no stream of gray or mist or spark. Effie just leans, hypnotically, and I hear the sound of boulders on rewind.

It's a much duller, less terrifying sound once I know what it is.

It's the sound of Naema's glistening, eternally moisturized skin hardening. Of her long eyelashes going pale, along with her hair and her eyes and the rest of her.

The gray eats her up. It traps her. Now that I'm watching the process, it isn't like something she becomes, it's like something taking her hostage.

Good.

Serves her right.

What have I done . . .

"Gargy," I call over my shoulder. "Get us out of here."

XVIII

EFFIE

When I wake up, we're flying and Tavia and Garg are arguing.

I try to hear what they're saying and at first I can't make it out. Sound is throbbing between my ears, like it's going in and getting stuck right past the gate and can't make it to my brain to be processed. Closing my eyes again helps. Gargoyle flight is pretty smooth, I guess, and instead of seeing the night sky and the city lights, I can just focus on picking out the words.

She's telling him it's the only place I'll be safe right now.

He's saying she can't possibly know.

It isn't up for discussion, according to Tavia. He's got to take us to whoever assigned him in the first place. Whoever it is, it's the only person we can trust. Or at least it's our best bet at not being found by everyone else.

I guess that's where we're going, because they're quiet after that.

The river's black beneath us. It's like a track down below and we're speeding along it. The bridges whiz past, and every time we come to the next one, Garg swings up and then brings us level again. I guess when you're not cleared for air travel and you're not privy to traffic control, best to play it safe. I wonder what would happen to a police or news chopper if it collided with a gargoyle.

I wonder whether gargoyles can die.

Maybe I'll revisit that wondering when I'm not soaring with one.

I groan at a sharpness that's running down the length of my body, and they realize I'm awake.

"Eff," Tavia says and reaches for me across Garg's broad torso. He's got each of us tucked under an arm while we fly over PDX. "I'm right here."

Our fingers find each other's, but it takes too much energy to hang on.

"Effie, your legs!"

I hadn't even noticed. My tail is gone. Beneath my dress, my legs are dangling, bare and silky. Not like when my skin peels like silk out of the end of a worm; they look amazing. Like I just had a serious spa treatment, the works. My whole body looks that way. It's pretty sad, but I almost forgot what healthy skin looks like on me. I reach up to feel my face and I can't stop. I can't decide which feels better, the supple tips of my fingers or the smoothness of my cheek. Even my scalp feels brand new and when I reach to find a twist, I find it's natural hair again; the scales are gone. Maybe forever, maybe just for now.

"How'd you do it?" Tav asks me.

"I don't know," and then something catches my eye down below. "Wallace—Garg." I have no idea what to call him. "Are we going to the faireground?"

We're well past Cathedral Park, but up ahead is the Vancouver site. For the life of me I can't figure out why we'd be heading there.

Garg doesn't respond (if he's salty over the exchange he had with Tavia, he shouldn't take it out on me), but that's definitely where we're going. He swoops low and we come right up the midway, between the tents shuttered until morning. That's one of the shops where Elric's dad (and now Elric) sells his wares. Over there's the mead stand and picnic tables.

We could walk from here (if I reach out, I could probably touch the dew-slick grass), but Garg keeps us in his arms. We're gliding through the unoccupied faire, and even after what happened with Elric, I have to admit: I miss it. I almost regret not attending opening day, and I wonder how many people have come looking for me (okay, or at least asked around), and how many will before the season ends.

Maybe if I'd come, things would be different now. I'd have been in the water where I'm supposed to be.

But how can this be my fault? I've accepted that the man at my mom's grave is my doing . . . but what about the others? The ones who must've been turned while Tav and I were waiting with Garg in the wetlands. Even if someone else *could* Compel me to transform people (which is the only way I figure I could be responsible for the people I don't remember seeing before the newscast), Tavia didn't know that until tonight, until she knew I was a gorgon.

Gorgon. I keep rolling that word around in my mouth. It's like learning my own name. My real name.

Anyway, she wouldn't make a habit of that. And she was stuck in the same reserve as me. Someone else hurt those people. They must've.

I still cringe. Because there are others I've hurt. I've stolen people from their families, from their lives. Children are stranded in a park, memorialized on lists about "keeping Portland weird" because of me. Their parents and siblings get older, but they never will.

It doesn't matter which ones I didn't change, I'm never gonna forgive myself for the ones I did.

Garg is hesitant to put me down because my Docs split back in the courtyard and I'm barefoot. But he brought us to the Hidden Scales pavilion, my personal holy grail, so the threat of wet feet isn't really a powerful deterrent. Anyway, the rolling fog that always decorates the tent hides my naked feet and ankles as soon as he gingerly sets me down.

"Don't tell me they leave the fog machine running through the night," I say because no one's said a thing yet. "That's dedication to the aesthetic. And also probably stupid expensive."

Tavia doesn't know what to think so she just looks between

259

us. It's not the first time she's been here, but she's staring like she's never seen the scallop trim and stripes before.

"Tav? You okay?"

"The walking water you see. It has something to do with this place."

"What are you talking about?"

"They call it the walking water on the Hidden Tales. You've never heard of it?"

I have, at least once. But it isn't what I see.

"I've seen that mirage everywhere, not just on the faireground," I tell her, but she isn't trying to convince me of anything. She's staring. Studying. She's putting it together the way she does when she's diagramming an argument for her Theory of Knowledge class. She's not ready to present, but she's figuring it out.

When I turn to Garg, he's still a massive stone beast, except in the eyes. If I look hard enough, I'm starting to see the guy from the pool. Whatever I thought about the gargoyle being my real dad flies out the window, thank God.

"Why are we here, Wallace?"

Like my calling that name's a trigger, the gargoyle starts to shrink. First his monstrous shoulders seem to buckle and his torso pulls his chest down. He's melting into a human form, the gray blooming into that tanned brown, his claws retracting into more human-like hands. Until he's just a guy. Covering his unmentionables. Because his prom attire has gone the way of my Doc Martens.

Tavia coughs and turns away to give him some privacy. (I probably should too.)

"Um." She's not facing us, but I can tell she's doing that thing where her eyes go wide and she pulls her lips into her mouth to keep from laughing. "I thought you were taking us to your boss."

I, on the other hand, have been staring at his hands, and he just noticed.

"One second," he says, and then it looks like he's concentrating. His human skin (or what looks like it, anyway) starts to protrude in the shape of clothes, like he's somehow put on a T-shirt and shorts underneath his flesh. And then the bulges change color and their edges get defined and they take on texture . . . and he's wearing his trusty old Southwest Community Center uniform.

"You really like that place, huh?" I smirk.

"It's where I met you."

With her back still facing us, Tavia coos.

"And it's the only clothing I know well enough to mold." That explains why he was always wearing it.

"This is where I'm from," he says once I've given Tav the all clear. "This is where my master lives."

"Okay. But surely not at this hour." I swivel my top half to glance at the tent before swiveling back. "Do you know where he lives by day? When he's not at the faire?"

"Effie, you don't understand." Wallace comes closer. "He's always here."

"Always," I repeat even though my skepticism's clear. "This guy lives in a circus tent? I just don't feel like studio apartments are that expensive. Don't tell me you've perched on this thing? You're light on your feet, but you're not that light."

"The fanfic is true, then." Tavia steps back toward the tent now that we're all properly dressed.

"It'll make sense when you're inside," Wallace says to me, but there's something hesitant about it.

"Okay." I rock onto the balls of my feet and back. (For a moment, I forgot I was barefoot, but no, my toes are definitely getting cold.) "So let's go."

"I'd better not."

"Wallace," I say. "What's going on with you?"

While he takes a deep breath, his eyes never leave me.

"I didn't follow his orders. Not exactly." Tav and I wait, and after a moment he explains. "I was charged with your protection, but. Only in my true form. I was never supposed to be . . ."

"A real boy?" I offer half a smile. "You weren't supposed to be Wallace, too."

261

He runs his hands over his shorn scalp and I step into him. Even though Tavia's right there, I stand as close to him as I can, lay my hands on his arms until he lowers them. He isn't me; I know that. He's not going to tear his skin apart. He probably doesn't feel an itch so deep he thinks he can't stand it. Come to think of it, neither do I. Not anymore. Not since Tavia Awakened me. I just want him to know I'm glad he made his choice.

"I wasn't supposed to watch you swim," he tells me. His eyes are hopping between mine like he can't decide which of my eyes to focus on. "I wasn't supposed to keep you out of his reach, or introduce myself, or . . ."

He's still doing it. His eyes are still sliding back and forth and they're dipping a little so I know he's looking at my mouth, too. It's stupid, but I feel like I know what he wants to say. And it sort of would be ridiculous, if *I* said it. *I've* only known him for a short time. But it turns out he's been falling for me a lot longer. I guess it makes sense that his feelings are a little stronger.

(Tummy tumble complete.)

"I won't let him hurt you," I say, and I slip my arms around him. His mouth breaks into a smile, but I know he isn't coming. And if he's this nervous, I don't want him to. I don't wanna find out that gargoyles don't last forever. "It's okay. Tavia's with me. She'll keep me safe."

And then he kisses me, right in front of my sister. There's a cloud of eternal fog around my ankles and I'm standing outside the Hidden Scales in the middle of the night, and Wallace is dressed like a lifeguard. It's amazing. It's like prom never happened. Like we didn't leave a bunch of stone statues in the courtyard of Beckett High. Like we're not about to meet some mysterious gargoyle master so he can tell us what Wallace has been protecting me from.

When I bat my eyes open after what I can only describe as a fairy-tale kiss, I remember Tavia's the real princess. If it had been her and Priam kissing (the way it was once or twice) I would've coughed or snorted or something and made it super awkward.

262

And mostly it would've been involuntary. Tavia's precious; she's just looking around the quiet fairgrounds with her hands folded together against the front of her ball gown like she's wandered out of an animated movie. When she senses that we're finished, she glances back.

"Ready?" she asks.

I nod once and take the hand she's offering.

"This is gonna feel disorienting," she tells me, like she's done this before. But I don't ask her how she knows. I trust her.

When she reaches out and opens the tent flap, we both step through into what I assume will be darkness. But Tavia was right.

We're someplace else.

We're standing somewhere that resembles the marshy place where Wallace carried us after the protest, but greener. Wetter, too. I can smell the water, stronger than back at the wetlands. And there are lights. Big and small orbs of light, just hovering. I don't know if they're living things or it's just what light is like here, but they sway like lanterns in a very gentle breeze.

"No wonder Wallace liked the courtyard so much," I say as Tavia and I look around.

Behind us, the pavilion canvas and double-flap closure is standing out against the earth and the foliage, but the rest of the tent is gone. It's a doorway, but we're obviously not inside it. This place feels endless. I can't see the sky because of fog and tree canopy and vines, but I know it's higher than the peak of a pavilion.

I breathe deep. This air is so refreshing. This place is so enchanting. It's making my chest swell in a way that only ever happens when I'm in my tank. Or when I was at home, with Mom. I just wanna stand here forever and take it all in.

With our hands locked together, Tav and I start walking. Not too quickly; I want to enjoy this feeling. I want to imagine my mom here, all the times she came inside. All the times I thought she was sitting at a table in a small tent, with a weight (literal scales) between her and the other story makers.

This isn't what I thought it'd be.

I wonder what you have to be or do to get to this place. I wonder if a fairegoer who'd gotten past the gray guard would've found a rickety table and a scale. If Tavia got here because she's a siren or because she was holding my hand.

I stop walking when my brain starts playing tricks on me. First I hear (in that sonar, sensing way) Mama Theo, or I think I do. I'm holding still to listen, but just before I close my eyes to concentrate, I see the mirage that's plagued me. The watery distortion in front of me, shivering on the glittering water in front of Tavia and me.

"The walking water," Tavia says.

I "hear" Mama again. I don't go with my first assumption (that the mirage is Mama, and that she's something more than I've known all this time), seeing as the last time I thought I'd stumbled onto the truth it had to do with my boyfriend's natural form being my father.

Instead I crane my neck in the mirage's direction and say, "Hello?"

My heart is racing, and I don't touch them to check but I'm pretty sure my twists have come to life again. I feel shaky on my feet and I hold Tav's hand a little tighter.

"Is someone there?" I ask even though I know there is.

It feels like forever since we've signed, since we were hugging at the Philipses' staircase before they split us up. Now I spell something out for Tavia and ready myself for when she speaks.

I stand with my feet together, like that'll make it easier. Like it's a medical procedure that follows logic or needs my help. It isn't. When Tavia repeats my question and wraps it in the Awaken call, my legs bleed into each other, the color of my scales pulsating until my tail appears behind it.

My eyes change; I know because my sight sort of adjusts. What I'm seeing doesn't become any less clear, but the scope rounds and the things with life seem to throb. It all happens pretty quickly, and when I'm in my natural form, still holding my sister's hand, there's another being where the mirage was—and he looks just like me.

His hair is dark and alive, like mine. If he were just another man, it'd probably look dreaded, but I know better. In this form, his hair is scaled and even though they're tied at the back of his head, the ends float and curl over his shoulder at will.

"The Hidden Scales." And until Tavia says it, I hadn't put it together.

There are no weights. There is no meeting table, no twenty-sided die. He is the hidden scales. He decides the stories.

"I'm not fond of sirens," he says. "For precisely this reason."

He's looking at Tavia, but he's speaking to me.

"I asked her to use that call," I tell him. The suspense is killing me. "Okay, so. Um, who are you?"

If Tavia weren't shell-shocked, she'd roll her eyes at me and say my name like a command.

Floating hair.

Long, thick tail.

Walnut-brown skin.

But I'm tired of being wrong. There's no way I'm accusing some stranger of being my kin no matter how much we look alike. No matter how obvious the truth is. He can tell me himself.

He slides forward, but only till he sees how I recoil.

"I'm your father." It looks like he hikes himself up a bit. He uses his tail to get a little taller. Like he's proud of that fact. Like he's pleased about me. "I'm the only one who could be."

I don't know if I'm blushing or if in this form it's any more visible than usual. Which is not at all.

"I'll have to take your word for it." (Why. Why did I say that.)

"No, you won't. There's someone else here."

Mama Theo. She *is* here. Which means she knows what *here* is, has known—

I can't start down that path again. Yes. We'll have a lot to work through when everything's said and done. For now, I just want to hear her say that this is really my dad. I want to know everything there is to know.

"Where is she?"

For the first time, his gaze slips. Or else he's looking at the water.

"Wait, she's under there? How?" I raise on my tail the way he did. "Is she alive? What did you do to her?"

I rush him before I know I've moved at all. It's just like in the courtyard; I move so much faster with a tail than I ever did on legs. Luckily I let go of Tavia's hand first, because when I barrel into my father, we go under. We tumble beneath the surface of the water and just like coming into the pavilion, it's a different world than the one I expected.

Nothing changes about the way I breathe. It's like air and water are interchangeable, and it must be because I'm in my gorgon form. There's definitely something new about the way I move. I thought I felt free underwater before; it was nothing compared to this.

My dad pulls out of my grasp and watches me discover my tail all over again. The way it carves through the water, fully extended. I'm still amazed at the length, by the way I can move the water when I coil it, the way I flip and twist like an acrobat with each motion. The way I can basically use the length of my tail like a jump rope, holding the very end of it while the rest encircles me.

But in the depths, I see a stone house like a *real* pavilion, like something out of the ancient world. It's got columns wrapped in seaweed and a roof, but there are no walls.

I take off in that direction, and I can sense him following.

There's a glass box down here, and Mama Theo's in it. In a tank of her own, only this one's filled with air. She's sitting when I descend, but by the time my hands are pressed against the glass, she's rushed to me.

"Mama," I whimper.

"Don't be scared, baby." She moves her hand like she's caressing my forehead and then my cheek. "It's not my first time in this stupid cage."

"Can you breathe?" I wanna bang my fists against the tank, but I don't want it to break.

"Well, I can talk, can't I?" She smiles at me. "Your daddy may be a liar, but he's not a monster, at least. Not completely, anyway."

I freeze. So he is my dad.

"If you'd stop coming to my world, I'd stop putting you in it," he says to her.

"You were supposed to stop coming to mine. You weren't supposed to send a stone demon to watch her every move, to make her think *he* was her kin."

That's what chased her off when I was locked in my bedroom. She knew what I thought, and that I was wrong. But maybe I was getting close. Maybe she knew I wasn't gonna stop searching now, and Garg was a direct path back to my father. To this place.

"You said it was gonna be up to Effie, not that you'd keep showing up trying to trigger her."

"I made that promise to Minerva, not to you. Effie should be with me."

He's talking to her from behind me, and when his hand falls on my shoulder I have to figure out how I feel quick. Dr. Randall told me that if it was hard to know how I feel, sometimes I could figure it out by studying what I do. Maybe that advice was only meant for little Effie, but it turns out I still need it. I'll judge my feelings by what I do—and I don't move away.

"You promised the choice was gonna be Effie's," Mama says to him again.

To my dad. The man I've never met before now, but who has been the watery mirage I've seen so many times. The gorgon guy beside me with his arm around my shoulder. Something tells me his name isn't really James.

"The choice *is* Effie's; that doesn't mean I didn't want to see her at all!"

267

"No matter if she had an episode every time you came around or not!"

"So you house her with a siren?"

"Checkmate," she bites back. "I knew the threat of her voice would keep you away."

"But you didn't know what her voice would do to my child."

"She's as much my child as she is yours."

"No, Theodosia. She isn't."

He calls her by her full name. This argument's been going on for years, I can see that, and at this rate it might go on a few years more.

"Well. That's what happens when you choose scales over fatherhood."

"That's your view of what I did. It wasn't Minerva's."

"Just because you hypnotized her into buying that story—"

"I didn't hypnotize anyone, give your daughter some credit for once."

"—doesn't mean she could sell it to me. She was gonna stay on land and have the baby and the two of you were gonna have this make-believe world where you run off into a tent to play house because you can't stand to live with legs."

"Because this is my natural form, Theodosia."

"But right in the middle of it is this precious baby who has to wait till she comes of age and finds out what her natural form will be, and then what? If she's a snake like you, then you'd all be together, right?"

"That was Minerva's plan, not mine. And I respected it, which is more than I can say for you."

I turn in the water, notice suddenly the way my tail is coiled with my dad's.

"Did the Chosen part of Mom's title mean chosen by you?"

Even under here, I can see the way his eyes fog. He can only nod.

"Chosen to raise her baby on her own," Mama says through

a scoff. "Chosen to be torn between two worlds. Chosen for a life nobody could want."

"Except her," I say, finally. "It's the life *she* wanted." I turn back and put my hand against the glass again. "And it hurt my feelings when you said 'snake' like that. I mean . . . look at me."

Mama Theo does. She runs her eyes over the (impressive) length of me and maybe the way I'm breathing just fine down here, just like him. I'm about to speak until she bites her lip. There's a lot more I want to say, but it's too new. There are certain things—certain complaints—I'm just not gonna make in front of someone else. Even if he is my dad. Mama Theo's been trying to pull my strings, they've both been going to war with each other while I spin in the middle without a clue—but she's still Mama.

There's no choice to make. They're both my family.

"Tavia," I say to myself. Because no matter why we were put together, she's my family now too. She's back on the shore probably worried sick. "It's time for you to go home, Mama."

Now her face crumbles, but she buttons it quick. It's something I could never accomplish when I was a kid and I'd get myself into trouble and the tears would come.

"Button it up," she'd warn me. It meant cut off the waterworks, hide the upset, make it look like I was fine. I never knew why that was the command, or what it was supposed to teach me. And even when I'd almost manage to swallow it, it'd just come sputtering back to the surface the moment she turned her stern gaze away. Sometimes she'd pretend she didn't notice and let me cry it out. Sometimes she'd swivel back and stare my tears into submission.

"Button it up," I tell her, but I'm smiling. When I kiss the glass, she leans in and kisses it too. Because neither of us know when I'll be coming home.

Neither of us know when I can.

XIX

TAVIA

It's always worrying when—after the two of you pass through a tent portal in an abandoned faireground to find yourself in some kind of second world or dimension—your gorgon sister attacks a man who might be her father and they both disappear into a mysterious body of water you can't see into.

What's even more worrying is when they come out of that unnaturally dark sea like they're the best of friends. And then further out in the water, something else crests and then it bobs a couple of times before drifting with pretty impressive precision to our area of the shore. The "something" turns out to be a see-through container, and Theodosia Freeman's inside. When it's almost entirely out of the water, anchored in the spongy earth and ultra-vivid and colorful flowers and groundcover, it opens along a corner seam and Mrs. Freeman steps out.

Effie unwinds her tail from her dad's (yeah . . .) and hugs her grandma, who cups my elbow without a word before walking past me toward the tent flaps.

Everyone's handling all this strangeness *really* well, considering, but I'm just a little confused.

"Eff," I say when her grandma's gone. "Can I talk to you a minute?"

Her dad is holding one of her hands, and it's not that it isn't really a heartwarming picture, what with their matching hair and tails and eyes. It's more the way the end of his tail is still submerged, and he seems to be sliding further in that direction. While he's holding on to Effie.

He kisses the back of her hand and squeezes it once between both of his before she comes to me. It almost makes me twitch. They don't look like strangers anymore. Hell, they don't even look like me and *my* dad, but how do I say that without sounding envious? It's happened once already today, me reframing Effie's circumstances as a comparative analysis with mine. Yes, she gets a "fresh start" with her dad, but that's because she suffered sixteen years without knowing him at all.

I'm afraid anything I say will sound as toxic to Eff as it does to me. But I have to say *some*thing.

It isn't until she's standing in front of me that I realize I've never seen this look before. Not her with him; just her. Granted, I haven't seen most of Effie's looks when she's in her gorgon state, but I feel like it'd be unique even without the scales at the corners of her round eyes. She seems so calm right now, even serene. She seems so suddenly optimistic and relieved.

Still.

"Aren't we going with Mama Theo?" I ask, and she shrugs.

"How can I?"

"No, I get that. But. Do you really wanna stay here, hidden away with him?" I drop my voice because I don't know anything about the strength of gorgon hearing. "*Just* him? When you've only just met?"

"Tav . . ."

I'd completely get it if she clapped back at even this tame interrogation of Brand New Dad. It's not like she doesn't know a thing or two about unconventional family dynamics. Why would this throw her off? Why would I want it to? But that's not where she's going at all.

"You know what I've done. You know they won't forgive me." She's right.

Now what. Think, Tavia.

"What about the ones you didn't do," I blurt as soon as it comes to mind. "What about the statues you didn't make?"

She starts to chew on the inside of her lip. I have to be careful here. I want her to think this through, but I don't want to upset her. I don't want to lose her for real this time. I don't want to say there's *no* safe place for her, because I know what that's like.

"Someone turned those other people to stone, Eff. All those statues in the streets of Portland, who were changed while we were stuck in the wilderness with Gargy? Someone did that. And it wasn't you."

What did her dad say? He's the only one who could be her father? Then he's probably the only other person who shares her power.

Effie inclines her chin, reaches for a scaled twist that jumps away from her touch at first and then pecks at it like it's kissing her hand.

"Why'd Wallace think he had to protect you from him?" I pause. "And where's Isabella?"

I've rolled my eyes at enough packaged teen dramas to expect Effie to erupt at me. Now, especially. She'll demand to know why I'm doing this, why I'm asking these questions. Why I don't want her to know her father. Why I can't stand to see her with a family of her own. Why it matters what he's done when I Compelled her power without her consent. Just like everybody says sirens will do.

But this is Effie. This is the girl who's been coming apart at the seams all year, and all it made her do was wake up earlier and swim longer and try harder. And want more than anything to know what she is.

"I have to apologize to you, Effie. I don't know why you should trust me after what I made you do at prom, and I'm not saying you should. But you don't hide, Eff," I tell her. "You never do. I know you want to know the truth about him."

"Yeah." She's swaying on her tail, looking down but not at anything in particular. "I really want him to be a nice guy."

"I know. Me too."

"But I gotta know, right?"

I drop my head in agreement and release a deep breath.

"I'm not mad at you," she says, still looking down. "I'm not saying it's okay. Just that I'm not angry."

I take my sister's hands in mine; it's more than I deserve.

"I just freaking love you, sis," I tell her.

"I just freaking love you, too."

And then Brand New Dad speaks.

"Euphemia," he says without approaching. Because he's been listening all this time.

"Your name's not really James, is it?"

"What?" His eyes volley from side to side. "No. My name is Jacoby."

"Yeah," she nods once, "that sounds about right. Okay. So is my friend Isabella down there too?" Effie asks through a sigh. "In another glass box?"

I didn't feel strange when Effie and Wallace kissed outside, but this—how quickly she asked the hard question—makes me feel like I shouldn't be here. If she knew him any better, this would be the epitome of uncomfortable, the way it always is when a friend argues with their parents in front of me. This is different, obviously . . . but still. I wish I could do that water-mirage thing Brand New Dad does, just ripple from the outside in and disappear from sight.

"She's free to leave now, Euphemia, but let me tell you why I brought her, at least, and why I had to turn those people to stone."

This is gonna be bad.

"Okay." I can tell by the way she says it that she's thinking the exact same thing. But he doesn't start immediately. He's a strong-looking gorgon, unnerving even, but he looks nervous. "Is it because you got caught up in your chess match with Mama Theo?"

Whatever she means by that, he's looking like she's onto something.

"It is, right? She didn't want me to be a gorgon, so you wanted everyone to know I am? Even if they'd be afraid of me?"

"Is that for real?" I can't help myself. He gives me the side of his eye, so, yes, this guy is really not fond of sirens. Sorry, sir. That's not exactly unique. "Were you trying to frame her? So she'd *have* to come here?"

Parents, amirite? Just wow.

"Oh!" Effie sounds like Priam watching the home team intercept. It's sudden, *way* louder than she speaks (ever), and her newly round eyes get even bigger. "I skipped the faire. And"—she almost says Wallace—"the gargoyle did too. I misbehaved and your guard betrayed you."

It's quiet while we wait for his confession, except for a charmingly ethereal tinkling that might be coming from the water or the canopy or from the bright plants and flowers. I thought I heard it while Effie and Brand New Dad were gone, but it wasn't this constant. It's not normal for me to be this easily distracted, but I have this sudden urge to walk up to the water's edge. Even though Effie and I just pulled a major sister-detectives moment and Brand New Dad is in the hot seat. I shake off the urge, but for some reason that involves blinking a few times, quickly, and when I do, the indigo's on the other side.

Right now, really?

My grandmother is the most.

I stop blinking altogether and try to focus on Effie's dad. I want to be here with her. I want to hear what he has to say for himself. I want to know why my grandma has such amazing timing.

It only takes a few minutes for my eyeballs to feel like they're staring down an open fire and, just as I suspect, the next time I blink, I'm in the blue. The Hidden Scales–Narnia world changes; deep-indigo trees with lighter shades for the plant life and the orbs of light.

This time it's different. Effie and Brand New Dad are still here.

It's like I haven't been transported. Instead the blue is closer now, close enough to melt into the real world instead of taking me out of it.

My sister and her dad are still speaking, their lips moving slow, no sound coming out. They're beautiful, their scales even more iridescent against the blue-scale color of this place.

Gramma's around here somewhere and I keep feeling drawn to the water, so I go to the edge and step in. And I drop like I stepped off the Santa Cruz bluffs at West Cliff Drive. There's no steady decline; I fall into the depths, but I don't feel wet. Now that I'm in the water, it's not so unnaturally dark. I can see the light moving through the water, it just doesn't feel like I'm in it. I wonder if that's how Effie feels when she's under the surface, like nothing's changed at all. But then why would she love it so much?

"Gramma?" And she's there. "Why don't you ever just show up when I show up?"

Hush, she mouths, and waves me off.

"I have to get back to Effie," I tell her. "Her dad's trying to talk her into staying in the tent with him." I don't have time to explain that it's not as end-of-the-world prepper as that sounded.

Awaken, she says.

"No, I know, but. That didn't really work so well. I mean, that's also my fault for siccing her on Naema."

I wish I hadn't just told her that. I wish the entire prom was just a dream, not the reason my sister is never coming home. Not the reason a girl I didn't like but didn't hate isn't either. Instead she's destined to become another tourist attraction on some website.

No. Naema's an eloko. She might be the first Black girl whose "disappearance" (or whatever they'll call it now, and I'm guessing it won't be "sculpture") will spark a national incident.

I guess she was right. She *isn't* like the rest of us.

Vivi! Grandma's not making a sound when she talks to me, but when she says my name, I snap out of my thoughts. When I'm looking at her again, she smiles. **I didn't say to Awaken *her*.**

I gasp and suddenly I'm not in the water anymore. I'm standing next to Effie and her dad's standing across from us, and the blue is gone.

"We have to go," I blurt, slapping her arm more times than I mean to. "I know how to fix this, we have to go."

~~~~~

I've never been to Triton Park before today. I've stalked the statues and the tourist blogs online with Effie, but there was never a good time to ask my traumatized sister for a personal tour. Now we're here together and I really hope I'm right.

Until it's done, I tell Effie to be a mirage, the way her dad was. She takes to it as quickly as she learned to move with her tail, the image of her rippling into invisibility on the first try.

"Ugh," I say to her, careful not to let anyone else hear. "You're seriously the coolest."

"I know," she whispers back. "I'm also terrified right now, Tav. How'd you get everyone to come?"

"Easy. I told them I'm a siren."

Before Effie can shriek or otherwise give herself away, I step away from her and come closer to the parents and the sculpture of the kids.

Ashleigh.

Mere.

Wiley.

Tabor.

Their families are here because I said I know what happened to them. I said I'd tell the world the truth about how they were changed, and I told Effie to record the whole thing. It turns out I didn't have to; someone called KATU and the field reporter's been off to the side filming intros and outros with little to no shame.

When I step closer, they stop. Everyone does. The whispering quiets and all that's left is the sound of the breeze between the sequoias, and something else. Some electricity I can't place.

This must be what it really feels like to be a siren, to have a captive audience. To be heard. So instead of giving any introduction, instead of making them wait another moment, I open my mouth to speak. I think I hear faint whispers, but my audience is silent, expectant. Hopeful but afraid. Whatever it is—the electricity and the faint whispering—I quiet them with one word.

My voice is power.

"**Awaken**," I tell the children. I say the word again and again, turning from one child to the next until I've told each of them.

And they do. Their skin blushes back to life as though it's the breeze making it happen. Ashleigh's ponytail swings down, completing a motion interrupted years ago. Tabor settles from his place a tiny bit off the ground. Each child draws in a deep, long breath, and the sound of it starts responding gasps from the watching adults. Finally, the children's joined hands swing as if the game is still in session, and then they realize they're awake.

When it's done, there's a moment in which no one makes a sound. Parents and siblings are touching children they haven't spoken to for the better part of a decade, but they don't know what to say. And then Ashleigh's mother lets it out.

She howls. She pulls her child into her chest—the daughter who should be as tall as she is now, but isn't—and she sobs like words couldn't do it justice. It makes tears spring to my eyes, makes me take a step back and completely fail at suppressing a shudder.

They're saying I set them free. That if I weren't a siren, they would've died without getting their babies back. That I'm a hero.

That the game is done.

Except none of the parents or the children are saying that part, and when it carries on the wind, we're all looking around for the source.

"*The game is done, the game is done,*" the wind chants.

The sprites. They must be gliding in the space between us, close enough that Ashleigh's mother grips her awakened child to her chest while her eyes search the sequoias.

"*Red Rover, Red Rover,*" they sing, "*Red Rover, Red Rover.*"

"Red Rover, Red Rover," the children reply, standing on tiptoe

277

like they're trying to reach the disembodied voices. They smile, Ashleigh, Mere, Tabor, and Wiley, and look to their parents as if for permission. Parents who for years have thought the sprites responsible, and can't know it isn't true. They hold the children tight while the sprites sing above our heads.

I don't know how to put them at ease, what to do next, until the reporter takes my arm.

She's been on her phone, calling the station. This wasn't planned as a live broadcast (no one trusts a siren), but they're putting it on the air. Right now. They're asking me to stay so they can do an interview, but I have to get out of here.

It's real now, the pain and the loss they never talk about on those tourist websites and TV segments. There is no happy ending, just relief and, as far as I can tell by the looks on the parents' faces, a lifetime of fear, of searching the sequoias and the sky for a threat they cannot see. I wish I hadn't wasted the time it took to make sure it was a spectacle. I needed it to be, for Effie's sake and my sake, but these families and their hurt matter more. I have to get to the others, to the ones in the courtyard and the one at Minnie's grave. I have to let them out. I have to set their families and loved ones free.

The kids are crying now because they're being told. That game was years ago, that's why their parents look so much older. (That's part of why.)

It's so much harder to watch than I thought it'd be, and I guess the same is true for Effie. Without warning, she ripples out of mirage mode and she's visible, gorgon tail and floating hair and all.

That wasn't part of the plan.

Everything stops again, except the camera man, who spins remarkably well despite his equipment, and the sprite chorus.

"*Effie, Effie!*" the sprites whisper-sing, enchanted the way that I was when I first saw her true form. "*Do the trick! Play again!*"

As for the rest of our audience, the videos from last night are suddenly proven true. There was speculation about elaborate VFX pranks. Someone trying to gain some sort of notoriety by making up a story about a mythical creature you could barely see in those short, shaky clips. Maybe Effie Calhoun Freeman was in on it, paid to play along because of her original connection to the statue/sprite story. It was only a matter of time before the footage was somehow verified, before someone figured out this was no impressive use of Photoshop. Now there's no need.

"It wasn't the sprites," Effie says through tears, while the reporter pokes the cameraman like it'll ensure he catches it all. "It was me. I didn't know it, I didn't know what I was. I'm so sorry."

I'm waiting to see how the adults react, but I don't have to hold my breath for long. Ashleigh runs to her, and Mere and the others follow. Effie's balancing on a tail longer than a python's, with scaled twists that can't stop dancing, but they hug her without flinching.

"Effie," Ashleigh says with her nine-year-old's voice, "you're okay!"

Eff lets herself slide down so they're the same height, even though it means her still human-looking torso is almost on the ground. Wiley's the first to run his hand along a coiled part of Effie's tail, and she laughs. It must be like being back at the faire.

Eventually everyone closes in, because nothing inspires forgiveness like relief. Effie was just a child herself, Ashleigh's mom tells the reporter while they film the reunited friends over her shoulder. Together they're admiring the flowers and the wreaths and the plaque that says their names.

They'll replace the children with a sculpture, I bet. A real one. It's Portland, so it might even be of Effie in her gorgon form surrounded by the kids. I can hope, at least. What matters—besides reuniting families and Awakening all the statues—is that we can go home now. After this, I think everything will be okay.

XX

EFFIE

Ms. Fish gave Isabella and me full credit on our sprite project because she saw Tav's Awakening on the news.

We lived our assignment, she told Isabella, and I'm pretty sure she did something obnoxious and extra with her hands when she said it, but I wasn't there.

Anyone else would've used the trauma of a gorgon kidnapper and being trapped in a glass box to get out of the last weeks of school, but Isabella's not like most people. She still texts me, for one thing. Asks if *I'm* okay.

She hasn't suggested any get-togethers, but I can't really blame her. Maybe she's had her fill of gorgon company, and maybe she just needs time. Either way, she deserves some space. Which is why I'm not going back to Beckett High.

Maybe things would've been different if my dad had shown similar restraint. He was supposed to back off until I got my tail, in case I didn't. Mom had brought me to the faire so we'd both be near him, but she made me a mermaid so my story couldn't suddenly be relocated to the tent. (Funny that Mama Theo disapproved of my mer life when it was specifically designed to do just what she wanted: keep me in the real world.)

"He was supposed to watch me from a distance," I tell Tavia

when she's back inside the tent. "And every time he got too close, my inner gorgon spiked and I blacked out. Or what I thought was blacking out."

Tav's just watching me, listening. She didn't get to hear my whole conversation with my dad, and I know she's worried about the two of us. Or me being with him, anyway.

"He should've backed off," I say like I'm conceding. "Especially in Vancouver."

"You could've turned a lot of people." She says it gently. "Thank God Gargy was there."

"He got tired of waiting. He's made some mistakes. Serious ones that hurt people. And me."

"You don't have to explain anymore," Tavia says. "I get it. He's your dad."

"Even if he was manipulative and selfish? And has control issues?"

"Yeah, I don't know any other dads like that," she says through a snort. Even though she knows her dad is a saint compared to mine. "You don't want to be him, Eff, you want to know him. It makes sense. I just wanted you to live at home. With me."

"I know. But even if I hadn't had the prom freak-out, I really think this gorgon thing's gonna work better if I'm a recluse." I don't mention my suspicion that despite Isabella's kindness and the all-is-forgiven, Portland-is-love fest going on, when the rose color clears, someone's gonna have questions about me and the fabled "walking water." I don't say my dad was smart to make his existence a myth, to never come out in the open, to have an enchanted world of his own so that only those he invites can find him. Instead I just settle on, "The world'll like me better."

"So will the fairegoers, I bet. That whole Hidden Scales thing seems like a hit."

"Yep."

"So." She sighs. "You're keeping your tail?"

"Dude, have you seen this thing?" I wrap it around and

around itself, balancing coils on top of coils so that when I'm at the top, I'm as tall as three grown men standing on each other's shoulders. The acrobats and their tower might have some competition next year.

Tavia's smiling, but she looks so heartbroken.

"Hey," I say to her as I glide down like my tail's an escalator. "I'm still gonna be your sister. We're still best friends."

"I know."

"And no matter where I am, it's you who set me free." When she starts to shake her head, I grab her. "Hey. You did. And you didn't Appeal to them, so it won't wear off. At least in Portland, by the people I stole from, I'll be forgiven. You gave me that."

"I'd do anything for you." She's trying not to cry, but it can't be helped. "How am I supposed to do senior year without you?"

"You were never the one who needed me," I say.

"I do, though," Tavia says when she rests her head on my shoulder. "I told you you're my everything."

When I tighten my arms around her, even my serpent-twists can't help reaching for her.

TAVIA

When I walk in the front door, it feels like I've been gone for years. I've been to two news studios today and spent an hour on the phone with some interviewer from Eugene before stopping by the Renaissance faire.

Wallace was there, hanging out near the Hidden Scales, eyeballing the dudes cosplaying gargoyles while they stood guard outside of it. They looked ridiculous and should be ashamed of themselves, and I told him as much. He just smiled and folded his arms.

"I guess you're not back in his good graces yet?" I asked him.

"I'm stuck on the outside. But it'll pass."

"Eff won't let him shut you out forever." I pet his arm. "Anyway. If you're stuck wearing a human face, at least it's a good look."

That made him grin.

"Thanks, Tavia."

"For what?"

"For being my first real friend."

"You're welcome."

We stood there in comfortable silence for a moment, like we were back on my roof in the middle of the night.

"You still have to take me up sometimes, you know? Nothing's changed."

"No, I know. I have a lot of free time now, so. I'll come back and visit your dad."

I burst out laughing. For a guy chiseled out of stone, Gargy's humor's pretty good. I'll miss his talons scraping on my roof.

The seriously surprising bit came when I passed Elric on my way out of the faire. I was all ready to give him the cold shoulder when he bounded after me.

"Good day," he said, all smiles. "And a fairer one now."

"Oh, um. Good day, blacksmith."

"What a way to greet your sister's beloved," he replied, one gloved hand on his chest.

"I haven't wounded you, I hope." I laughed.

"In time, I'll recover. When I see Euphemia next." And he removed his heavy work glove before gesturing for my hand. Which he kissed.

"Well. Bye," I said, cutting my eyes at him and shaking my head while he jogged away.

It's good to know he was never the bastard I thought he was. He was always in character; he just didn't know Effie'd gotten (temporarily) confused.

After all the excitement, my house seems pretty quiet. Almost depressingly so. Sure it's back to being an only child, but I try to remember things are very different now. My dad might still be scared, but he's the only one. At least in this town. And this town is where I live.

I'm halfway up the stairs when I hear his voice.

"Hey, Vivi." When I turn, Dad's coming up to meet me, but he stops before he gets there, lays his hand on the rail and tightens it once.

He wants to tell me this won't end well. That no matter how many people call me "hero" right now, it'll go bad, like it always goes bad when you're a siren. He wants to tell me that I'm being stupid and this isn't safe. I shouldn't have started my own channel, like Camilla, about sirens who've lived in the open and about the calls, and about how much re-education we all need. He wants to say that I need to think about how it feels for everyone else. For him.

"What is it, Dad?"

"Oh, I just. I got a call today. Somebody wants to do a documentary about the kids. Effie's friends and their families. And you."

He pulls a scrap of paper out of his pocket and offers it to me.

"I told them you'd let them know."

"Thanks," I mutter, looking at the number and his careful handwriting.

"All right."

"What about my family?" I ask before he can go back down the stairs. My dad lifts his chin like he doesn't understand. "They called me after they spoke to you. Which reminds me I'm gonna have to change my number. Pretty sure someone put it online or something; my phone's been blowing up all day. Anyway. Yeah, they know sirens run in families, so they said you could be in it too. If you wanted."

Dad puts his hands in his pockets. Takes one out and rubs the top of his head. He nods . . . and then he nods again.

"Okay. That sounds good."

"Okay." I try not to smile and not to breathe too quickly. "I

284

Acknowledgments

A Song Below Water is about the lifesaving power of Black sister-hood, and as such there are a number of friendships—budding and years long—that I have to acknowledge. But first I have to speak to the sister because of whom this book exists: my tiny big sister, my unofficial twin separated by two years, Jen French.

I told you in DM, jokingly if I recall, that my voice is power, and then followed it up with, "Omfg, what if all sirens were Black girls?" I knew immediately it would be my next project, and we spent days talking about a character you'd imagined named Effie, and what it might be like to write something together. Something we hadn't done since our grade-school days, writing about twin sisters, Megs and Pegs. (I had to. Now they belong to the ages.) We didn't end up getting to write it all together, but you gave Effie a personality and a passion, and I tried to keep her true to both. I hope you love her as much as I do, because I consider this story ours. Sha-boing-boing-boing.

I have to interrupt my own acknowledgments to say there's no way I'm not putting Ezra Morrow near the top. It is beyond amazing to have a son I adore this much reach an age and level of insight where you became a beloved CP. Thus far, you've read this book the most times out of anyone who wasn't paid to read this book, and son or daughter, you will always be part of my primary audience. Thank you for filling my life with music and art and passion, and yes, for "basically being the same person."

To the Black sisters who have given me life for years and this year: Anastasia Clemons, Tonya Clemons, Serrana Smith, Nnekay Fitzclarke, Bianti Curry, Rubis Iyodi, Karen Strong, Leatrice Mc-Kinney, Tracy Deonn, Dhonielle Clayton, Saraciea Fennell, Patrice Caldwell. Thank you for the safe spaces we create; I need them. All my love and admiration, and my boot ready to be applied to necks, as needed.

Thank you to Victoria Marini, who understood, and who partnered with me to find the right home for my girls.

Thank you to Diana Pho, my editor, who has been on my team a lot longer than we've been working on this book. Thank you for the continued invitation, and the confidence, long before anyone else knew my name. To that 2014 tweet, and the fact that we finally got to work together.

Thank you to the team at Tor Teen, for your early and sustained support, and to Alex Cabal, my amazing cover artist who brought the girls to life. This cover will always have a special place in my heart.